T0668461

# SHADOW BOYS

ALSO BY HARRY HUNSICKER

The Jon Cantrell Thrillers
*The Contractors*

The Lee Henry Oswald Mysteries
*Crosshairs*
*The Next Time You Die*
*Still River*

A JON CANTRELL THRILLER

# SHADOW BOYS

# HARRY HUNSICKER

 THOMAS & MERCER

Text copyright © 2014 Harry Hunsicker
All rights reserved.

Published by Thomas&Mercer, Seattle

www.apub.com

Amazon, the Amazon logo, and Thomas&Mercer are trademarks of Amazon.com, Inc., or its affiliates.

ISBN-13: 9781477825754
ISBN-10: 1477825754

Cover design by *theBookDesigners*

Library of Congress Control Number: 2014939678

Printed in the United States of America

*To Alison*

*Little Mexico*
*Dallas, Texas*
*1981*

This fear has no name.

Raul Delgado, eleven years old, wishes it did.

With a name it would be easier, like dealing with the barrio toughs down the street or with Papa after he's had too many cervezas.

But the terror is nameless, a dark coil that wraps around Raul's insides and squeezes until there's nothing left, just a hollowness without end.

Everything that is good in Raul's world—his mother's tamales, Christmas morning, lunch at Pike Park after Mass—all that has disappeared into the blackness.

Raul's brother, Carlos, huddles next to him in the hall closet. Mama's winter coat dangles above their heads, fragrant with her perfume and the metallic tang of mothballs.

Raul wonders if Carlos feels the fear in the same way. He decides not.

His brother is different. Mama and Papa say so, as do their teachers.

Carlos is twelve, a year older than Raul. Carlos is smart and quick with his words. He is the instigator, of course. His actions have caused this nameless fear. It is all his fault.

Raul's teeth chatter. He smells the sweat on his body and the dust in the closet, overpowering the illusion of safety created by the aroma of his mother's coat.

Carlos touches his arm, tries to reassure him, but tears leak from the corners of Raul's eyes. He recites a Hail Mary in his head, the only prayer he can think of at the moment.

His brother shifts his weight slightly, puts his lips near Raul's ear. He speaks in a voice so quiet it is like a daydream.

"It's okay," Carlos whispers. "Just be cool."

Raul nods, too scared to speak.

The wood floor of their house on McKinnon Street creaks. The light at the base of the door changes; someone is in the hall.

*Hail Mary, full of grace.*

Raul stares at the ribbon of light. It is a Tuesday in July, early afternoon, and nothing good can be outside the closet. Mama is at her second job, cleaning the house of a rich family in Highland Park. Papa is at a bar somewhere.

The knob before them squeaks as it turns. Raul takes a sudden breath, presses against his brother.

The door opens.

Light floods in, silhouettes two large figures in the hallway of their home.

*La policía.* Two gringos in blue uniforms, guns on their hips.

A stocky man with red hair and one who is bald with thick blond sideburns.

The officer with the red hair nods slowly as if this is what he's suspected all along, two kids hiding in a closet. He reaches down, grabs Carlos's shirt, and pulls him into the hall.

The bald cop sticks a cigarette between his lips.

"You little shit," the red-haired cop says. "Where's the money?"

Carlos shrugs, and the cop slaps him across the side of the head, palm walloping the boy's ear. Raul cringes.

Carlos grunts and falls to the floor, but he doesn't speak. After a few seconds, he pushes himself to his hands and knees. A growth spurt has left him tall but painfully thin. In a sleeveless cotton shirt and his frayed Ocean Pacific shorts, he looks frail.

"Damn wetbacks." The bald cop pulls Raul from the closet.

Carlos stands, shoulders squared. He rubs the side of his face where the officer struck him. He looks at both policemen, face determined. He says, "Get out of my house."

The fear inside Raul spikes as high as the tallest building in Dallas and then lessens, replaced by something else: pride, and more than a little envy. He is proud of his brother, the strength he possesses, the way he stands up to the gringo cops. He is also envious because he knows this strength will never be his. He is weak, a follower. Not a leader.

The red-haired cop, the older of the two policemen, stands absolutely still.

There is no movement inside the house. Even the specks of dust seem to have stopped their dance in the light from the living room window.

Outside, the Popsicle man rings the bell on his *paleta* cart. A dog barks.

The bald cop chuckles, lights his cigarette with a Zippo.

"The Delgado boys. Hard-ass criminals." The red-haired cop shakes his head. "Looks like we're gonna have to take us a little a ride."

He grabs the brothers by the neck, shoves them toward the front door.

Raul's knees are wobbly. He knows his brother has had encounters with the law before, but he is startled to hear their family name mentioned. His stomach rumbles and he worries that he might wet his pants. Or worse.

A few seconds later both boys are in the back of the squad car parked in their driveway, hands cuffed behind them.

The peeling paint on the side of their house appears dirtier than usual. Heat waves shimmer above the air conditioner mounted in the front window.

The street is empty. Police cars in this neighborhood tend to do that. The Popsicle man is nowhere to be seen.

Raul blinks sweat from his eyes. Then he begins to cry.

The bald cop sits in the passenger seat. He looks in the back and says, "Pussy."

Carlos Delgado is quiet as the red-haired officer pulls out of the driveway and speeds down McKinnon Street.

The neighbors' houses pass by, clapboard shacks ringed by chain-link fences. Some are white, others painted a riot of different colors—green and purple, bright yellow, orange.

This section of Little Mexico is Raul's home, the only place he knows. His parents moved to Dallas from the Rio Grande Valley when he was a toddler, ten years ago, and South Texas is not even a recollection now. He wonders if he will ever see any of these houses again.

The red-haired officer cuts across Harry Hines Boulevard, a large street that leads to downtown and the police station. He keeps driving, zigzagging his way toward the deserted area by the railroad tracks.

"Where are you taking us?" Carlos says, alert.

Neither officer replies. The houses become smaller and grubbier the closer they get to the railroad. There are more vacant lots, the packed earth covered in trash and cast-off junk, car parts, refrigerators, mattresses.

A few hundred yards in front of them looms the twin smokestacks of an old power plant, long closed. To the right of the power plant sits a huge concrete structure, a grain silo.

"Y-you can't take us here." Carlos's voice cracks. "W-we have r-rights."

The bald cop chuckles as the squad car rattles over a series of train tracks.

A few moments later, they stop by a grove of cedar trees shading an abandoned building.

The red-haired cop rolls down the windows, turns off the ignition.

The engine ticks as the bald cop lights another cigarette.

No people in sight, just the four of them in a hot squad car.

"Where's the cash?" Red Hair looks in the mirror at Carlos.

Carlos blinks. His skin has grown pale. But he doesn't speak.

Red Hair glances at his partner. "How many times we busted Carlos Delgado?"

Bald Cop shrugs and blows a smoke ring.

"And what's your name?" Red Hair looks at Raul in the mirror.

"Leave my brother alone," Carlos says.

Raul tries to speak but nothing comes out. He wants to tell the two policemen where the money is, the twenty-three dollars they snatched from the cash register of the convenience store an hour before. The theft had been Carlos's idea, as usual. A little movie money, if they could ever get a ride to Northpark Mall.

Red Hair sighs. He turns in his seat, pulls his pistol from its holster, extends it over the top of the seat, and presses the muzzle against Raul's forehead.

The weapon is a big black slab of metal. The hammer is already cocked.

Raul feels the wet warmth spread out from his crotch.

Bald Cop tosses away his cigarette and swats at a bug.

"Where's the fucking money, Carlos?" Red Hair flicks a lever on the pistol with his thumb. "Don't make me hurt your little brother."

The steel of the barrel is hot against Raul's skin. He shakes uncontrollably.

Red Hair laughs, enjoying himself. Raul wonders if he will ever laugh again.

Carlos hangs his head, defeated. He reaches into his pocket and removes the wad of currency.

Red Hair takes it with his free hand, chuckling, too. He moves the muzzle from Raul's head, but the gun's still looming in front of him, the muzzle like a cold, dark eye.

Bald Cop lights another smoke, waves away a fly buzzing around the interior of the car.

Raul realizes this has all been a big joke to the two officers. He is just a dumb Mexican kid, and the police have such power that they can threaten his very life for nothing but their own amusement. Anger mixes with his fear.

Carlos stares at the floor of the squad car. He hates to lose, even money he has pilfered.

"I got shit to do today." Red Hair wags the gun at Carlos like it's a finger. "If I didn't, I'd run your ass down to juvie right now."

Bald Cop swats at the fly as though pissed at it.

His hand accidentally strikes Red Hair's shoulder, and in that moment all that was in Raul's world is no more.

Sunlight and thunder burst forth inside the car, an explosion brighter and louder than anything he has ever experienced.

And water. Salty, warm water all over Raul's skin.

His ears don't work right. From a long way off, he hears Bald Cop yelling, his voice high-pitched, filled with terror.

After a period of time—he will never know how long—Raul opens his eyes, blinks away the thick liquid on his face.

The first thing he sees are the ghosts, two white-faced figures staring at him. Since one has red hair and the other is bald, he realizes they are the two police officers, their faces drained of all color, their souls altered in some way he cannot comprehend.

He looks to the left for his brother but no one is there, just a bloody lump of flesh wearing Ocean Pacific shorts. This is not his brother, of course. Carlos was just here; he'll be along any moment.

Raul tries to make sense of the thunder and the sunlight, but he can't.

He calls out for his mama but hours pass before he is allowed to see her. Instead he encounters more police officers, men in blue uniforms and gray business suits. The policemen are followed by reporters, dozens of people with notepads and cameras and video recorders.

Raul Delgado scans the crowd for his brother but he is nowhere to be found.

# - CHAPTER ONE -

*Dallas, Texas*
*Present-day*

Springtime on the Grassy Knoll. The city's only true tourist attraction.

The air was thick with pollen and the chatter of Japanese visitors.

I sat on the concrete steps at the top of the infamous hill, the Texas School Book Depository behind me, Reunion Tower off to my right.

My position offered a view of the sloping lawn that led to Elm Street, the strip of asphalt where President John F. Kennedy had met his demise a half century or so before.

A Japanese group stood between where I was and the street, clustered over a patch of Saint Augustine turf. They were snapping pictures, frantically pointing to several shiny objects on the ground.

No one was paying any attention to me, so I reached into the paper sack on my lap and grabbed another handful of empty rifle cartridges. I pitched them off to the right.

A little hobby of mine, tossing spent rounds on the Grassy Knoll. Gave the tourists something to talk about.

Amazing how much fun you can have with the simplest things.

My name is Jon Cantrell, and my mantra these days is to enjoy life whenever you can. Because you can never tell when the good times might end, a hard lesson I'd learned firsthand watching too many people die over the years.

A Latino man wearing a trim gray suit strolled down the sidewalk. He was headed toward Stemmons Freeway, following the route Kennedy's motorcade took. When he reached the spot on Elm where Oswald's first bullet had struck the president, he stopped and stared at the chalk marks on the road's surface marking the location.

Then he looked up the Grassy Knoll and walked my way. As he moved, his jacket shifted, displaying a holstered gun on his belt opposite a gold shield.

He was a Dallas police officer, a deputy chief. Something of a public figure, for reasons having nothing much to do with his rank. He was also the reason I was sitting on the steps at the top of the Grassy Knoll.

A meeting, at his request, subject unknown.

I put the bag on the ground and waited.

He stopped in front of the steps and glanced inside my sack.

"So you're the bullet guy," he said. "You know that drives the tourism people nuts."

Olive-skinned, maybe six feet tall, a trim 170. My age or thereabouts, midforties. He was good-looking in the way determined people are, bursting with energy and self-confidence, the type of man who attracts others by his personality as much as by his appearance.

"Everybody needs a hobby," I said. "This is mine."

He sat next to me, stared down the knoll at the Japanese group.

"I talked to some people on the force who knew you back in the day," he said. "You come highly recommended."

I shrugged. "I had my moments."

Unfortunately, one too many of them were indictable.

Neither of us spoke for a few moments. The Japanese boarded a bus and were replaced by a group of Germans.

"There's a problem that's recently come to my attention." He straightened his tie. "I think you'd be a good fit to handle it."

The Germans noticed the empty cartridges. Lots of hand gestures and *achtung*-ing.

I didn't reply. What service could someone like me provide a high-ranking police officer? An indiscretion that needed tidying up? Perhaps a bit of street justice for someone who had escaped the clutches of the legal system? Neither option appealed to me in the slightest.

He pulled an envelope from his pocket.

"I'm trying to locate a certain person. He's gone missing."

Two German men scampered up the hill, cameras in hand. They began taking pictures of their fellow tourists who were taking pictures of the empty cartridges I'd scattered earlier.

"My suggestion is you hire a private detective." I looked at the deputy chief. "Or—here's a thought—call the police."

The two photogs began talking to each other in their native tongue. Loudly.

Why were the Germans always the most obnoxious tourists? Must be something in their DNA, like the need to start wars.

"I'd rather not get the department involved with this," he said. "And most PIs, well, they're desk jockeys. This situation requires someone with a certain amount of street savvy."

I was an ex-Dallas police officer as well as a former federal agent. I had street savvy out the wazoo and the scars to prove it. But I didn't want to work the streets anymore, or be involved with people like the deputy chief.

I didn't say anything.

"Your background," he said. "You know what doors to knock on. How hard to knock."

In the distance, another bus stopped and disgorged a herd of tourists. This group was morbidly obese, so I figured they were good old-fashioned Americans.

"I'm not an investigator," I said. "This is not my area of expertise."

Neither of us spoke for a few moments. Instead we watched the tourists take pictures.

After a period of time, he said, "I wonder what motivates someone like you."

I picked up my sack of shells.

"Can't imagine it being money," he said.

My employer was a law firm based in Washington, DC. They specialized in the legal issues private companies encountered when doing business with the federal government. My compensation package was generous.

"From what I hear," he said, "you're the best-paid janitor in town."

I rolled my eyes but didn't speak. The word "janitor" implied cleanup, which was such an unseemly term.

The law firm where I was employed needed certain situations handled in a discreet manner. The bulk of my work was to make sure property was returned to its rightful owner. This oftentimes required a delicate but firm hand. Feathers needed to become unruffled. Umbrages redressed. Inconveniences made less so, problems turned into opportunities.

"Oh, sorry." The deputy chief chuckled. "You don't like the term 'janitor.'"

"No, I don't."

My business card read "Special Projects Facilitator and Collections Agent."

That's what I'm all about: facilitating and collecting. Thank goodness I don't work at a sperm bank.

"Afraid I'm going to have to pass," I said. "My company doesn't like their people to moonlight."

The Germans were getting yet more obnoxious. I resisted the urge to tell the loudest to shut his strudel hole.

"I talked to your boss. Theo. He's willing to make an exception." The deputy chief paused. "You know, in the interest of good relations with the local authorities."

Subtext: if you don't want to have your people hassled, let Jon Cantrell take this assignment.

I sighed. "Well, since you asked nicely, I guess my answer is yes."

"Look at you." He clapped his hands softly. "Making the right choice."

"Tell me about your missing person."

"He's from West Dallas. Thirteen years old. Lives with his half-blind grandmother."

"People disappear every day," I said. "Maybe he ran away to join the circus."

"He's African American and autistic."

I rubbed my eyes as the weight of another lost cause settled onto my shoulders.

"How long has he been gone?"

"About a week."

"Odds are good that he's dead."

The deputy chief shrugged. "Then I need to know that he's dead."

"Why are you so interested in one kid from the wrong side of town?"

He didn't speak for a few moments. The glint of self-confidence in his eyes had drifted away, replaced by a shadow of something else, a darkness that I was more familiar with than I cared to admit.

"I used to be a kid from the wrong side of town," he said. "Maybe I'm trying to make sure the same mistakes don't get made."

The words were softly spoken but echoed loudly in the dark corners of the city's history.

"His name is Tremont Washington." He popped a mint in his mouth. "I believe you knew his father."

The air in my lungs got hot, throat clenched. He'd saved the best for last.

Tremont's father had been an undercover narcotics agent with the Texas Department of Public Safety. Ten years ago, he'd stepped in front of a drug dealer's machete that had been swinging toward my neck. I lived; he didn't.

"They told me his family was taken care of." I shook my head. "Relocated to California."

"They lied." He handed me the envelope. "Here's everything I have on him."

I held the package at arm's length. After a moment, I stuck it in my hip pocket.

He turned, started to leave, then stopped and said, "How's Piper?"

The one person we currently had in common. My former lover. The deputy chief's on-again, off-again girlfriend. Piper had set up the meeting. She'd obviously told him about my employment situation, given that he'd checked in with Theo.

I didn't reply.

"Tell her I said hello." He smiled. The expression had no warmth.

With that, Deputy Chief Raul Delgado walked away, threading his way through the tourists on the Grassy Knoll.

# - CHAPTER TWO -

Captain Mason Burnett pondered his surroundings, Dallas City Hall's green room, a well-appointed lounge behind the area where press briefings were held.

Leather sofas soft as butter. Mahogany-paneled walls. Coffee and bottled water on a side table. A fifth of Wild Turkey discreetly hidden in the corner in case someone needed a shot of courage before facing the media glare on the other side of the doors.

Taxpayer money at work.

The room was empty except for Mason, who was the commander of the SWAT team, and his boss, the chief of police.

The chief smiled at Mason but didn't speak. It was the smile of an executioner right before the noose tightened.

The top cop in Dallas was an ingratiatingly insincere man with the political instincts of a medieval pope.

When the chief came after you, the knife always went into the exact center of your back, no chance to save yourself. Even if you could reach the handle and muster the will to go after the man, you had to take into account the fact that he was half black and half Asian, the equivalent of being born with bulletproof skin when it came to city politics.

Mason was a twenty-five-year veteran, one of the few Caucasians in the upper echelons of the force. He'd realized several years ago that he would never advance to the next level, assistant or deputy chief. He'd like to blame that on his ethnicity, but he'd come to understand that the next level required a certain degree of political skill, finesse that he did not possess or care to. This realization did not lessen the bubble of anger he felt at moments like these.

He served as head of the Field Services Division, a catch-all department that handled special operations like the SWAT team, among other functions.

In normal times, no one got too close to Captain Mason Burnett or to his people, which was how he liked it.

In normal times, most people were afraid of Mason Burnett.

An aura of danger clung to him, something he cultivated.

But these were not normal times.

The crime rate in Dallas, which for the last decade had been on a steady march downward, had recently done the abnormal: it had risen.

This meant that all the affirmative-action gerrymandering and political machinations the chief could muster were for naught. More crime meant that the chief's ass was on the line, and that fact didn't bode well for those under him, especially a white guy who'd never really been a team player.

Mason stood, walked across the room, and opened a bottle of water.

The chief's assistant, a lieutenant named Hopper, entered the room.

Hopper was in his early forties and average in every way. Pale skin, pale gray eyes, close-cropped hair that was neither blond nor brown nor gray, but a mix of the three. A trim six feet tall.

He held a whispered conversation with the chief and then approached Mason.

The chief had an interesting management style. He never talked with those below him in the command structure, his deputy chiefs or captains. Not in person or on the phone, or via e-mail. Not a word.

He used one of his assistants, usually Hopper, to communicate. He told them what to say and how to say it.

Lieutenant Hopper stopped in front of Mason, scanned his outfit, and smirked.

Mason was not dressed in a regulation uniform. He wore navy-blue fatigues, black combat boots, and a custom Colt .45 semiautomatic pistol on one hip. No one ever said anything about his clothes, however. Part of the aura. You did not jack with Mason Burnett—though Hopper was almost doing so with that smirk.

"The chief has a message," Hopper said.

"Yeah?" Mason took a drink of water. "And what would that be?"

"Don't fuck up." Hopper turned and left the green room.

———

The mayor and the chief stood as far away from the podium as possible, a wide gulf between them and Mason. Several other members of the command structure—deputy chiefs, captains, a handful of ranking sergeants—stood along one wall.

Rule one of city politics: stay as distant as possible from potential train wrecks.

Hopper hovered a few feet behind the chief, his pale gray eyes never leaving Mason's face. The man never seemed to blink.

The press conference had been scheduled for the lunch hour, a move that indicated they didn't want a high attendance but at the same time they didn't want to bury the briefing on a Friday afternoon.

If the plan tanked, the powers that be weren't on the hook for making a big deal about it. They'd point to the sparsely attended press conference, making sure everybody focused on Mason Burnett. Then, they'd fire him.

There were maybe ten reporters present, about half of them Mexican, reflecting the makeup of the city—an unfortunate new reality, in Mason's mind.

"Hello, everybody." Mason adjusted the microphone upward.

He was a tall man in his midforties. Six-three, barrel-chested, muscular. His blond hair was close-cropped, slowly going gray.

"Thank you all for coming out today." He smiled at the assembled people.

No response. One of the print guys was eating a hot dog. He spilled some mustard on his shirt.

Mason made it quick. He talked about the spike in offenses, how even though everyone thought it was just a momentary blip, the DPD was committed to lowering the rate of violent crime for the safety of the citizens. He told them about the new program: highly visible SWAT officers patrolling certain neighborhoods in an effort to dissuade violent crime.

He did not mention that the idea was not his, but a scheme foisted upon him by the chief, a man who knew about as much about actual police work as a stripper did about particle physics.

He did not dwell on the fact that SWAT officers were often viewed as soldiers in cop clothes and this initiative would effectively militarize the streets of Dallas.

Mason paused in his delivery, glanced at the mayor and the chief. The chief made a gesture like a gun cocking, aimed at Mason—not an image of support.

Mason wrapped up the presentation, asking if there were any questions.

After a brief Q and A, the press conference broke up.

The chief nodded once and left.

The reporters turned their cameras off, put notepads away.

In the back of the room sat an African American man in his early twenties, not part of the official press contingent. He wore a red beret and camo fatigues, the sleeves ripped off the jacket.

He raised his hand.

"Yes?" Mason flicked off the microphone.

"You gonna patrol in West Dallas?" the man asked.

Mason left the podium and sauntered toward the young guy in the red beret.

"I'm sorry," he said. "I didn't catch what organization you're with."

The man crossed his arms, tried to look tough. "I represent the People's Blog of Southern Dallas County."

Mason put a foot on the chair in front of the man, leaned an elbow on his knee, and looked down at the representative of the People's Blog. The effect was intimidating. He'd practiced the stance to get it just right.

"What was your question again, son?"

"Your fascist troops." The man raised his voice. "Are you going to occupy territory south of the Trinity River?"

Mason shook his head, spoke softly. "I'm not at liberty to discuss operational matters at this point."

One of the TV reporters glanced at them, obviously trying to see if a shouting match might erupt that would make his trip to city hall worth the trouble. Hopper glided over and engaged the reporter in conversation, glad-handing him toward the exit.

Neither Mason nor the man in the red beret spoke. They stared at each other until the TV reporter left.

When the room was empty, the man said, "Then maybe you can tell me how come the police don't investigate missing persons cases."

Mason kept his expression blank.

"I'm not sure what you mean," he said. "Could you be more specific?"

"The readers of my blog, they'd like to know what the police are doing to locate a certain missing person." The man paused. "He disappeared a week ago."

Mason forced himself to ask the question. He already knew the answer.

"This missing person. What's his—uh, or her—name?"

"Tremont," the man in the red beret said. "His name is Tremont Washington."

# - CHAPTER THREE -

After meeting with Deputy Chief Raul Delgado, I left the Grassy Knoll and headed toward my Lincoln Navigator, a company car. I found my SUV in the Sixth Floor Museum parking lot, then tossed the sack of spent cartridges in the rear and got in the driver's seat.

My phone, battery removed, was in the console.

I slid the battery into place, powered on the device, and dialed my boss, Theo Goldberg, Esquire, managing partner of Goldberg, Finkelman, and Clark, PC.

I'd never actually met Theo Goldberg. He'd hired me by e-mail, based on my experience as a government contractor and skill set as a former law-enforcement officer. Theo was but a voice on the phone, Charlie to my Angels.

He answered after the first ring. A gruff hello followed by voices in the distance.

"You could have let me know about the deputy chief," I said.

Kids screaming in the background, a coach's whistle.

"Do you have any idea how much child psychologists cost?" he said.

This reply was so far from anything I was expecting that I had no comeback.

"Isaac, my youngest, he's been taking archery lessons since he was in the second grade."

Theo's voice was more high-pitched and whiny than usual. He dropped his *r*'s, too—the result of growing up in Boston.

"I thought we had an agreement." I started the Lincoln. "After the mess in Omaha. You promised to tell me *everything* about a job."

Omaha had been a simple retrieval (my bread and butter), a misappropriated shipping container full of property belonging to the Department of Energy. Unfortunately, the shipping container was in the possession of a man who owed money to some very dangerous people in Chicago. Theo Goldberg, a tiger in the courtroom, was naïve in the ways of the street, and failed to mention the Chicago connection. Luckily, I was able to keep the body count low and most of the ensuing meltdown out of the media.

"Isaac shot a classmate," Theo said. "With his bow and arrow. In the buttocks."

"Anything else I need to know about Raul Delgado?" I slid the transmission into drive.

"Thank God the child he hit is all right," Theo said. "A minor puncture wound in his privileged WASP ass."

"Focus, Theo. *Fo-cus.* Let's talk about this guy in Dallas, the deputy chief—"

"The kid he shot, his father is an undersecretary at Homeland Security."

I headed toward the exit.

"Homeland Security, one of our biggest clients." He made a tsk sound. "Not good, Jonathan. Not good at all."

I gave up on my topic. Best to let Theo get it all out of his system. He'd get back to the reason for my call in due course.

"So what's with the psychologist?" I said.

"The school. They recommended a therapist to deal with any anger issues Isaac might have. Three hundred dollars an hour."

From his end of the phone, kids yelled like they were at a soccer game. I hoped it was a soccer game.

"The deputy chief," Theo said. The background noise got quieter. "This Gonzales fellow—"

"Delgado," I said. "His name is Raul Delgado."

"Whatever. Listen, he's someone we want to keep an eye on. We want to *know* about him."

Theo Goldberg was in the knowing business, as he liked to put it, knowledge being the currency of power in twenty-first-century America.

"Gotcha."

"Find his missing whatever," Theo said. "Establish a relationship."

Another biggie at Goldberg, Finkelman, and Clark. *Relationships.* The currying of favors. He who has the biggest Rolodex wins.

"That other thing," Theo said. "You're gonna take care of that, right?"

"On my way, even as we speak." I drove past the conspiracy theorists at Dealey Plaza.

Wind noise from the other end of the line. Huffing. Heavy breathing. Footsteps, running. Theo yelled, "Isaac! Put the fucking cat down!"

"You're busy," I said. "I'll let you go."

He came back on the phone. "Be careful, Jonathan. You're like the son I never had."

I was pretty sure we were the same age, in our forties. I didn't mention this. Instead I said, "What about Isaac?"

But the line was dead.

———

My assignment from Theo Goldberg this fine spring morning—that "other thing" he'd spoken of—was to facilitate the return of some property that belonged to the United States: a laptop computer. The laptop had been issued to a government contractor who was reluctant to return it.

In Texas, there were two groups of people that you absolutely didn't screw with, no matter what.

In order of importance, they were 1) Baptists and 2) the Dallas Cowboys.

The computer was in the possession of an ex–Dallas Cowboy named Tommy Joe Culpepper, son of the pastor of the Waco Baptist Church in McLennan County. Tommy Joe's mother was heir to a Permian Basin oil fortune, to boot.

That's about as close to royalty as you can get in Texas.

Tommy Joe, who fancied himself an Internet entrepreneur when he wasn't nailing divorcées at the country club, had an office in a renovated warehouse that housed tech start-ups and IT companies.

The building was on Stemmons Freeway, just on the other side of downtown from the School Book Depository. A few minutes after watching Deputy Chief Raul Delgado saunter away from me down the Grassy Knoll, I parked the Navigator between a Ferrari and a Toyota Prius with a Mister Spock bumper sticker.

I was wearing dark jeans, a black dress shirt, and brown lace-up boots. From the rear of the Lincoln I grabbed a black sport coat and shrugged it on.

*Look the part.* A saying of Theo's. I was trying for Internet-savvy investment banker but likely came across as a Silicon Valley dope dealer. Oh well.

Tommy Joe's office was on the ground floor at the back, a large open area with polished concrete floors and exposed wiring so it looked all techy.

I walked in without knocking and found the Dallas Cowboys' third-string wide receiver (in 1993) hunched over his desk, tamping a nugget of crystal meth into a pipe.

"Hello, Tommy Joe." I smiled.

He looked up, mouth agape. He was a big guy, six-three or -four, most of the football muscle having gone to fat. He wore a starched white button-down, a gold Rolex, and the Super Bowl ring he got for sitting on the bench and keeping an eye on Michael Irvin's cocaine stash.

"My name is Jonathan Cantrell. I'm with the law firm of Goldberg, Finkelman, and Clark."

"Whuh?" He frowned.

"We represent the government of the United States."

He put the pipe down.

The room smelled like burnt ammonia, so it was a safe bet that this wasn't going to be his first hit of the day. Partially packed moving boxes lay scattered about.

"You signed a contract," I said. "With the Department of Immigration and Customs, remember?"

Several computer-nerd friends of Tommy Joe's had developed an algorithm to spot likely illegal-alien crossing points. Tommy Joe had formed a company and sold the idea to Uncle

Sam. Unfortunately, neither the nerds nor Tommy Joe could deliver. Probably because the algorithms didn't work out. Too many variables, not enough data points. Who knows? A contributing factor might have been that Tommy Joe was pond scum.

"The laptop," I said. "The one they provided you. I need it back."

The computer contained government protocols and encryption data for federal contractors, information to be kept secret and returned upon request.

The Department of Immigration and Customs Enforcement had retained my employers to retrieve the laptop after Tommy Joe had ignored their letters and phone calls.

He stood up. "I don't gotta give nothing back."

"Yes, you do. Your contract is null and void."

His nostrils flared with each breath.

"Paragraph two, sub-paragraph C," I said. "Quote: 'In the event of this agreement being terminated, all properties provided to the contractor are to be returned forthwith.' End quote."

"You know who I am?"

"You're the big man on campus." I shook my head. "But they don't care about any of that in DC."

Tommy Joe came around the side of his desk, face contorted with rage.

I held up a hand. "Stop."

He stopped.

"I know what you're thinking right about now, Tommy Joe."

He began to hyperventilate. Face purple.

"You're thinking you're a badass and there's no way you're gonna let some cat like me waltz in here and tell you what to do."

He didn't say anything.

"Maybe back in the day you were a badass. Maybe back in the day you could have stopped me." I lowered my voice, barely above a whisper. "But not today, Tommy Joe."

He might as well have sent a press release to announce his next move. His right hand clenched and unclenched several times. He finally made a fist, reared back.

"Don't do it, Tommy Joe. I do not want to hurt you."

He swung anyway, a roundhouse toward my jaw, the kind of punch that looked impressive in the movies but was totally impractical in real life.

If you see it coming you have oodles of time.

I caught his wrist, yanked it forward and then up behind his back. Then I kicked his feet out from under him and slammed him to the floor, face-first.

He roared like a grizzly bear and bucked against me.

Astride his back, I grabbed his other arm and brought it to meet the first, then cuffed him using a plastic zip tie from my jacket pocket.

"Where is it?" I said.

"Screw you, ass-munch."

I sighed. Then I twisted one of his ears until he screamed.

*"The d-d-desk d-drawer!"*

I let go. Dragged Tommy Joe to the wall and rolled him upright with his back pressed against his bound hands, legs spread. Then I walked around the desk and opened the largest of the drawers.

The laptop was there, resting on top of a small plastic bag containing six or seven pencil-eraser-sized chunks of methamphetamine and a pint bottle of vodka.

I dumped the meth into an ashtray, added an ounce or so of vodka, and lit the whole thing on fire with Tommy Joe's lighter.

"See you around." I tucked the laptop under my arm and headed for the door.

"You are fucking toast." Tommy Joe tried to sound menacing. "I'm gonna hunt you down like a—like a—"

I stopped. "Like a wild dog? A feral pig?"

He didn't say anything, so I left.

———

*Dallas police headquarters*
*1981*

Raul Delgado, eleven years old, closes his eyes for a moment. He tries to erase the image of blinding light and the thunderclap that seared itself into his brain and left a constant ringing in his ears.

Even with his eyes shut, however, the light and the ringing remain. The only result is that the smell of urine and cigarette smoke becomes stronger.

He's still wearing the same clothes he had on in the backseat of the police car, the ones he peed in when he became so scared.

When the cop pointed the gun at him.

Right before the huge explosion that changed everything.

He opens his eyes.

The cigarette smell comes from a man in a light-blue, Western-style suit, a Dallas police badge clipped to the jacket pocket. His face is cratered like the pictures of the moon Raul has seen in school.

The man is smoking Pall Malls and drinking coffee. He is also leafing through a folder, which Raul imagines has something to do with himself and his brother, Carlos.

36

The two of them are alone in a small room. The room is furnished with a metal table and three metal chairs. The walls are brick, painted a pale green. The floor is gray concrete.

The man with the pockmarked face sits across from Raul. He hasn't spoken other than a gruff hello when he entered a few minutes ago.

Raul rubs his nose with the back of his hand. His face and shirt are still speckled with blood. Raul can't quite figure out why. He knows he isn't hurt, not cut anywhere. He's pretty sure the two cops who were in the front seat, the red-haired one with the gun and his bald friend, weren't hurt either.

Therefore the blood must be from his brother, Carlos.

But that makes no sense.

Carlos is invincible. He is incapable of being hurt. If only he will show up, he'll put all this to rest.

The cop closes the file. He lights another Pall Mall and blows a plume of smoke across the table.

"How many times you been arrested, Rah-ool?"

The cop's accent is thick, like his mouth is full of marbles.

He is the kind of man Raul's mother has warned him to avoid, a redneck who doesn't like Mexicans or Negroes. To Raul, he represents a slice of Texas that is exotic and vaguely dangerous, like prison rodeos and chicken-fried steak.

Raul shakes his head, unable to form words. He wants to talk, to tell the man that he's never been arrested. That was his brother, Carlos, and then only a couple of times.

The man taps his Pall Mall into an ashtray. "You Delgado boys cut a wide swath across Mex-Town, I'll give you that."

Raul wishes he could speak. He needs to tell the officer it was all just for fun. Just for something to do.

"A couple of real Pancho-fucking-Villas," the cop says. "You and your brother."

Words finally come.

"No. You don't understand—" Raul is shaking his head, eyes welling with tears.

"Don't sass me, Rah-ool." The cop stabs out his cigarette. "Don't ever do that, you hear me?"

Raul swallows the lump in his throat. Quits shaking his head.

"A couple of armed robberies on Maple Avenue, liquor stores," the cop says. "We're gonna need you to tell us about those, all right?"

Raul doesn't speak. His mind races, breath comes in gasps.

He and Carlos have never robbed a liquor store. They grabbed money from the cash register at 7-Eleven, stole coins from the car wash. Never anything with a gun. Never.

The cop arches an eyebrow. "Cat got your tongue, Rah-ool?"

Raul shakes his head. Then he remembers what the man said about sassing him. So he stops. If only Carlos would arrive. He could explain everything. He is good with words. And with people.

Raul swallows several times, works up the nerve to speak again.

"Where is my brother?" His voice is ragged. "He can help you."

The cop stares at him, face blank. He pulls a Pall Mall from the pack. Sticks the cigarette in his mouth but doesn't light it.

There is only one way into the room, a door by the cop. From the other side of the door, over the ringing in his ears, Raul hears raised voices, people arguing. Then, footsteps followed by silence.

The cop looks at the door for a moment. He drops his cigarette on the table and grabs a briefcase off the floor like he is in a hurry. He opens the case and pulls out a plastic bag containing a revolver.

The weapon has a short barrel and is battered, the wooden grips chipped, the metal dotted with bits of rust that remind Raul of the cop's scarred face.

"This here's your gun, right?" The cop drops the sack on the table. It makes a loud thud.

"No-no-no." Raul shakes his head, no longer worried about sassing. "We never touch guns."

The cop takes a drink of coffee but doesn't speak.

"Where is my brother?" Raul is crying now. "He will tell you. We never use guns."

"Damn, boy." The cop scratches his chin. "They puttin' stupid sauce on your tamale or what?"

"Please. Just ask Carlos." Raul wipes his cheek. Smeared blood stains his hand.

The cop opens the sack, drops the gun on the table.

"Don't worry," the cop says. "It's unloaded."

Raul stares at the weapon.

"This is a Smith and Wesson." The cop points to the revolver. "The one you and your brother used when y'all robbed them liquor stores."

Raul feels his stomach churn. The room looks like it's growing smaller.

"Maybe you could pick it up," the cop says. "That might jog your memory."

Raul doesn't move.

"G'on." The cop points to the weapon again. "Put it in your hand."

For some reason—maybe it's the officer's tone or the small-ness of the room or the fact that his brother is nowhere to be seen—Raul is more fearful now than when he was in the back of the police car.

He shakes his head. Tears stream down his cheeks.

"I need you to pick up the fucking gun, Rah-ool." The cop stands. "You don't want to make me mad."

Raul crosses his arms, hugs himself, head shaking.

The cop walks around the table, fists clenched.

Raul is trying to make himself small, when the door is flung open and a man in a blue uniform steps into the room.

"What in the hell is going on in here?" He looks at the cop with the pockmarked face.

The cop doesn't say anything.

"Is that a gun on the table?" The man in the uniform points to the battered revolver. "You brought a firearm into an inter-view room?"

"I'm in the middle of questioning a suspect." Pockmark points to the door. "Why don't you give us a little privacy until we're done?"

"The hell you say. A *suspect*?"

No one speaks. The feeling in the room is tense, but Raul is relieved to see the man in the uniform.

He is in his forties, with lots of ribbons and badges on his shirt. His hair is cut short like an army man. His Texas accent isn't as thick as Pockmark's.

More important, his eyes are not like those of the man with the scarred face. They are angry now, but they also appear to have a hint of kindness, of concern.

The man with the pockmarked face has eyes like a dead fish. Empty but scary, all at the same time.

"You're done now." The uniformed officer points to the door. "Get out."

Pockmark, with his dead eyes, stares at the officer for a moment. Then he says, "My boys ain't gonna take the fall for this."

"One of your *boys* shot an unarmed juvenile." The uniformed officer shakes his head. "There's gonna be hell to pay for that, and there's not a damn thing you can do about it."

# - CHAPTER FOUR -

I parked the Navigator in a gravel lot, underneath a billboard advertising discount lap-band surgery.

Cop bars. What an interesting concept.

Angry people with guns and badges, drinking.

One of the main watering holes for the Dallas PD was an ugly concrete building a few blocks down from the county jail. It was on a street that used to be named Industrial Boulevard but was now called Riverfront Drive in an effort to spur redevelopment of ugly concrete buildings.

Sam Browne's sat between a strip joint that featured dollar drink specials and a place called Jimmy's Bail Bonds and Title Loans.

The rebuilding push wasn't working so well on this section of Riverfront/Industrial.

Sixty minutes after Deputy Chief Raul Delgado disappeared down the Grassy Knoll, I pushed open the door to Sam Browne's and stepped into a narrow room that stunk of cigarettes and pine disinfectant.

Smoking is illegal in restaurants and taverns in Dallas, but hey, what are you gonna do, call the police?

I carried Tommy Joe's laptop in one hand. It wouldn't do to get it stolen from my SUV. Theo Goldberg would probably have an aneurism.

The bar was at the back, presided over by a cop whose real name nobody remembered since he'd opened a bar called Sam Browne's. Now everyone called him Sam.

The place had a couple of pool tables with some booths along one wall, tables in the middle, and a jukebox by the front. The decor was a combination of sports memorabilia and pictures of John Wayne being a Real American. The big-screen TV by the door was tuned to a rodeo, bull riding.

I let my eyes adjust to the darkness after the noon sun outside.

Maybe ten customers. A group of exceptionally fit men with long hair and beards—the narcs. Three or four uniformed cops at the bar, working on shots and beers, their faces flushed and veiny.

And a woman in a booth in the corner, sipping a cup of coffee.

She was in her early thirties, a willowy five foot eight.

Even though we'd known each other for years, the first glimpse of her face always managed to make my heart catch in my throat just a tiny bit.

Piper Westlake. Currently a sergeant with the Dallas police, assigned to the property unit, otherwise known as the "department they stick you in when they don't know what else to do with you."

The bartender nodded hello and kept polishing beer mugs.

I ignored the day drinkers and wandered over to where Piper sat. She looked up, a faint smile on her face.

"Shouldn't you be at work?" I slid into the opposite side of the booth.

She tapped a file folder. "I'm inventorying cold-case evidence boxes even as we speak."

"Fun."

"Beats watching bull humping on TV or whatever the hell they're showing."

Silence settled over the table for a few moments. Then:

"Did he ask about me?" She glanced up from her files.

I lied, shook my head.

Crowd noises from the TV. Something important happened at the rodeo. Maybe a bull started humping one of the cowboys. The uniformed cops at the bar let out whoops of encouragement.

Piper looked up again. "So. What did he want?"

Silence.

*He* would be Deputy Chief Raul Delgado.

"You want to get involved?" I asked.

"I'm making conversation. That's what people in polite society do."

Piper had eyes that were as blue as a spring sky and hair the color of wheat. Her features were attractive but possessed a haunted quality that was hard to define, like a fashion model weary from being on the lam for a murder she didn't commit.

"I don't want to get in the middle," I said. "You know, of whatever is going on between you and your boyfriend."

"He is *not* my boyfriend." Piper's voice raised a click higher than what was needed for a quiet conversation. She pushed the file away.

Deep inside both of us lay a wellspring of anger. We were the sum of our choices, a lifetime of bad decisions combined with actions beyond our control, events that had been thrust upon us.

Sam the bartender approached, wiping his hands on a rag.

"Everything okay over here?" he said.

Neither of us spoke for a moment.

"It's fine, Sam." Piper pulled the file back. Picked up her pen.

We were like gin and tonic, better together but a dangerous mix in certain circumstances. We could finish each other's sentences. Cover each other instinctively in a firefight. Know when to talk and when to remain silent.

"You doing okay, Jon?" Sam smiled. "Haven't seen you around in a while."

Sam had a gentle, kindhearted way about him that masked an innate ability to handle any situation. He was well into his seventies but had forearms like Popeye's.

A month ago I'd watched him toss two bikers out who were harassing an off-duty waitress from the Waffle House down the street. The bikers were forty years younger. He'd broken the nose of one of the men.

"Everything's peaches and cream, Sam." I tried to sound like I meant it. "You can go away now."

Piper sighed loudly and dropped her pen.

"Aw, c'mon, Jon." He shook his head. "Why you gotta be that way?"

I didn't say anything, more than a little ashamed that I'd let nothing turn into something.

"Spray a little more gas on the fire, why don't you." Piper shook her head. "Sam, it's all good. Really."

Sam mumbled under his breath but left.

After he was gone, Piper said, "Were you born an asshole or did you take lessons?"

"I'm doing well today, thanks for asking."

Piper drank some coffee.

"Your boyfriend wants to hire me to find a missing kid."

*"He's not my boyfriend."* She kept her voice to a whisper this time.

Piper had dated the deputy chief for a few months, a period of time punctuated with several breakups, as neither she nor Delgado were well suited to stable relationships. Not to imply that I was.

"Tremont Washington," I said. "That name mean anything to you?"

A police radio from the bar clanged, an alarm of some sort. Two uniformed officers paid their tab, lumbered to their feet, prepared to leave.

After they were gone, Piper looked at me. "Do you miss being a cop, Jon?"

I lied again. "No."

I missed the sense of belonging that came from wearing a blue uniform. But I'd feathered my own nest and there was no going back.

Piper pulled out a smartphone, tapped the screen a few times.

"A patrol unit entered the name Tremont Washington under its daily activity log," she said. "Note says, 'possible runaway.'"

A daily activity log was where the police kept a record of calls and actions that didn't warrant a formal police report. The log meant the responding officers didn't believe the caller or didn't care.

I removed a single sheet of paper from the envelope that Raul Delgado had given me. Tremont's physical description and address.

"He lives in West Dallas with his grandmother." I gave her the street and number.

She squinted at the screen. "Yeah, that's the address they used. The projects."

I nodded. "So why's a deputy chief interested in a kid from the hood?"

"He's a deputy chief," she said. "Everything the brass does is a riddle wrapped inside an enigma."

I folded the piece of paper Raul Delgado had given me and put it back in the envelope.

"Lysol Alvarez," Piper said. "That's his turf."

Lysol was a street thug who had the IQ and work ethic of an investment banker. At one point he controlled a large swath of South and West Dallas.

"He's still alive?"

"Hard to kill somebody that mean," she said. "I'd start with him."

Neither of us spoke for a few moments.

"I'm not asking for your help," I said.

"Then why did you come here?" She slid from the booth. Tossed a few bills on the table.

I watched her walk away. After a few steps she turned and looked at me.

"Don't be late this afternoon."

# - CHAPTER FIVE -

## THE PIMP

Tink-Tink Monroe surveys his empire.

A parking lot behind a two-story apartment building on Audelia Road by LBJ Freeway.

He stands on the balcony of the upstairs unit he's currently using as an office, a Swisher Sweet in one hand, a Schlitz Malt Liquor in the other.

A feeling of contentment washes over him. He is the master of his domain, the captain of his destiny. The King.

Life is good here in Dallas, so is business, much better than either had been in the Ninth Ward before Katrina blew through New Orleans.

Beyond the rotting wooden fence that surrounds the parking lot hums the commerce the city is known for, a ball of energy unlike any he's ever experienced in all his thirty-four years.

Even the air smells rich, a pleasant aroma that is a combination of the Popeyes Chicken next door and his cigar.

Tink-Tink Monroe is an entrepreneur, a man determined to escape his humble origins and make something of himself. He is the youngest of five children, his mother a working girl in one of the hot-sheet brothels in Algiers, across the river from the French Quarter. He never knew his father.

Now, he is the King.

In the parking lot of the Dallas apartment are six campers, registered under the name of his number-one lady's grandmother. Each trailer has a girl who's earning for him. Ten, twelve hours a day, six days a week.

Below his feet, on the ground floor, he has a half dozen two-bedroom apartments, a girl to each room. Across Audelia, there is a massage parlor that he controls, too. Another three or four girls there at any given time.

The Empire of Tink-Tink Monroe.

His ladies are quality, clean and healthy for the most part. A class operation all the way.

The word on the street is that he's the biggest pimp in Dallas, certainly the biggest in Little NOLA, as the area where the Katrina refugees have settled is called.

One of his guards steps onto the balcony. He says, "Pizza's here, boss."

Tink-Tink tosses his cigar onto the asphalt below. He points to the far end of the parking lot, where a navy-blue Crown Victoria sits nose-out, under a leafless elm tree.

"You see dat car ovah in da corner?"

The guard nods.

Tink-Tink drains his beer. "Find out who's parking in my parking lot wit'out axing me first."

"Yeah, boss." The guard grabs a baseball bat from the corner and leaves.

Tink-Tink pitches his empty beer can off the balcony, too, and steps inside the apartment.

The place doesn't have much furniture, a black leather couch from Rent-A-Center, a glass coffee table, and a flat-screen TV.

In the middle of the coffee table sits a pepperoni and sausage pizza from Mr. Gatti's—his favorite—and a cold Schlitz.

A girl perches on the armrest of the sofa. She's seventeen, pretty like a dancer in a Rihanna video, wearing a halter top and a pair of Daisy Duke shorts. One eye is still a little swollen.

He nods, happy to see everything where it should be. The bitch is learning. He's in the process of turning her out, but she's been all kinds of uppity.

"You got my change, girl?" He sits, opens the box.

"Right here, Daddy." She hurriedly hands him a wad of cash.

Tink-Tink puts the money in his pocket. Then he grabs a slice, sticks it in his mouth.

From the hallway leading to the front door, a figure emerges. A white guy in a black tracksuit with a ball cap, pulled low. The jacket is zipped up around the lower half of his face.

"The fuck do you want?" Tink-Tink wipes pizza grease from his chin.

His guards are just outside. They're fixing to be in a world of shit because Tink-Tink has told them about a zillion times not to let cats like this in without calling first.

"What happened to her face?" Whitey points to the girl.

She crosses her arms, nervous, looks to her pimp for guidance.

Tink-Tink puts the slice down. Nothing about this is right. With his elbow, he touches the nine-millimeter in his waistband, looking for a measure of comfort.

Whitey speaks to the girl. "Get out of here. Now."

She gulps, eyes wide with fear, but complies, scampering from the room. A few seconds later Tink-Tink hears the front door open.

Then he hears the girl scream.

Tink-Tink reaches for his weapon. "You're making a big mista—"

The gun appears in Whitey's hand out of nowhere, a pistol with a silencer on the muzzle.

"I got money," Tink-Tink says. "We can work sumpin' out."

The first bullet hits him in the stomach.

It feels like a two-by-four slammed into his gut. No pain, just a throbbing sensation. The taste of blood fills his mouth.

*"Noo."* He holds up one hand, grabs his nine-millimeter with the other.

The second round punches a hole in his palm. Light is visible through the wound.

Time seems to stop as Whitey pulls the trigger for the third time.

A blip of light, and a bullet that appears to be traveling so slowly Tink-Tink Monroe can track its progress as it moves toward his head.

He thinks about his mother and the empire he's created.

Then, everything is black.

# - CHAPTER SIX -

After meeting with Piper, I put in my weekly appearance at the Dallas headquarters of Goldberg, Finkelman, and Clark, a smartly decorated half-floor in a downtown skyscraper.

My office was a cramped six-by-ten, but it offered a stunning view of the southern half of the city. Fair Park and the Cotton Bowl lay twenty stories below, pale smudges surrounded by a green tarmac of vegetation. A gauzy layer of gray haze blanketed everything.

No one paid me any attention. My supervisor/boss, such as Theo Goldberg was, lived a half continent away. Everyone in the Dallas office gave me a wide berth.

I left the laptop with the managing partner's assistant, told him to overnight it to DC. Then I got a cup of coffee, sat at my desk, and looked through the mail, most of which was junk or related to my current employment, such as a statement for my 401(k) account.

After dispensing with the mail, I perused various databases, looking for mention of Tremont Washington.

Nothing, as I expected. Tremont had no criminal record, no driver's license or other form of state-issued ID. He was in the Social Security database as receiving disability payments, the checks going to his grandmother's address—information I already had.

I closed my computer and stared out the window, enjoying the view.

The phone on my desk rang, startling me.

That phone never rang. I was still getting used to having one there. Heck, I was still getting used to having a desk.

It was the receptionist.

"Mr., uh, Cantrell?"

Her voice was timid, like she didn't know how to handle talking to that strange man in the little office.

"Yes."

"This is Carolyn at the front." She was whispering now.

"Hi, Carolyn-at-the-front. What's up?"

"There's a man here to see you."

"That's not good, Carolyn. People don't come to see me. It's the other way around."

"He says his name is Tommy Joe." She paused, lowered her voice further. "And he's really, um, scary."

"Call security, Carolyn. And then tell him I'm not here."

"Uh, Mr. Cantrell . . . you are the number for security."

I slumped in my chair. "Okay, I'll be right out."

The reception area for Goldberg, Finkelman, and Clark was wood-paneled like an English gentlemen's club. Leather chairs, Persian rugs, the occasional painting of a fox being killed.

Tommy Joe stood by a coffee table. He'd changed clothes. He was now wearing a pair of ratty jeans and a gray T-shirt. His face was drawn and pale. His Super Bowl ring was gone.

I approached him warily, arms loose.

He watched me get closer, eyes blank.

From the corridor behind the reception area, several attorneys had come out, the office grapevine evidently telling them there might be something worth seeing about to go down.

I stopped about five feet away from Tommy Joe.

"What do you want?"

Tommy Joe reached for his back pocket.

"Don't move your arms." I stepped closer. "Or I'll break them."

The distance between us could be cleared in about a half second. If he had a weapon, I planned to grab it with one hand, leverage his elbow with the other. Wait for the cracking sound. Then throw him to the ground.

That would neutralize the problem and give everybody a good show.

He stopped, licked his lips. "It's just a piece of paper."

"Turn around," I said. "Slowly."

He did as requested. No telltale bulge in any pocket or under his shirt.

"Two fingers only," I said. "Take the paper out."

He pulled a folded sheet from his pocket and put it on the coffee table.

"You're gonna want this, too," he said.

"What is it?"

"I'm going to rehab."

"Good for you."

"Everything I touch, it turns to shit." He rubbed his nose.

I picked up the paper. It contained an address in North Dallas, what looked like a commercial building.

"I don't want this on me, too." He pointed to the paper.

"What does that mean?"

"They're waiting for me downstairs." He shuffled to the door and left.

I slipped the paper in my pocket and turned around.

A small group of attorneys and support personnel were standing in the hall watching me.

My sport coat felt tight and the paneled walls of the reception area seemed to be closing in.

They were staring at me like an exhibit at the zoo, the strange guy who wasn't a lawyer, the one with the hard eyes and impassive face. I was exotic, outside the bell curve of their experience.

I didn't belong here and everyone knew it. I ignored them all and went to my office.

———

*Dallas police headquarters*
*1981*

The police officer with the kind eyes and the ribbons on his chest leads eleven-year-old Raul Delgado from the interview room.

He takes him down a hallway full of other officers, hard-looking men wearing short-brimmed cowboy hats and guns on their hips. The air in the hall smells like cigarette smoke, coffee, and sweat.

The men move aside and watch them go by. They don't speak.

Raul can't be sure but he feels like they are angry with him for some reason. He doesn't understand why.

The officer with the kind eyes leads him to a tiled room with rows and rows of lockers and a large shower area in the corner. The room appears empty.

He goes to a locker, opens the door, and pulls out a gray sweat suit.

"You're gonna have to roll the sleeves and cuffs up, but these'll fit you pretty good."

Raul nods, understanding that the man is offering him a chance to change out of his pee-soaked pants and blood-spattered shirt.

"You should take a shower, too," the man says.

Raul looks at the dark corner where the faucets sprout from the wall like silver tree limbs. It is an open area, no privacy.

"Nobody's gonna bother you," the man says. "I cleared everybody out."

Raul nods.

"I'll stay outside, guard the door." The man smiles.

A question forms in Raul's mind, but he is afraid to ask. Instead he just stands there, staring at the officer's ribbons and medals.

The man says, "Your name's Raul, right?"

"Yes." Raul nods, glad the man doesn't pronounce it like a redneck.

"My name is Bobby." He holds out his hand. "Nice to meet you, Raul."

They shake. The officer's skin is rough like wood that needs to be painted.

"I'm a lieutenant with the Dallas Police Department." Bobby hitches a thumb in his gun belt. "Back there, in the interview room. I'm sorry about that."

Raul swallows several times. After a few moments, he says, "Carlos. My brother. Where is he?"

Bobby's face is expressionless. He waits for a long while before speaking. Then:

"Your mother had a seizure or something when she heard."

Raul clutches his stomach.

"She's gonna be all right," Bobby says. "But she's in the hospital."

Raul shakes his head, trying to will away the bad news.

"Trouble is, we can't find your daddy nowhere."

The room is silent for a moment.

"Carlos," Raul says. "Where is my brother, Carlos?"

More silence.

Raul scratches his arm like he always does when he's extra nervous.

"You need to understand something." Bobby sits on a bench so they're eye to eye. "Lot a people in this department want to blame what happened on you and your brother."

"I don't understand."

"They're gonna say you were armed. You were a threat to the two officers who had you in the car."

Raul struggles to catch his breath, his words jumbled. "We—we—we were just trying to have fun. We weren't trying to h-hurt anybody."

Bobby nods like he understands. Then he grabs the boy's hand and says, "Quit scratching yourself, son. You're bleeding."

Raul looks at his arm. His nails have rubbed a raw patch. Blood seeps from the skin.

"I gotta ask you something." Bobby's voice is soft.

Raul stares at the man blankly, chest heaving.

"In the back of the police car," Bobby says. "Did you have a gun with you?"

Raul shakes his head.

"Did you take that money from the store?"

Raul hesitates. Then he nods.

"Stealing's wrong, son. Don't you know that?"

"I—I'm sorry." Raul wipes tears from his cheek. He is truly sorry. He doesn't want to disappoint this man.

Raul scratches the raw patch on his arm again.

"Quit that now, all right?" Bobby pulls his hand away. "That ain't gonna bring Carlos back."

Raul frowns, trying to make sense of the man's words.

"You should get cleaned up." Bobby points to the showers. "Your mama needs you."

"What did you say about my brother?" Raul raises his hands, trying to deflect the message that is coming right at him like a bowling ball. "Carlos—where is Carlos?"

Silence in the locker room except for the drip of a shower-head in the corner.

"Aw, son. I'm sorry." Bobby pats Raul's shoulder. "You're brother, he's dead."

The weight of the universe seems to catch in Raul Delgado's throat. His skin becomes icy, his stomach hollow. He shivers once and falls to his knees, weeping.

The reason for the flash of light and the ringing in his ears becomes clear, as does the enormity of what has occurred.

His brother is gone.

A wall plants itself into his mind, dividing his life into two separate but unequal halves.

Before Carlos, and after.

He cries and cries as Bobby pats his shoulder and tries to comfort him.

# - CHAPTER SEVEN -

At 5:01 p.m. I walked into a windowless office in the Preston Center section of North Dallas, a small suite of rooms decorated like a girl's bedroom in a 1950s romantic comedy—lace and doilies and overstuffed chairs, everything frilly and pink.

Preston Center was in the geographical center of North Dallas—ritzy shops, expensive high-rises, swanky restaurants. A former president officed a couple of blocks away.

In a room behind a small reception area, four white leather chairs circled a coffee table, exactly equidistant from each other, no one position superior to the other. On the coffee table, three bottles of water bracketed a box of facial tissue.

Piper sat in one of the chairs. Otherwise, the room was empty.

"You're late," she said.

"It's barely five o'clock."

Piper opened one of the waters but didn't speak.

"Where's Corinne?" I sat across from her.

Corinne was a psychologist in private practice. She had a contract with the Veterans Administration to provide counseling services to former members of the armed forces.

Here are a few facts that are important to know at this juncture:

Corinne specialized in couple's counseling. Her contract with the feds stipulated that she would treat only vets and their spouses.

Piper and I were not a couple. Also, in the eyes of the government, we were no longer regarded as vets.

If Piper and I stopped seeing Corinne, we'd go to prison.

A sticky wicket, as the Brits say.

We sat in silence for a few moments, neither of us knowing what to say. Introspection: not our long suit.

"So, how was your afternoon?" I said finally.

Piper clenched her fists, blinked several times.

"What? I'm just making polite conversation."

"Always pushing my buttons, Jon. That's a great way to start therapy."

"Therapy?" I looked around the office. "This is a boondoggle, remember?"

Piper and I were former government freelancers, private law-enforcement contractors at one time employed by the DEA. At the end of our tenure as narcotics agents, we'd committed a small number of felonies, most of which were the result of our efforts to stay alive. Our trouble at the time sprang from a series of greater felonies being committed by men hiding behind the thin veil separating the federal government and corporate America.

When the dust had cleared and the prosecutors were looking for somebody to charge, they'd trained their sights on us.

After much discussion at the Department of Justice, a decision was reached, one that was a quintessential mess of bureaucratic compromise.

We would not be prosecuted if we entered into counseling for an unspecified period.

The benefits package made available to us only provided for "relationship therapy sessions"—even though we'd barely been in what could've been called a "relationship" at the time of the activities that had resulted in this boondoggle, and certainly weren't now—and then only at a select few counselors. I could have used the insurance provided by my current employer but none of their mental-health providers were on the DOJ's approved list.

There was no way we could afford to pay for our own therapy, so like many a good American, we adapted our situation to fit the available insurance. If we needed to pose as a couple to get out of this particular mess, we would do so.

Ergo, our current meeting.

The door on the far side of the room opened and Corinne entered.

Corinne was in her midthirties. She wore a tweed skirt and black lace-up shoes. She had the air of one who enjoyed a good game of softball back in her college days.

She greeted us and sat down.

"How are things this week?" Her voice was soft and soothing.

Piper snorted.

I said, "Things are fine."

"Piper, you seem to have something you want to say." Corinne leaned forward, all earnest.

"No." Piper glared at me. "Things are . . . fine."

Piper's record had actually been cleared, which was why she was able to get a job with the Dallas Police Department. I had something of a more checkered past, so law enforcement was out of the question for me. That's when Goldberg, Finkelman, and Clark had found me. They didn't care about my past. They cared about results.

Corinne scribbled some notes.

I yawned, tried to look interested.

"How is everyone sleeping?" Corinne looked at each of us in turn.

Neither Piper nor I trusted the confidentiality of any health care professional, especially when it came to some of the more unseemly issues we'd dealt with. So we spoke in circles, talked in code and double entendres, which I suppose people who really are in therapy do as well.

One thing we did talk about openly was our sleeping or lack thereof. The insomnia was worse when we were apart, which was all the time now.

"In your bedroom," Corinne said. "Have you removed the TV like we talked about?"

At the same time, Piper said "No" while I said "Yes."

Corinne arched an eyebrow.

"I took the TV out," I said, "but Piper brought it back."

Corinne nodded thoughtfully.

"I tried to implement a sleep-friendly environment," I said innocently. "Like you suggested we do."

Piper stared at the floor, lips pursed, venom dripping from her pores.

Corinne tapped a pen on her knee. "Piper, is the television more important than getting a good night's sleep?" A long pause. "Or your relationship with Jon?"

"I like to watch those true-crime shows." She cut her eyes toward me. "Especially the ones where the wife kills the husband."

Corinne stopped tapping, a surprised look on her face. She quickly regained her composure and jotted something down.

I tried to keep from laughing. Piper hated TV.

No one spoke. The silence stretched out, a few seconds became a minute or more.

Finally Corinne flipped through her notes. "How are the nightmares, Jon?" She glanced up. "Are you still dreaming about your father's death?"

I didn't speak. Piper looked away, sipped water.

Corinne leaned forward. "Jon? Do you still dream about your father's death?"

I shook my head.

In the dream, which came every time I slept, my father and I are walking down a narrow street at night, the asphalt glistening from rain. We have no destination. At the end of the street a fire burns brightly in an oil drum. We keep walking but never get closer. Blocks and blocks go by, and I realize my father is bleeding from a gunshot wound, and I am holding the weapon in my hand. That's when I wake up sweating, tangled in the sheets, unable to go to sleep again.

Corinne gave me a tiny nod that said *I know you're lying but I'm not going to push it now.* Then she turned to Piper.

"How is Jon around the house these days?" she said.

"All he does is watch westerns on cable," Piper said. "*Bonanza* and *The Big Valley* for Pete's sake, and drinks beer until he passes out."

"How would you know?" I said. "You're always at work."

I hated westerns. Drank two beers a month, maybe.

Corinne wrote something down.

"And you never shut up about your boss," I said.

Piper took a quick breath, nostrils flaring. Corinne didn't seem to notice.

"Raul this, Raul that." I arched an eyebrow. "If our relationship wasn't so rock solid, I might be jealous."

Piper scratched her face with her middle finger.

"Jon, let's talk about your drinking," Corinne said. "How many alcoholic beverages do you consume each day?"

"I usually have some gin with my cornflakes. After that it's a blur."

Corinne steepled her fingers. "Admitting you have a problem is the first step toward fixing it."

I sighed, looked at my watch, anxious to leave even though I had nowhere to be.

"Our hour is not finished yet," Corinne said.

I tried to relax. We sat in silence for a long while.

Finally, Corinne asked Piper about her "kids."

Piper, an orphan, collected parentless children as a hobby-slash-form of self-therapy. Dozens of them, maybe more. She sponsored war orphans in the Balkans, the offspring of AIDS victims in Africa, street urchins in South America. Pictures of the children served as bonding substitutes, adorning the walls of her living space. She sent presents to each and every one for holidays and birthdays.

It was sweet and endearing and just a little bit crazy.

Piper and Corinne talked about her orphans for a period of time. Then our session was over. Corinne smiled and said she looked forward to seeing us next time.

Piper and I left together. We walked silently down the hall.

In the elevator, we were alone.

I pushed the button for the ground floor, turned, faced Piper.

"I put some feelers out for this Tremont kid," she said. "You go down to West Dallas, be careful, okay?"

I nodded.

She slid into my arms, tilted her face toward mine, and kissed me. We stayed that way, intertwined, lips together, until the door opened in the lobby.

"I'm sorry, Jon."

"For what?"

"We always seem to be on different pages."

I mentally conceded the point.

Back when we were together, if one of us wanted to stay at home, the other wanted to go out. She liked zombie movies; I preferred comedies. The only time we came together emotionally, thinking and operating as a single unit, was when our backs were to the wall. But if you built a relationship on seeking out danger so two could be as one, then neither would live very long.

"At least we're in the same book," I said.

She stared at me for a moment and then darted from the elevator.

# - CHAPTER EIGHT -

Mason Burnett debated the tools at hand: an ASP retractable baton or the more traditional billy club.

The gangbanger with the teardrop tattoos on his face stood before him at the foot of the swayback bed, arms crossed, giving Mason the stink eye.

They were in the second-floor bedroom of a boardinghouse a few blocks south of Jefferson Boulevard in Oak Cliff. One of Mason's SWAT officers stood in the doorway, keeping any curious residents at bay.

The gangbanger's stink eye demonstrated a lack of respect, something that Captain Mason Burnett had never put up with during his long career.

"You hablo English?" Mason decided to go with the billy club. It became a classic for a reason.

"Whatchoo want with me, homes?" The gangbanger was about twenty-five. His skin was the color of roasted walnuts, greasy black hair held down by a bandana tied around his head.

"The *botánica* on Jefferson," Mason said. "You hit it?"

The boardinghouse was old, built in the 1940s, wood-framed. The windows were open since there was no air-conditioning, and the warm air wafting through the room did little to cut the smell of marijuana and stale sweat. This odor was preferable to the stench of urine and mold in the hallway.

"What the fuck is this?" Gangbanger looked at the man in the door and then back to Mason. "You guys aren't real cops. You're dressed like soldiers or some shit."

"We're SWAT," Mason said. "And yeah, we are real cops."

"I want my lawyer." The hood cocked his head to one side. "You feel me, mister SWAT man?"

Mason popped him in the forehead with the end of the billy club. Not a hard blow, just enough to get his attention.

The hood swayed on his feet but didn't fall.

"The fuck you doing?" He rubbed his skull.

"Who you banging with?" Mason asked. "Is it gonna be old homie week when you go back to the joint?"

The tats on the hood's arms indicated he was affiliated with an offshoot of the Mexican Mafia, or La Eme, originally a prison gang.

The hood shook his head several times, blinking, clearly trying to focus. After a moment, he appeared to recover. He gave Mason a sneer and a hand sign—thumb, index, and middle finger pointed down.

"You do that again, I'll break your fingers off and grind 'em up into taco meat."

Mason tried to look as angry as he sounded. Despite being a clusterfuck, the chief's new anti-crime initiative—putting SWAT officers in high-crime areas—was actually pretty fun. He was on the street, busting up punks like the old days.

The hood shook his head. "I ain't robbed no *botánica.*"

Mason sighed. He was having a grand time rousting beaners, but this particular incidence, the aggravated robbery of a *botánica,* was causing him something of a dilemma. *Botánicas* were stores that sold herbs and potions for use in Santeria rituals and other voodoo mumbo jumbo. In Mason's mind, if a store that sold devil shit got robbed, who really cared?

Unfortunately, the owner was injured during the course of the robbery, which meant Mason and his people had to act like they gave a shit. Also, a video camera at a nearby business had a pretty clear image of the suspect, a punk who looked a lot like the gangbanger with the teardrop tattoos.

"The old guy at the *botánica,*" Mason said. "You busted him up pretty bad. Why'd you gotta go and do that, huh?"

"Voodoo shit they sell there," the hood said. "Gives me the creeps, yo."

"You broke his arm."

Gangbanger shrugged, an indifferent look on his face.

A quarter century on the force, Mason Burnett knew an admission of guilt when he saw one.

"I didn't break nothing," Gangbanger said. "Didn't rob nothing neither."

Mason swung his club, striking the hood just above the elbow on the arm he'd raised to protect himself. Mason used more force this time, and the hood fell back on the bed, clutching the arm and bellowing.

From the doorway came the sound of a police radio, a voice asking for Mason's location. Mason looked at his SWAT guy and nodded an okay. Then he turned his attention back to the hood.

"Where's the money . . . *homes*?" He swatted the gangbanger in his kidney with the club.

"Leave me alone." The hood was frantic. "I'm not resisting or nothing."

"Here's how it's gonna go, ass-munch." Mason grabbed the man's ear, pulled him from the bed. "You don't tell me about the robbery, I'm gonna rip off your head and skull-fuck you."

*"Owww."* The gangbanger scrambled to follow Mason as he was pulled toward the windows.

The street was narrow, lined with other old homes, junker cars, and unkempt yards. Mason's Suburban was parked in front near a pair of SWAT officers milling about.

A similar Suburban turned the corner, idled down the street, and stopped behind Mason's.

Raul Delgado got out.

What in the hell? The appearance of Commander Warm-and-Fuzzy sent a spike of anger surging through Mason's system.

"Where's the money?" Mason walked the hood toward the largest of the open windows.

"Fucking-a, man. You're gonna pull my ear off."

"No. You weren't listening. I'm gonna pull your head off," Mason said. "Or you can tell me where the money is."

The man was by the open window now, the backs of his knees pressed against the sill.

"Alright-alright-alright. The cash is in the closet." He pointed to a door in the corner.

Out the window Mason could see Raul Delgado talking to his officers. Why the hell was a deputy chief on the street any-way? Trying to get in touch with his *people* or some shit, no doubt.

In the bedroom, Mason's SWAT guy opened the closet and pulled out a paper bag. He looked inside and then nodded to Mason.

"Please," the gangbanger said. "Let go of my ear."

"Okay." Mason did as requested.

The gangbanger sighed in relief, rubbed the side of his head.

Mason gave the hood's chest a hard shove and watched him tumble out the window.

Screams followed by the sounds of branches breaking from the hedges lining the building.

Mason leaned over the windowsill and looked down, a feeling of satisfaction welling in his chest. The gangbanger lay in a tangle of twisted limbs and broken branches. He was clearly alive but not in the best of shape. Probably wouldn't get to play on the prison basketball team or anything.

Deputy Chief Delgado was staring up at Mason, aghast.

"Hello, Rah-ool." Mason smiled. *"Cómo estás?"*

Delgado hated when people mispronounced his name. It was also a breach of protocol to not address him by rank in this type of circumstance. Which was why Mason did both.

"What the hell happened here, Captain Burnett?" Delgado called up to him.

"Suspect appeared to be high on angel dust. Thought he could fly." Mason shook his head. "What a dumbass."

Delgado pulled a two-way radio from his belt, called for an ambulance.

"We're all okay, by the way," Mason said. "No officers were hurt."

Delgado stared at him for a long moment.

"In case you were wondering," Mason said.

Below him the gangbanger groaned and tried to roll out of the bushes.

# - CHAPTER NINE -

After the DOJ-mandated counseling session with Piper, I bought some tacos at a place on Mockingbird Lane and headed toward White Rock Lake in the eastern section of the city.

The wind had picked up as the day had waned, and the surface of the lake rippled, a blanket of tiny waves that glistened in the afternoon sun like so many shards of broken glass.

Jogging trails surrounded the lake, a thin ribbon filled with young, attractive people walking and running.

Beyond the trails lay a series of expensive homes owned by people who sought a view of the lake and the illusion of coolness that the proximity to water provided.

I turned into the driveway of a large stucco home, an old Spanish colonial with whitewashed walls and arched windows.

The structure sat atop a bluff, overlooking a lawn the size of three or four football fields. I steered the Lincoln up the gravel drive, parking in front of the house next to a late-model Toyota Camry. A large Ford van with handicap plates was in the attached garage.

Up close, the home appeared in a state of mild disrepair, like the owner had lost interest. The tiles on the front patio were cracked, missing in a few spots. Weeds filled the flower beds. Grass spiked through the rocks in the driveway.

I got out—the container of tacos under an arm—took the steps two at a time, then rang the bell to one side of the carved wooden door.

A few moments later the door opened and a woman in her late twenties appeared. She was maybe five foot six, pretty like the hostess at a mall restaurant. She wore a caregiver's uniform—baggy white pants, matching top, and a pair of Nike running shoes.

"You must be Jonathan," she said. "I've heard a lot about you."

"You're the new nurse?"

"The agency sent me over a couple of weeks ago." She stepped to one side. "Please, come in."

I entered the foyer. Terrazzo tile covered the floor. The plaster walls were the color of old bones. The air smelled like a hospital—rubbing alcohol and disinfectant.

"The judge is in the parlor." She took the tacos off my hands and pointed to a cavernous room to one side of the entryway.

Bradshaw Landis Clark, the third named partner at Goldberg, Finkelman, and Clark.

He was a descendant of a man who arrived in Texas with Stephen F. Austin in the 1830s, one of the original settlers of the state. Retired from the federal bench ten years ago after a drunk driver hit his Jaguar head-on and left him paralyzed from the waist down. He'd been with Goldberg and Finkelman ever since.

Judge Clark sat in his wheelchair by the front window, staring at the lake.

He was in his midsixties, hair thick and gray, left long so it brushed the collar of his shirt.

"Hello, Jonathan." He spoke without turning around.

"I brought dinner. Tacos." I sat in an easy chair by the window. "*Carnitas* and *barbacoa*."

The view was spectacular but sad at the same time, considering the condition of the man in the wheelchair. Sailboats slicing through the scalloped waves, people running along the jogging trails, others riding their bikes. Judge Clark had been a marathoner and a mountain climber until his accident.

"I wasn't expecting you." He cut his gaze my way.

His eyes were unblinking, a deadpan expression perfected after twenty years on the bench.

"I was in the neighborhood."

Before becoming a judge, Clark had defended my father, a sheriff in a nearby county, against charges of drug trafficking. He'd been a family friend and mentor ever since.

"You want a drink?" I stood, walked to the bar on the far wall.

Clark didn't reply.

I took that as a yes and poured two fingers of Glenlivet into a crystal highball. No ice, no water. I returned to the window and handed him the glass.

"How is everything at the office?" he said.

I shrugged but didn't speak.

Clark took a sip of scotch. After a few moments, I told him about Tommy Joe Culpepper. I didn't say anything about the lawyers clustered around the hallway, watching me. That didn't matter, however. The judge could read between my lines.

"The other people at the firm," Clark said. "You think they don't like you, don't you?"

I didn't say anything. I'd given up a long time ago caring what other people thought about me.

"That's because they need you but don't want to admit it." He paused. "And because of that, they fear you."

We were silent for a while.

"Do you know who Raul Delgado is?" I told him briefly about my meeting with the deputy chief and his request that I locate the missing teenager, Tremont Washington.

"Thirty years later, I still remember the TV reports." Clark grimaced. "Little Raul Delgado, his face covered in his brother's blood."

"What do you think he wants with a kid from West Dallas?" I said.

"Everything he does is for one reason." Clark swirled the scotch around his glass.

"And that would be?"

"He wants to wipe away the blood and bring his brother back."

"How about in the short term?" I said. "Like, say, in this lifetime."

Clark drained his glass. "He has a future in politics. People talk about him running for mayor. Or even governor."

I stared out the window. That was more than enough reason for Theo Goldberg, my boss and the managing partner of the firm, to want eyes and ears on the man.

"He's a charismatic person," Clark said. "Plus he's Hispanic, which fits the current demographic shift in Texas nicely."

"And he's an underdog." I nodded thoughtfully.

"Risen from circumstances that would have broken lesser men," Clark said. "Embraced the very organization that destroyed his family."

"Like a made-for-TV movie."

Clark chuckled.

Before I could say anything else, the nurse entered the room, carrying two plates of tacos. She'd changed into Lycra running shorts and a skintight tank top that stopped just above her belly button. Her stomach was ripped, a sinewy six-pack.

"Anybody hungry?" She handed us each a plate.

Judge Clark and I sat in silence, staring at her.

"I'm gonna take a run." She tapped a rectangular bulge between her hip bone and shorts. "I've got my phone with me if you need anything."

She left. We watched her stretch on the front patio, then jog down the driveway.

"Where do you get nurses like that?" I said.

"My friend owns the agency." Clark craned his neck to follow her progress. "He supplies employees who fit certain criteria that I specify."

"Doesn't that drive you nuts? Since—" I didn't finish the sentence.

*Since you can only look.*

"And how is Piper?" Clark picked up a taco. "Speaking of things that drive me nuts."

The judge hated Piper. Thought her crass and uncouth. Which she was, bless her heart.

I took a bite of my food.

"Why don't you stay the night?" he said. "The upstairs guest room is made up."

I was renting a townhome in North Dallas. A one-bedroom unit decorated with a big-screen TV and a plastic ficus tree. All the modern conveniences, but an empty abode.

"We could take a drive," he said.

I could smell the loneliness in his voice.

"Sure, I'll shack here tonight." I smiled.

The least I could do. The man had saved me from prison.

———

*Dallas, Texas*
*1984*

Three years after the racist cop blew his brother's head off, Raul Delgado, fourteen years old, again found himself in a squad car, this time in the front passenger side.

He was not handcuffed.

And this was not his first time in this particular vehicle. But today the texture of the vinyl seats and the crackle of the radio brought back unpleasant memories of that summer afternoon when everything about his life changed.

Bobby, the lieutenant with the kind eyes, was driving. Bobby's eyes weren't very kind right now. They were angry.

They'd spent a lot of time together these past few years, and Raul knew Bobby as well as any person he'd ever met, maybe even better than his brother or mother. Raul saw anger in the man, but he also saw sadness draped over him.

But mostly there was the anger.

They were leaving the fairgrounds just east of downtown Dallas.

It was October and the state fair was in session.

Carny barkers on the midway, stuffed animals for prizes, roller-coaster rides, and a giant Ferris wheel. People having fun.

Bobby drove down a pedestrian esplanade past the booths selling corny dogs and cotton candy. The squad-car lights were on, flashing red and blue, but the siren was off.

Fairgoers moved out of their way, staring at the squad car that contained a gringo cop in his forties and a teenage Hispanic boy riding with his arms crossed and a scowl on his face.

Raul wished he gave a shit how Bobby felt, like he used to, but he didn't.

He still liked him—the man saved Raul from those in the DPD who would have crucified an eleven-year-old boy for merely being a Mexican American—but he realized Bobby was also part of the problem.

Bobby worked for an organization of oppression, according to speakers Raul had heard at the Chicano Liberation Center on Oak Lawn Avenue. The Dallas Police Department was a tool of the white man, designed to enforce the imperialist policies of the federal government.

Why everyone didn't acknowledge this was beyond Raul Delgado's comprehension. It was all so clear if you knew where to look.

"You really stepped in it this time," Bobby said.

Raul didn't speak.

"Nearly broke that boy's jaw."

Raul pointedly turned away from his mentor and stared out the passenger window.

"You wanna tell me why?" Bobby stopped to let a woman push a stroller across the esplanade.

A few moments passed.

Raul said, "He called me a wetback."

The boy whose jaw might or might not be broken—Raul didn't really care one way or the other—was from North Dallas, the most racist part of the city. He was a symbol of all that is wrong with the system. The boy was a *preppy*. Dressed in a pink knit shirt with a tiny lizard on the breast, khaki pants, Top-Sider boat shoes.

The preppy had been a few years older than Raul. He'd been drunk, of course. Many gringos had issues with alcohol, according to the books Raul had read.

The problem started when the preppy had made a remark about Raul's Che Guevara T-shirt, and Raul had decided to teach him a lesson.

"If more Chicanos stood up for themselves," Raul said, "then perhaps the mistreatment of my people will lessen."

"Your people?" Bobby cut his eyes to the passenger seat.

"The Latino has been denied a place at the table." Raul tried to keep his voice from rising. "Texas was settled by Chicanos hundreds of years before the white man came."

Bobby sighed. "Son, I'm all for you getting in touch with your roots—"

"Then why did they stop me?"

"Aw, c'mon." Bobby shook his head. "They had to stop you."

Raul didn't reply.

"You were beating that kid's ass into the ground," Bobby said. "Has nothing to do with you being Mexican."

The Dallas police maintained a large presence during the state fair. Several officers had pulled Raul away from the preppy kid before he could do any permanent damage. The officers had learned Raul's name and knew enough to call Bobby.

Bobby was an important figure in the Dallas Police Department, and he had made it known that if anything concerning Raul Delgado occurred, he was to be notified immediately.

This fact infuriated Raul for several reasons.

One, he was nearly fifteen and perfectly capable of taking care of himself.

Two, Bobby was a kind, decent man and should not be working for an organization of oppression.

And last but certainly not least, the motherfucking Dallas Police Department killed his brother.

Bobby said, "You got to let the anger go, son. It'll eat you up if you're not careful."

"I am not your son." Raul spoke the words with icy deliberation.

Bobby didn't reply. He continued driving.

Raul's father had been deported. His mother was an invalid. A stroke felled her when she'd heard the news about her eldest child, Carlos. She was cared for by the extended family in their neighborhood in Little Mexico.

Raul pretty much came and went as he pleased, very little adult supervision.

Except for Bobby.

Raul was sorry for what he'd just said to the man, the way he was treating him. For the past three years Bobby had been a constant in his life—taking him to school, buying him clothes and little gifts, coming by to make sure he was doing okay.

They left the fairgrounds, and Bobby turned off the squad lights. They were on Haskell Avenue, a street of dingy bars, washaterias, and pawnshops.

Bobby used the radio to notify dispatch that he was going to get some lunch.

Raul had spent so much time in the company of police officers, Bobby and his friends, he recognized the codes and even the dispatcher's voice.

"You want to get some pancakes?"

Raul didn't reply.

It was early afternoon. Bobby was a big fan of breakfast, didn't matter the time of day. Something about working deep nights during his early years on the force. He knew all the good places that were open twenty-four hours.

After a moment, Raul shrugged and nodded.

Bobby turned the squad car toward downtown and drove for a few blocks without speaking. Then he said, "I won't be around forever—you know that, don't you?"

"What do you mean?" Raul felt a flash of fear. "Are you sick?"

"'Course not. I'm as healthy as a horse." Bobby turned on Ross Avenue. "I mean I'm gonna retire at some point."

Raul nodded like he understood the implications of this statement.

"That means I won't always be around to look out for you."

Raul turned away. He stared out the passenger-side window at the buildings of downtown. His eyes welled with tears, and he didn't understand why.

"You need to make peace with the Dallas Police Department," Bobby said. "And whatever else is eating you up inside."

Raul wiped his cheek. He hoped Bobby hadn't noticed the tears.

They were in the heart of downtown now, amid the towering office buildings.

With a start, Raul realized where they were headed.

A smile creased his face.

"Junie gets outa school early today," Bobby said. "Thought she might like some pancakes, too."

Junie was Bobby's daughter, his only child. Twelve years old, the apple of her widower father's eye. She had auburn hair and a spunky temperament. Both Raul and Bobby doted on her, just in different ways.

Bobby headed toward her school, and for a moment Raul felt the anger go away, as if everything was right in the world once again.

## - CHAPTER TEN -

I drove the judge around White Rock Lake in the handicap van, the windows down. The activity appeared to please him. When we returned, Clark had another splash of scotch in his living room and regaled me with stories of Dallas in the 1980s, a time rife with cocaine, discos, big-haired women, and rampant over-building of commercial real estate.

Then my beeper beeped.

Theo Goldberg. My boss. Clark's partner.

I pulled my battery from one pocket, the phone from another.

Clark excused himself so I could speak in private. He wheeled off to find his nurse.

Theo answered immediately. In the background, I could hear the zing-zing of a video game. I imagined him in a sub-urban family room, a large area decorated with pictures of his kids, somewhere in Alexandria or McLean.

"Everything go okay today?" he asked. "The thing this after-noon. We're good, right?"

"The item is on its way back to you."

A woman's voice, his wife I presumed, telling the kids it was time to go to bed.

I looked at my watch. It was nine thirty on the East Coast.

"I heard the contractor came by the office this afternoon," Theo said.

"Yes. Nothing serious, though."

A rubbing noise, fabric on the mouthpiece. Then Theo's muffled voice: "Isaac! Do not stick that in the wall plug!"

A crashing sound. Theo swore.

"Everything okay?" I asked.

"The nanny, she accidentally doubled his dose of Ritalin." He sighed. "Don't have children, Jonathan. The little devils eat your soul."

I waited.

"What did he want?"

"Who?" I said. "Tommy Joe?"

"Does everyone in Texas have two names?"

"Only royalty."

Another crashing sound.

"He was on his way to rehab, and not a minute too soon. He gave me a piece of paper with an address on it," I said. "Told me something about how he didn't want that bothering him, too."

An intake of air on the other end of the line.

"Bad news?" I asked.

"The deputy director was on vacation."

"I'm not following."

"His administrative assistant placed an order while he was gone. A mistake. Drop-shipped to Tommy Joe Culpepper at that address."

"What was in the order?" I said.

"An equipment package." He paused. "For a new FOB."

I rubbed my eyes.

The Border Patrol, the department Tommy Joe had been doing business with, fell under the purview of the Department of Immigration and Customs Enforcement and had developed a novel strategy to combat illegal border crossings in remote areas. They set up a series of FOBs, forward operating bases.

These were self-contained defensive units—forts—designed for the military where Border Patrol agents could live and work for extended periods.

The FOBs themselves were modular buildings, modern-day Quonset huts. They were heavily fortified with bulletproof yet ultralight materials—tactical-grade carbon fibers and blast-resistant ceramics, polymers developed by NASA. The buildings were dropped in by chopper or transported by eighteen-wheeler. They were supplied by private companies, as were many of the agents who staffed them.

The standard equipment package, also capable of being airlifted or shipped via traditional ground transportation, was enough to outfit a small company of soldiers: twenty or so M-4 carbines, the standard military rifle. A carton of handguns. Ammunition, medical supplies, food, communication equipment, et cetera.

"I just found out a few minutes ago," Theo said. "The client, he's very upset at his admin. But the civil service rules, you know—he can't fire her."

"And no one thought to question why a package like this was being sent somewhere so far from the border?"

As soon as I spoke the words, I realized how silly they sounded. This was the US government we were talking about. Inefficiencies oozed from every pore of Uncle Sam.

"It was supposed to ship to Del Rio." Theo chuckled. "Besides, if the feds started doing their job right, we'd be out of business."

"Okay." I tried to figure out the closest place to get coffee. "I'm rolling."

"Just make sure the shipment is secure. We'll send a pickup team later this week."

"Gotcha."

"That type of, uh, equipment in the wrong hands." He clucked his tongue. "Not good."

I ended the call and yawned.

———

The piece of paper Tommy Joe Culpepper had given me contained an address on the far north side of town—a small office building on Dallas Parkway, a major thoroughfare which split that section of the city in two, near Arapaho Road.

The location was part of a two-building complex, one-story offices next to each other, separated by a walkway and narrow courtyard. Nineteen-eighties construction, brick with big mirrored windows, landscaping dead from lack of water.

It was dark when I got there. Commercial buildings dominated the area. They housed low-end businesses—personal-injury attorneys, one-man ad agencies, mortgage companies. Most were dark as well, parking lots empty.

A "For Sale" sign was in front of the address Tommy Joe had given me. Both buildings appeared to be vacant, like they'd been that way for a long while.

I parked in front of the correct address and got out, a flashlight in one hand.

The front door was locked, as was the rear. No signs of forced entry.

I shone the light in a window.

The building was empty. I could see the other end. No walls or other interior finish. And no crate marked "Property of US Government."

On a hunch, I went to the sister building, thirty feet away.

This structure had a loading area at the rear, a metal roll-up door wide enough to drive a truck through.

All the entrances were locked as well, no signs of entry.

At the rear, by the loading door, I flicked on the light and peered through a dusty window.

The building still had interior walls, but not many.

At night, without the sunlight streaming through the empty structure, the crate was hard to see, sitting in a corner of the utility area by the cargo door.

A big ten-by-twenty box.

Stenciling on one side marked it: "Border Patrol—Forward Operating Base. Do Not Open Unless Authorized."

That'll keep the bad guys out of it.

I checked again, made sure the doors were secure.

Tommy Joe must've been planning a move. I remembered the packing boxes at his office this morning. He'd probably recently bought these buildings and was using the one next door as the mailing and delivery address. When the crate arrived, he stuck it in the building with the loading door.

The shipment was secure for the moment. I'd call Theo in the morning and arrange a pickup. For now, I was tired.

I got back in the Lincoln and, after a moment's hesitation, headed back to the judge's house.

———

Judge Clark was ready for bed when I arrived. He asked me if everything was okay, the wording such that it was clear he didn't want details.

I nodded. We visited for a while and then he wheeled himself to his ground-floor room.

I went upstairs.

A king-sized bed and a top-of-the-line air conditioner. The second-floor guest room had all that I could want.

There was also a sitting area with a TV, common space in the middle of the bedrooms.

About midnight, I was watching *Letterman* when Clark's nurse wandered out of her room.

She wore a Dallas Cowboys T-shirt that barely covered her ass. I had on a pair of boxers and a Jerry Jeff Walker concert shirt that had seen better days, part of the stash of clothing I kept in the Lincoln along with various toiletries.

I nodded hello, and she sat next to me, a few inches separating us.

"He's a nice guy, isn't he?" She pointed downstairs.

I nodded again, turned up the volume a little.

"He thinks the world of you, you know?"

I shrugged.

She yawned and stretched, her leg touching mine.

"So . . . are you involved with anybody?" she said.

Kids today. So much more forward than when I'd been in my twenties.

"Look, it's not that I don't think you're attractive." I lowered the volume. "But I'm old enough to be your, well, significantly older brother."

"I like men of a certain age." She ran a finger down my thigh.

"I'm not *that* old."

I stood. Her hand fell away from my leg.

We were silent for a few moments.

"There is somebody else, isn't there?" she said. "Must be something special."

She was indeed special, in ways I couldn't articulate. I wondered where Piper was at that very moment.

# - CHAPTER ELEVEN -

The next day, I got up and made the judge a pot of coffee. He looked tired and old in the harsh glare of the morning light. This made me melancholy, sad for the people in my life who were slowly going away.

We visited until the nurse came in to make breakfast. She and I ignored each other for a few minutes until I finished my coffee. Then I went to my townhome and showered and dressed. Since I was going into the field today, I wore Levi's, a dark T-shirt, and Nikes.

I called Theo Goldberg and left him a message about the shipment, telling him it was secure for the moment. Then I set out to find Tremont Washington.

Because of my past employment with the DEA and the Dallas police, I was familiar with the neighborhood where Tremont lived, a hardscrabble section of the city that had fallen out of the poverty tree and hit every branch on the way down.

West Dallas was originally an unincorporated area known as Cement City, named for its largest employer, the Portland Cement Plant, a cesspool of pollution rendered only slightly less noxious by its proximity to a lead smelter. For much of the twentieth century, the very air in West Dallas was dangerous.

Singleton Boulevard, the main drag, ran due west from downtown, the street populated with tire stores, fried chicken restaurants, taco stands, and pawnshops.

According to the information Raul Delgado had given me, Tremont Washington lived with his grandmother in the Iris Apartments on Hampton Road, across from the bucolically named body of water known as Fish Trap Lake. The Iris was HUD public housing, well maintained as those types of properties went but not a good place for a white guy to venture even in broad daylight. The police only responded to calls there in groups of three or more, one of whom was armed with a fully automatic weapon.

I drove past the Iris Apartments and then down an interior street.

The wood-framed houses were small, probably much like they'd been when Bonnie Parker and Clyde Barrow had called the area home a century before.

It was midmorning, a sunny day. Every block or so, I passed someone sitting in a lawn chair on the corner, watching what little traffic there was, cell phone in hand. Human radar for the man I was going to see.

At the intersection of Borger and Vilbig sat a brick house larger than most, surrounded by a freshly painted picket fence. A Cadillac Escalade was parked nose-out in the driveway, a young African American man in a wifebeater shirt and calf-length shorts leaning against the hood.

I parked across the street and got out. I kept my hands visible. Moved slowly but deliberately.

The young man stared at me but didn't seem alarmed. I knew others were watching from the houses nearby.

The man stuck a cigarillo between his lips.

"Whatchoo want? Crackertown's across the river."

"Lysol around?"

"Who's asking?" He crossed his arms.

"Tell him Jon Cantrell's here."

He cocked his head to one side like he was trying to figure out what planet I'd come from.

I said, "Tell him I'm not looking to jam anybody up."

Lysol Alvarez was the head of a street gang that ran most of West Dallas. He was half black, half Nicaraguan, one hundred percent dangerous.

The young man gave me his best tough-guy glare before he pulled a cell phone from his pocket and sent a text. A moment later he looked up.

"Yo. Front door's open."

I nodded thanks and strode toward the house.

The yard was tiny but immaculate, manicured like a putting green. Palm trees grew on either side of the walk leading to the porch.

I pushed open the door and stepped into a living room that looked like it had come from the gangsta edition of *Architectural Digest*.

Black leather furniture, polished hardwood floors, white-washed plaster walls. An abstract painting of Tupac over the fireplace, the color scheme green and orange. On the opposite wall was a flat-screen TV tuned to a basketball game. The sound was muted so as not to compete with the opera music playing on the ceiling-mounted speakers.

Nothing like a culturally sophisticated street thug.

Lysol wore a maroon seersucker suit and woven sandals. No shirt. The open jacket accentuated the definition of his pecs. He was sitting on the couch, tamping a wad of pot into a bong that looked like a glass skull.

In the corner stood a beefy man in an Adidas running suit, holding an AK-47.

I surveyed the room, particularly a spot on the floor in front of the fireplace.

"Looks like you got all the blood cleaned up." I sat in a chair by the coffee table.

Lysol was in his early forties. His head was shaved, the lobe of one ear missing from a botched assassination attempt a few years before.

"Ancient history." He lit the bowl with a cigar lighter. "You came here to talk about that?"

Several years before, we'd had a minor tussle over a CI, a confidential informant. Things hadn't worked out all that well for the informant and he'd lost a lot of blood on Lysol's floor.

Probably all his blood, come to think of it.

"Lysol hears things." He exhaled a plume of marijuana smoke. "Like you're no longer in the business."

"This is true." I stifled a cough. "Joe Citizen. That's me."

"You're an attorney now?" He arched an eyebrow.

I shook my head. "I'm associated with a law firm. Let's leave it at that."

"So what brings Joe Citizen I'm-not-an-attorney to West Dallas?"

I'd never busted him, though I'd had plenty of opportunities. There were always bigger targets or people who served a larger strategic goal. He was aware of this fact.

Plus, I liked the guy. He'd grown up in a crack house a few blocks away and managed to survive, some might say thrive, in an environment that had destroyed other, lesser men. The eldest of his six children was starting SMU next year.

"Can't an old friend just stop by to say hi?"

"Lysol has no friends, Jon, just people who need things. Some of these people he tolerates." A long pause. "Others he does not."

From the rear of the house came the click of heels, a female walking.

A few moments later a woman in her twenties entered the room. She was brunet with porcelain skin, about six feet tall, wearing a short black sundress that accentuated her thighs.

She deposited herself beside Lysol on the sofa, legs curled underneath her.

"Hey, baby." She nuzzled his neck. "Sawyer needs to go shopping."

"And what does Sawyer need to get?" Lysol pulled a wad of currency from his pocket.

"Something to make herself pretty for her man." She took the money.

The woman was stunningly attractive already, pretty like a Cowboys cheerleader who'd married well.

"Sawyer should just buy clothes." Lysol grasped her arm. "No coke. Lysol doesn't like people around him who do blow."

The girl smiled but her eyes looked fearful. Lysol had that effect on people.

"Sure, baby." Her voice was tight. "No blow."

Lysol let go. The girl scampered away, headed toward the rear of the house. He relit his bong, took another hit, and looked at me.

"You were getting ready to tell Lysol what you need."

I coughed. The secondhand dope smoke and third-person conversations were making my head hurt. Nevertheless, I played along.

"Does Lysol know a kid named Tremont Washington? He's from the neighborhood. About twelve or thirteen years old. Might be considered a little slow in the head."

Lysol looked at his guard, the man with the AK-47, and nodded once. The guard disappeared from the room, giving us a degree of privacy.

I waited.

Lysol took one final hit and put the bong down. "You ever watch MSNBC?"

"On occasion," I said. "Why are you asking?"

"You ever see the special on sex tourism in Thailand?"

"No. But I'm familiar with the concept."

"Certain men come to West Dallas to exercise their urges on the people here, much like they do in Thailand."

Poor people made good targets. It had been that way since the first caveman amassed a herd of woolly mammoths and decided to diddle his less-wealthy neighbor's kid.

"A white man was arrested exactly one week ago, near the Iris Apartments," Lysol said. "You should probably talk to this individual."

"Does this person have a name?"

"Lysol is not at liberty to disclose this information." He wagged his finger. "Lysol is being exceptionally generous already."

True dat. He didn't owe me anything, since I wasn't in the game anymore. Maybe he liked me, too. A fellow could dream, couldn't he?

"Thanks." I smiled. "Jon will look into this information right after he visits with Tremont's grandmother."

"At the Iris?" Lysol raised an eyebrow.

I nodded. "Stopped here first. A matter of courtesy."

"Lysol appreciates your show of respect. But you should be very careful at the Iris since Lysol does not control that particular piece of ground."

I stood. "Thanks for the warning and the information."

"You do still carry a gun, don't you?"

I shook my head. "Live by my wits these days."

Lysol nodded slowly. "That was always Jon's strong suit."

# - CHAPTER TWELVE -

I left Lysol Alvarez's compound, headed back to Singleton Boulevard.

At the corner of Singleton and Borger sat an old wooden building, boarded up, abandoned. The structure had a small canopy on the front. Weeds poked through the crumbling concrete. Beer bottles littered the ground.

The building used to be the Barrow family's service station, an early staging ground for young Clyde's foray into lawlessness.

It was forgotten now, not even a plaque commemorating the location's brush with infamy. The place could have been a metaphor for all of West Dallas: nobody much cared about the present. Why should they care about the past?

I turned west on Singleton and then north on Hampton.

The Iris Apartments appeared on my right. Eight buildings total. Constructed in the 1960s, garden-style. Two stories. Each unit opened onto a breezeway that ran the length of each building.

The breezeways were like canyons of crime, sheltered from outside view, protected from the elements, serving as a walkway to the homes of people who had for the most part lost hope.

Tremont's apartment was in Building Six, toward the back, unit 6225, the second floor.

I parked between a metallic purple Lincoln and a late-model C-class Mercedes, the nicest vehicles in sight. I got out.

Across the parking lot, a group of young men clustered around an unlit charcoal grill. They were smoking and drinking from quart bottles of beer hidden in paper sacks.

The leader appeared to be a guy in his thirties with dreadlocks and a diamond grill on his front teeth.

I'd heard of him before but couldn't remember his name. Supposedly he only spoke in a badly feigned British accent.

They stared at me, especially the guy with the dreadlocks.

I didn't stare back. Lots of bad things start with eyeball beefs, the implied disrespect that comes from looking too closely at someone.

I walked purposefully to the outside stairs leading to the second floor. Took the steps two at a time. Knocked on unit 6225 and then committed a felony. Not my first, probably not my last.

In front of the peephole, I held up a DEA badge and ID card with my picture. The credentials were legit, but I was not—no longer a federal agent. I figured a badge would go farther here than my business card from Goldberg, Finkelman, and Clark.

Movement from inside. The door opened a fraction, held in place by a chain, and a woman's face appeared in the gap.

She was in her seventies. Wrinkled, coffee-colored skin. Gray hair, eyes cloudy with cataracts. She squinted at my face.

"Yes?" Her voice was frail. "May I help you?"

"Are you Alice Simpson?"

She didn't reply, clearly trying to figure out why a man with a badge was coming to her door.

"What is it you want?" she said.

"I'm here about your grandson."

"Tremont?" A faint smile on her face. "You know where he is?"

"No. But I'd like to help you find him."

From behind me came the sound of footsteps and men talking. Loud, like they owned the place.

Alice heard them, too. She frowned for a moment and then closed the door a few inches. She removed the chain, motioned me inside.

I did as requested. She shut the door behind me, locked the dead bolt.

Her apartment was small but spotless. Avocado-green carpet, a beige sofa and matching easy chairs. Two framed photographs hung over the sofa: Dr. Martin Luther King and President Obama. The other walls were decorated with drawings and artwork that all depicted the ocean or a beach.

"May I see your badge again?"

I handed it to her and she grabbed a magnifying glass from an end table. After a couple of moments of scrutiny, she returned my credentials.

"Tremont is not into drugs," she said.

"Me neither." I stuck the badge in my pocket. "When was the last time you saw your grandson?"

"I called the police." She was trying to contain her anger. "Tremont's friend, that Delgado fellow, he said he'd help, but so far nothing."

I didn't reply. I'd figured that Tremont and Delgado knew each other. Would have been nice if he'd told me, however.

"There was a reporter. I told him, too." She snorted. "He said he'd write a story about it on the computer."

"A blog or something?" I asked.

"I dunno. The computer, what he said."

Neither of us spoke for a few moments.

"Tell me about the last time you saw your grandson."

She nodded, wiped a tear from her eye.

"A week ago this morning. He left for work. And I haven't seen him since."

Tremont had a job? There's a little tidbit that Raul Delgado's piece of paper failed to mention.

"Where did he work?"

Alice Simpson limped across the room to a buffet by the dining room table. She picked up a framed eight-by-ten photograph. The photo sat next to an American flag folded into a triangle and an open jewelry box that displayed a Purple Heart.

"His mother, my baby, she died in Iraq." She wiped her nose with a tissue. "Tremont's all I got."

I walked to where she stood and took the picture, an image of a gap-toothed grade-schooler next to a woman in Army fatigues standing in front of the Calatrava Bridge, which linked West Dallas with the rest of the city. Both mother and child were smiling.

I put the picture back on the buffet by a stack of mail.

"He's such a happy boy," she said. "Even when he heard about his mama, he tried not to be sad."

"What happened to his father?" I kept my voice neutral.

Damon Washington, Tremont's father and my friend, had been a Marine Recon officer, the jarhead's version of Special Forces. Smart as a rocket scientist, built like a linebacker, reflexes of a cat. Could have done anything after he got out—law school, a corporate gig, whatever. Instead, he became a cop, which is how we met.

"Worked for the state. The po-lice." She shrugged. "Died on the job."

"Narcotics officer, right?" I frowned like I was trying to recall. "I remember hearing something about that. Damon Washington, that was his name, wasn't it?"

In the end, all the brains and training in the world couldn't help with the disease that afflicted Tremont's dad.

She nodded, lips pursed, a topic she didn't care to discuss.

Damon Washington was an adrenaline junkie. Police barracks and war zones are full of them. Still, we were friends, something that neither of us took lightly.

I looked at the artwork.

"You like the beach?"

"We were going to go to the coast one day, me and Tremont." She smiled. "He's never seen the ocean."

I nodded.

"The doctors say that a change of scenery might be good for someone with his condition," she added.

"What is Tremont's, uh, condition?"

"Autism," she said. "A mild form."

I nodded, unsure of what to say.

"Last week," she said, "I walked him to the bus stop. At 8:00 a.m."

"Where was he going?"

"He catches the crosstown express." She crossed her arms like that answered everything.

I let the silence drag on.

"He was going to work. He liked to be busy."

"His job. Tell me about it."

"It was a program. They take people like Tremont and find them things to do."

She scurried back to the buffet and opened a drawer. She pulled out a small leather folio, removed a card.

"Here." She handed it to me.

The Helping Place, a 501(3)c corporation, address in a ritzy part of Dallas just north of downtown.

The back of the card contained their mission statement: to help disabled members of the community find employment and meaningful value in their lives.

"And you saw him get on the bus?"

Outside came the sound of a siren. It grew louder, then softer.

"Yes. Yes, I'm sure I saw him get on the bus." She sounded anything but sure.

"A hundred percent certain?"

She nodded once and stopped. Her eyes welled with tears.

"My mind, it's not what it used to be," she said softly. "I'm not sure of much of anything anymore."

"That's okay." I put the card in my wallet. "I'm gonna talk to the neighbors, see if they remember anything."

"I miss him so much. I can't tell you." She walked to the other side of the room.

I pulled a business card out. Dropped it on the dining room table.

Alice Simpson picked up a feather duster and looked around like she was trying to recall something that had slipped her mind.

I started to say good-bye but realized she probably didn't know I was still there. So I left.

# - CHAPTER THIRTEEN -

The Gunrunner

Irish Joe counts his money, the weekly take.

His favorite activity.

Stacks of twenties and fifties and hundreds. The bills are wrinkled and dirty, occasionally tinged with blood. He doesn't care.

Joe Callahan, Irish Joe on the street, is in a wood-paneled room at the back of his office on Harry Hines Boulevard, in the northwest section of Dallas. The room is filled with cartons of ammunition and boxes of firearms, stacked to the ceiling.

Chinese AK-47 knockoffs, both the street-legal semi-automatic versions and the illegal fully auto models. Cheap nine-millimeter pistols from South America. Military-surplus rifles from various third-world countries.

Every item has a market and a price. Irish Joe takes a cut as each passes through his hands.

He used to be a legitimate gun dealer. He had an FFL, the federal firearms license required to buy and sell guns, and a storefront down the street where he sold rednecks Benelli shotguns for duck season, bolt-action Remingtons for deer, and Ruger pistols for self-defense situations that would never transpire.

But the feds took away his license after the incident with his sister's daughter, so he turned to more lucrative endeavors.

His space is the middle unit of a three-store strip center. On one side is a pawnshop he has an interest in; the other is a discount cigarette retailer.

Irish Joe owns the strip center, too, a cinderblock building located in the no-man's land between those blood-sucking Korean hoods to the north and the Mexican gangbangers to the south.

Both groups leave him alone, except when they need his services.

Irish Joe Callahan, a fifty-eight-year-old native of Dallas and former deacon in the Carrollton Church of Christ, is the largest illegal gun dealer in the state, maybe in the Southwest. He doesn't think about these things or the people stupid or unlucky enough to get in the way of a bullet from one of his weapons. He only thinks about the money.

The illegal buying and selling of firearms, though extremely lucrative, is not his favorite activity. That distinction belongs to his side business, gun rentals.

For a small fee, Irish Joe will rent a firearm, untraceable of course, for whatever activity the customer requires. Plus a cut of the take. He will also provide advice on the proposed job. Which liquor store has what kind of security. Banks that save money by going without an on-site guard. Individuals who might be carrying a large amount of cash. That sort of thing.

This is a good life Irish Joe has forged for himself, free of all the government regulations he used to have to deal with.

It's midafternoon.

He's got an appointment in Richardson, a suburb north of town favored by Russian immigrants. He's to inspect a crate of Chechen sniper rifles, maybe make an offer.

He puts the cash into one of the safes along the far wall, next to the Kruggerands and diamonds from that deal in Fort Worth last week. He slides the nickel-plated Colt .38 Super into the holster on his hip. Covers the gun with his Windbreaker.

He turns on the alarm and leaves by the back door.

His Bentley is by the Dumpster. Across the lot sits a navy-blue Ford, a Crown Victoria. Otherwise the parking area is empty. Customers use the striped spaces in the front. Everyone else knows to stay out of the back.

Irish Joe is not stupid. He understands that his activities generate enemies. So he does what any prudent person in his situation would do. He draws the .38 Super from its holster, flicks the safety off, and aims at the Crown Victoria.

Slowly he advances.

The windows are tinted.

When he's about ten feet away, the driver's door opens.

Joe says, "Hands where I can see them."

A man in a black tracksuit exits, palms out, held high. His ball cap is worn low, shielding his eyes.

"Easy, Joe." The man smiles. "That any way to say hello?"

"Do we know each other?" Joe keeps the .38 aimed at the middle of the tracksuit.

The man looks vaguely familiar but Joe can't place him.

"My front pocket," the man says. "I've got ID. Okay if I get it?"

Joe hesitates and then nods. He keeps his finger on the trigger.

The man slowly reaches into his pocket and pulls out a wallet. He flips it open, displaying a badge.

Joe lowers his gun but doesn't relax.

The only thing he hates worse than Mexican gangbangers and Korean hoods are cops, especially bent ones, which this guy appears to be.

"A jewelry store got hit downtown," the man says. "I need to ask you about it, okay?"

Part of what Irish Joes sells along with the temporary use of one of his guns is confidentiality. Irish Joe does not talk to the police. Ever.

His best move is to give this cop the brush-off and set up a meeting for later, one with his lawyer present.

"I've got to be somewhere." Joe holsters his gun. "Maybe we can schedule something tomorrow."

"Sure, Joe." The man draws a silenced Glock. "Whatever you say."

Irish Joe Callahan claws at his hip for the .38 but it is too late.

All the money and guns and Kruggerands in the world will not stop what comes next.

A puff of smoke and he is facedown on the asphalt, a few steps from his Bentley.

As the blood pools beneath his body and his life slips away, Irish Joe tries to think of who will mourn his passing, but no one comes to mind.

This makes him sad. Then it's over.

———

*Dallas, Texas*
*1987*

Raul Delgado was seventeen years old.

Five years had passed since his brother died in the back of the police car.

A half a decade, as Bobby liked to say.

So much had changed, but so much remained the same.

Twice a week, Raul attended Mass at the Cathedral Shrine of the Virgin of Guadalupe in downtown Dallas. He went to confession and lit candles in memory of his brother as well as his mother, who passed the previous spring, may God rest her soul.

The neighborhood around the cathedral had changed. The wood-frame houses that Raul remembered from his childhood were disappearing one by one, replaced by office buildings and fancy stores.

Just across the freeway from the church, a few blocks from his old neighborhood in Little Mexico, a huge complex of buildings was under construction—a hotel, shopping mall, and office tower.

The Crescent, that was what they were calling it. The buildings looked like something from a movie set in Europe. Bobby told him all the new construction would add to the tax base, which was a good thing. Raul supposed that was right—Bobby was smart about stuff like that—but he was still sad to see the homes and other buildings that were part of his childhood being demolished.

He walked down the center aisle of the cathedral. The sun spilled through the stained-glass windows, casting colored shadows on the pews.

It was the middle of the day, so there were not very many worshippers. A few old women he recognized from the neighborhood, his mother's acquaintances.

They watched him pass, eyes like slits, faces disapproving.

It was the clothes, of course.

Raul didn't care. He was proud to be a Dallas Police Explorer, the youth program for those interested in a career in law enforcement. The uniform—dark pants, a light-blue shirt with a gold badge embroidered on the breast—provided him with a sense of pride and purpose.

Law and order. That was what this country needed. Not that Chicano revolutionary babble he used to be so into. What an idiot he'd been, listening to those people who came around after his brother died, the ones who wanted him to be the poster child for a new revolt against the white man.

He exited the church and stood on the curb on Pearl Street, waiting.

Better to work within the system. Better and safer.

Bobby arrived a few moments later, driving an unmarked Chevy bristling with antennas.

Raul hopped in the passenger seat and grabbed the microphone from its holder on the dash.

Bobby's strawberry-blond hair was thinning and going gray. The bags under his eyes, on the other hand, had grown thick and dark. But he still had a kind expression on his face, and it pained Raul to realize that the man who had been like a father to him was growing old.

Bobby pulled away from the curb.

Raul asked if he could call dispatch to tell them they were out of service.

Bobby smiled and nodded. Then he sped up as Raul held the mic to his mouth and gave the unit number of the squad car.

A few minutes later they were on Stemmons Freeway, speeding past the Hyatt Regency tower, where Bobby and Junie had taken Raul for dinner on his sixteenth birthday.

They headed toward Bobby's home, a ranch in Ellis County, just south of Dallas.

The place had seventy-five acres, maybe a dozen head of cattle. It was split by a creek, the terrain flat like Kansas. The only trees were the cottonwoods that lined the water.

Twenty minutes later, the Chevy pulled through an open gate and then down a caliche road that led to a wooden farmhouse built in the 1890s.

The grass covering the pastures was the color of sand, the result of the current drought, but the lawn surrounding the house was green and lush. Between the lawn and home lay a flower bed filled with roses and petunias.

Bobby parked in the garage next to a battered Ford pickup.

He and Raul got out and entered the home through the back door.

The air smelled like old wood and fried chicken. Comforting, safe.

Raul always felt good when he stepped into Bobby's house.

Junie was in the kitchen, cooking lunch.

Chicken and mashed potatoes. Green beans with sliced onion and a ham hock simmering on the stove.

Bobby kissed her forehead and poured three glasses of iced tea.

Raul said hello. Then he performed his chore: setting the table, the silverware and napkins placed on the oilskin tablecloth just like Junie had showed him.

Since his mother died, he'd been more or less living with Bobby. His *abuela*, Maria, had legal custody but she was old, well into her seventies, and did not object when Raul stayed away for days at a time.

Junie was fourteen. She had reddish-blond hair and legs that seemed to go on forever, at least when she was in those cut-off jeans.

Raul tried not to stare at Junie's legs or the swell of her breasts underneath the T-shirts she wore in the summer.

Raul missed his brother. He wished he could visit with him, explain what he was thinking and feeling. Raul and Bobby were close, but there were certain things he just couldn't talk about with the older man, especially when it concerned Bobby's daughter.

Junie fussed over the food. She was unusually quiet. Bobby and Raul looked at each other and shrugged. She was changing as well, becoming moody at times, stubbornly independent at others.

After a moment she turned to Raul and said, "Add another place at the table, will you?"

Bobby arched an eyebrow. "Who's coming for lunch besides the three of us?"

His daughter didn't answer, intent on maneuvering a plate of chicken out of the oven or maybe avoiding the question—Raul couldn't be sure.

"Hey, Junie." Bobby's tone was insistent, forceful. "Answer me."

Raul paused, a knife and fork in his hand—the extra place setting. The atmosphere in the kitchen was tense.

Junie turned around. A lock of hair dangled in front of her eyes, making her look older and more beguiling than her years.

"Wayne's coming to lunch, Daddy." Her voice was soft.

A sharp intake of breath from Bobby.

Wayne was eighteen, a dropout from a little town near the ranch.

Junie attended a private school in Dallas on a scholarship. But she lived here, in rural Ellis County, a world that was only a few miles from the big city but light-years different when it came to the types of people one encountered. Even at Raul's age, he understood the difference those few miles made.

Raul had met Wayne. He detested him, as did Bobby. Wayne had cruel eyes and an expression on his face like he enjoyed other people's misfortune, like there was humor to be found in someone else's pain.

Wayne wore his hair long in the back, short on the sides, and dressed in skintight Wrangler jeans and plaid shirts with the sleeves ripped off.

Bobby called him a punk, repeatedly pointed out to Junie that he'd been in and out of trouble with the law since he was thirteen.

For some reason, this seemed to make Junie want to be around Wayne all the more.

Raul heard the name and felt a little bit of his soul crush.

Junie was so pretty, so kind. Why would she want to hang around with somebody like Wayne?

Junie said, "He's just a friend, Daddy. That's all."

Bobby nodded once, his eyes cold and hard, like when he had to arrest somebody. He looked at Raul and said, "Set another place. Looks like Wayne's gonna be joining us for lunch."

Raul did as asked, wishing with all his might that Wayne would just go away and die.

# - CHAPTER FOURTEEN -

At the Iris Apartments, leaving Tremont's unit, I was halfway down the stairs of Building Six when I heard the screams.

First floor. The breezeway. A woman's voice, terrified.

The smart thing to do would be to keep going, head straight to the Lincoln and leave.

But I didn't do the smart thing; I rarely do.

At the foot of the stairs, I stopped. Turned. Looked down the row of ground-floor units.

Two men in baggy shorts and T-shirts stood over a crumpled figure.

A woman in a black dress, crying, hair mussed.

Sawyer. Lysol Alvarez's girlfriend.

Crap. Why did I look?

The larger of the pair, an overweight guy who looked like Fat Albert from the old Bill Cosby cartoon, smacked her face.

"Where's the rest of the money, ho?"

Sawyer whimpered.

"We gonna take that Mercedes, then," Fat Albert said. "Plus, you owe for the last eight-ball."

*"Noo!"* She held up one hand, pleading.

Fat Albert grabbed her fingers, bent them backward, an awkward, painful angle that would break bones if it went much further.

Sawyer screamed again.

The smaller thug laughed.

I stepped into the breezeway.

"Let her go."

Fat Albert and his crony, Little Albert, looked up. Sawyer yanked her hand free.

"Move away from the woman." I used my best cop voice. "Place your hands on top of your head."

I headed toward the three individuals, walking with as much swagger as possible.

"Who the hell are you?" Fat Albert put his hands on his hips.

"DEA." I held up my badge.

Little Albert pulled a gun from his waistband.

This was the point where a real DEA agent would draw his piece as well. But I was unarmed. So I kept walking.

"Bitch owes me two large," Fat Albert said. "You gonna cover that, mister DEA agent?"

"Put the gun down and let her go." I stopped about ten feet away.

"You ain't the five-oh," Little Albert said. "Where's your piece? And your backup?"

Fat Albert lumbered toward me, fists clenched.

When he got close enough to touch, I said, "I have the money she owes. You don't have to hurt her."

Fat Albert stood between me and his partner, blocking Little Albert's shot. He said, "Let me see the cash."

I reached for my pocket with one hand and popped him in the eye with the other, using the tips of my fingers. Nothing takes the fight out of a man quite like getting hit dead center in the pupil.

Fat Albert screamed, pressed his hands to his face.

Little Albert tried to peer around his partner's bulk to see what had happened while not getting too far away from Sawyer.

I kicked Fat Albert in the groin.

He screamed again and fell to the ground, landing on his side, his back to Little Albert. His shirt rode up, displaying a handgun wedged in the waistband.

I dropped to my knees and reached for the weapon.

Little Albert was holding a mouse gun, probably a .22 or .25 caliber. He gulped, trying to comprehend how things had gone downhill so fast.

Then he fired. And missed.

The bullet hit his partner in the buttocks.

Fat Albert was having a sucky day. I almost felt sorry for him. First his eye, then his nuts. Now he'd been shot in the ass.

Little Albert tried to fire again but the gun jammed.

I grabbed Fat Albert's piece, an off-brand semiauto nine-millimeter. I racked the slide back to check the chamber.

The gun was empty.

I dropped the weapon, jumped up and charged. Head down, arms out. Tackled Little Albert.

He dropped his gun and tried to fight, but I elbowed his ear twice, rendering him immobile for the next few moments.

After a second to catch my breath, I stood, tried to keep my knees from shaking.

"Are you okay?" I looked down at Sawyer.

She was hyperventilating, arms crossed, face pale.

From the parking lot came the sound of people yelling. From Hampton Road, the blare of sirens.

"We gotta get out of here." I pulled her up.

"You don't understand." She pointed to the nearest unit. "I need to go in there."

Little Albert groaned. The sirens grew louder.

"We are in the hot zone," I said. "We really nee—"

She opened the door and dashed inside.

At the far end of the breezeway, maybe fifty yards away, three police officers rounded the corner.

No choices left. I dashed in the unit after Sawyer, slammed the door shut. Hoped the cops didn't see me.

The apartment was a drop house. The living room was empty except for a duffel bag full of foil pouches, a boom box, and a couple of video games.

Sawyer was on the floor, rooting through the duffel.

I grabbed her arm, shoved her toward the back. She reluctantly let herself be guided away from the living room, a handful of foil pouches clutched in her fingers.

"Lysol told you no coke, remember?" I opened the bathroom door, dragged her inside with me. There was a window over the tub that led to the parking lot.

"Please don't tell Lysol what Sawyer did." She shut the door. Slid her arm around my waist. Drew us close. "Please."

Her breasts pressed against my chest, our faces inches apart.

"Sawyer will make it worth your while." She licked her lips. "She promises."

"Will Sawyer quit talking in the third person?"

"Huh?" She frowned. "Look, just don't tell Lysol where you found me."

I started to answer but the bathroom door burst open, and a uniformed officer aimed a pistol at my face.

"Don't move," he said. "Police."

"Shit." Sawyer slumped against the wall.

"Put your hands on your head," the cop said. "Both of you."

I did as requested.

Sawyer said, "I want my lawyer."

# - CHAPTER FIFTEEN -

Mason Burnett was running late.

He hated to be off schedule, but with the implementation of the chief's new anti-crime initiative and his other activities, he had no choice. Plus, he'd had to spend a lot of time filling out forms about what had happened to the gangbanger at the boardinghouse in Oak Cliff.

Mason hated paperwork. But since the pantywaist Delgado had been there, he figured he'd better make sure his version of events was crystal clear.

He found a spot in the parking garage large enough for his Suburban. The nearby cars were expensive, Mercedes and Cadillacs and BMWs.

All the wealth the city had to offer seemed to be concentrated into this small area, a five- or six-block complex of office buildings and stores known as Preston Center.

He jogged across the street, caught the elevator just in time, and walked into the nondescript set of rooms, only seven minutes late for his appointment.

The woman with the sensible shoes was waiting in the reception area. She smiled at him.

"Sorry I'm late," Mason said.

"You ready to begin?" She pointed to an inner office.

Mason nodded and followed her into a frilly sitting area, four white leather chairs around a coffee table. Two bottles of water rested on the table.

They sat in silence for a few moments. Mason opened a water, took a sip.

"How was your day?" She tapped a pencil on her knee.

Mason took several deep breaths, tried to compose himself.

The woman's name was Corinne. She was a therapist under contract with the city of Dallas, among other law-enforcement agencies. She specialized in couples counseling as well as treating first responders for stress-related maladies.

Mason had been seeing her for six weeks.

Ever since the incident with the prostitute in the platinum wig.

"My day." He put the water down. "It was fine. I had a good day."

"Everything okay at work?"

More silence.

The woman with the platinum wig had been working a corner on Fort Worth Avenue, south of downtown. Mason's people had been taking down a drug house a few blocks away. He had stopped at the curb to make a call when she'd approached him while he was still in his vehicle, offering him a date he'd never forget—round the world for only forty bucks.

Corinne cleared her throat, brought him back to the present.

"Work is fine," Mason said.

"Good." She nodded.

Mason looked around the room but didn't say anything.

"You can talk about whatever you like."

Mason nodded. Wondered what he should bring up today.

More silence. Then:

"You ever notice how brown this damn city is?" Mason asked.

"Excuse me?"

"Dallas used to just be coloreds and whites." He paused. "Sorry, I mean African Americans and their white oppressors."

Corinne stared at him like he'd taken a shit in the middle of her coffee table. Damn bleeding-heart bull dyke.

He continued. "Now half the billboards in town are in Spanish, and you can't hardly turn on the TV without seeing some Mexican soap opera full of big-titted sluts named Maria or Consuela."

Corinne scribbled furiously on her pad.

"We're confidential here, right?" Mason smiled.

She looked up and nodded, clearly trying not to curl her lips into a sneer.

"Not that I mind big tits." Mason winked. "You like a nice rack, too, dontcha, Corinne?"

She put her pen down. "What I like or don't like is not why we're here. Let's talk about you. Or your job, which is what brought you to me in the first place."

"Everything's great at work." Mason crossed his legs. "Except for the fact that the chief has me boxed in like a cow on the way to slaughter."

Corinne started scribbling again. "What exactly do you mean?"

Mason explained briefly: the new SWAT team program foisted on him by the chief in response to the spike in crime. He neglected to mention the gangbanger and the window.

Corinne interjected occasionally but for the most part let him vent.

While he talked, Mason envisioned the prostitute with the platinum wig. The way she stood, the color of her hair, the halter top that barely contained her breasts. All of it reminded him of his stepmother.

"What the chief did." Corinne tapped the pencil on her pad. "How does that make you feel?"

Mason chewed on his bottom lip for a moment, thinking.

"Fucked," he said. "Is that a feeling?"

Corinne got a thoughtful look on her face. Then she nodded.

The hooker had nearly died, right there on the sidewalk by his official DPD vehicle, a few hundred feet from the drug house.

Mason hadn't meant to strangle her, but the memories she stirred in him had been intense, a blinding spell of anger that he hadn't known existed.

One of his men had stopped him.

When it was over, he'd looked at the bruises on her neck, amazed that he'd caused such damage. The entire experience had been like a different person inhabiting his body.

Because he was Captain Mason Burnett, a twenty-five-year decorated veteran of the Dallas Police Department, a man feared by rank and file as well as the command structure, Internal Affairs had recommended counseling.

"How are the dreams?" Corinne asked.

"They're fine," Mason lied.

"You're sleeping okay?"

He nodded.

His father haunted his slumber. An angry, bitter man, full of whiskey and rage. Blue-collar and proud of it. No explanation why he married a woman who wanted more out of life than *Hee Haw* reruns and Sunday dinners at Luby's.

Shirley, Mason's stepmother.

A woman who fancied herself better than a two-room shack in Cockrell Hill. A woman who worked at an upscale French restaurant on Lovers Lane, serving rich men from North Dallas, sleeping with more than a few. Shirley with the golden hair and the breasts like melons, ripe and inviting.

"Are you taking the pills I prescribed?"

"Yes," Mason lied again.

The meds dulled the edges of his existence, smoothed over the rough patches.

Mason didn't like things smooth. As time went on, he realized how much he liked the anger, how comforting it felt.

"What are you thinking right now?" Corinne asked. "Your expression. You seem . . . upset."

Mason unclenched his hands, unaware of when he'd balled his fingers into fists.

Corinne said, "Are you all right?"

"I'm fine." Mason forced himself to smile.

She jotted something on her pad.

"My mind drifted. Where were we?"

Corinne put down her notes, crossed her arms tight. "Our time's up."

Mason stared at her for a moment, realizing that she was afraid. He chuckled and stood. "See you next time, counselor."

# - CHAPTER SIXTEEN -

Lew Sterrett Justice Center—the Dallas County jail.

I'd put who knows how many people in there over the years. Now it was my turn.

My expired DEA badge earned me a private holding cell on the second floor, down the hall from a guy whacked out on angel dust or bath salts. Lysol Alvarez's girlfriend Sawyer went wherever they took pretty young women who'd been caught holding a couple ounces of cocaine.

About an hour after they locked me up, Piper appeared outside my cell, a badge clipped to her waistband. Behind her stood a sheriff's deputy.

"Impersonating a federal agent." She clucked her tongue. "That's a no-no."

I'd called Piper, not anybody at the office. She could get me out quicker. And the office—i.e., Theo—didn't need to know about this any sooner than necessary.

"Don't forget the drugs," I said. "There was a felony amount in the duffel bag."

"Looks like that's gonna get stuck on the two hoods. The one who got shot in the ass squealed on his partner."

"Small mercies." I stood and stretched.

Piper looked at the deputy. "Cut him loose."

The deputy unlocked my cell. He said, "We hope you've had a nice stay."

Piper opened the door.

"If you have access to the Internet," the deputy said, "please consider rating our facility on Travelocity."

"Everybody's a comedian." Piper steered me toward the exit while the deputy laughed.

We walked past the cell holding the duster. He was naked, huddled in the corner, arms outstretched as if warding off the attacks of creatures only he could see.

Piper opened a metal door at the end of the hall and we found ourselves by the intake area for the south tower.

"What about Sawyer?"

"What's a 'Sawyer,'" Piper said. "Is that some jailhouse slang you picked up in the last hour?"

"Sawyer was the woman arrested with me." I lowered my voice. "She's Lysol Alvarez's girlfriend."

"Lysol—my favorite sociopath." Piper shook her head. "Why were you with his girlfriend?"

"I wasn't *with* her. I was talking to Tremont's grandmother and—look, it's too long to get into right now."

"It always is." Piper used her badge to cut to the head of the line at the checkout station. She gave the jailer my intake number and got a manila envelope that contained my personal effects.

"What's Sawyer's last name?" she said.

I shook my head.

"Just run the first name then." Piper spoke to the jailer. "Sawyer. Like Tom and Huck Finn."

He tapped a keyboard and then looked up. "Nada."

I remembered what Lysol had told me about a child molester arrested one week before. I leaned in front of the Plexiglas divider and said, "Can you do a search for people arrested last week on a specific date?"

The guy in line behind us, a biker the size of a Deepfreeze, told me to hurry the fuck up. Piper growled at him, literally.

The jailer looked at me over his reading glasses. "What do you think this is, a Holiday Inn?"

"How long would it take you—"

"C'mon, Dillinger." Piper dragged me toward the elevator.

On the ground floor, we navigated our way through the throngs of people coming to visit relatives or friends. Then we left the building.

Outside, it was early evening. The sun was setting across the Trinity River. The clouds above the Calatrava Bridge were orange and purple, clean and refreshing after the grayness of the jail.

I sat on a bench a few yards from the jail entrance and opened the envelope. It was almost all there: money, keys, cell phone, pocketknife. But no DEA credentials.

"They took my badge." I put everything in my pocket.

"You're not an agent anymore." Piper shook her head.

"I need you to look up somebody for me. A man who was arrested at the Iris Apartments a week ago." I explained briefly what Lysol had told me.

She pulled her smartphone out, tapped on the keypad. "The mainframe's down. Again."

"How about something to eat. Maybe grab a bite at Sam Browne's?"

"Can't. Sorry." Her voice was soft. "I, uh, have plans tonight."

"Plans?"

"Yeah. That's what people do. They make arrangements for an activity at a mutually-agreed-upon time."

"You've got a date with Delgado, don't you?"

"Jon." She knelt in front of me. Put a hand on my leg. "You and I are not together anymore."

I shoved her hand away. "What was last week then?"

A few beers at a Mexican food joint had led to dinner and then a hurried drive back to my place, where we'd shed our clothes and fallen into bed. Despite no longer being a couple, we somehow managed to follow this same pattern once a month or so.

She stood, looked across the Trinity River toward West Dallas.

"Why did you arrange a meeting with Delgado for me?" I said.

She didn't reply.

"This kid, Tremont Washington, he wasn't a loser," I said. "He wasn't a druggie either."

"Delgado knew about you already," she said. "He knew about us, too."

At the curb, a black Suburban stopped, blocking traffic. It was clearly an unmarked police vehicle.

"He asked if you'd be good at something like this." She paused. "I said yes. Then I set up the meet."

"Somebody snatched Tremont," I said.

"Or he looked sideways at the wrong gangbanger." Piper put on a pair of sunglasses. "And now he's dead in a ditch somewhere."

I didn't reply. She'd made the most probable assumption, but something bothered me about her scenario.

The driver's door of the Suburban opened and, speak of the Devil, Deputy Chief Raul Delgado stepped out. He was wearing a different suit, navy with charcoal pinstriping. He saw us and waved.

"Going to the opera?" I said. "Or a charity fund-raiser?"

"Do you think I just want to be friends with benefits for the rest of my life?"

The air seemed to get thin.

"That's what we are now, Jon. Two losers who bump uglies on occasion. Nothing more."

Delgado headed toward us, maybe thirty feet away.

"I'm a cop now, back where I belong," she said. "And you, you're all corporate with the law firm and your Armani suits."

"It's Hugo Boss," I said. "My sport coats. That's who makes them."

She smiled at Delgado and waved.

"I do have a couple of Zenga suits."

"Whatever, mister GQ." She spoke to me while looking at Delgado. "We decided this was for the best, remember? Time apart. Get to know ourselves. Yada yada."

I remembered. While the Justice Department was trying to figure out who to charge with what, we'd gone to Colorado, searching for Piper's mother and looking for a little peace and quiet. But tranquility was not part of our makeup, and trouble seemed to fill our lives like smoke in a pool hall.

Then the money ran out, and we headed back to familiar turf—Texas. She'd gotten the job with the Dallas police. Judge Clark had arranged for my position with the law firm, introducing me to Theo Goldberg, the managing partner.

Delgado approached, smiling magnanimously.

"I took care of things." He looked at me. "You won't be charged."

"Gee, thanks." I stood.

"Sorry you were arrested," he said. "I was unaware until Piper told me."

I didn't reply. Piper stared off in the distance. An awkward silence descended upon our little group, or perhaps that was just my imagination.

Several uniformed officers, muscular white guys with buzz cuts, were walking toward the jail entrance. As they went, they stared at us, not exactly friendly looks.

Little-known fact: cops invented the evil eye, a scowl that could draw blood. These guys were masters. With my record at the DPD, I figured they were looking at me.

I ignored them, as was my custom.

Raul Delgado did not. He stared back, his look matching theirs in animosity. The officers maintained eye contact until it was long past polite, their heads turned sideways. Then they looked away.

"Friends of yours?" I asked.

"Nobody likes the brass," he said. "Especially an uppity Mexican like me."

"Leave it be." Piper touched his arm. "They're not worth the effort."

Raul Delgado took several deep breaths, turned back to me.

"Your little adventure today," he said. "What have you learned?"

"Lots of things," I said. "Such as, you didn't tell me Tremont had a job."

Delgado crossed his arms. "I'm not familiar with every detail of the young man's life."

"Now would be a good time to tell me all the details you do know," I said. "Especially why you're so interested in him."

"Piper and I have an engagement in a little while." He looked at his watch. "A dinner gala."

Piper shook her head, rolled her eyes. Delgado didn't notice.

"A gala?" I glanced at my former lover. "How droll."

"Raul's giving a speech." She gave me a venomous look. Then she mentioned the name of a charity dedicated to empowering women in third-world countries, the kind of organization most cops couldn't even fathom existed.

"But there's a slot in my schedule right now," Raul said. "Perhaps we could go somewhere and talk."

"Here's to slots." I headed toward the unmarked Suburban. "I'm riding shotgun."

———

*Ellis County, Texas*
*1987*

Blood on his shirt.

The new Explorer uniform that Bobby bought him last week.

Raul Delgado tried to wipe away the stain, but the liquid just smeared, greasy and thick.

He was almost eighteen.

Six years since the last time blood coated his clothes, that of his brother, in the back of the squad car.

Now there was no vehicle in sight. There was nothing but the cottonwoods along the creek bank, their leaves rustling in the summer breeze.

Beyond the cottonwoods lay the gaunt expanse of Bobby's ranch, acres of pastureland, flat like an ironing board and baked brown by the sun, scarred by lines of barbwire fencing.

Raul's hands hurt.

He looked at his fingers.

They were swollen, knuckles bruised.

A few feet away lay Wayne, Junie's boyfriend-who's-just-a-friend.

Wayne was facedown in the mud at the edge of the water. He was shirtless. His pants were around his thighs.

As Raul watched, a trickle of blood seeped from Wayne's face, staining the mud red.

Raul looked at his hands again. Flexed. The movement hurt.

He wished he could figure out what he was feeling right now but couldn't. There was nothing inside him but emptiness. He tried to summon a mental picture of his brother, Carlos, someone he could talk to in his mind, try to explain what happened, but he couldn't even do that.

From somewhere nearby came a keening sound, a soft wail that was almost lost to the wind and the quiet babble of the creek.

Raul wondered if he might be in shock. He knew the wail was important but he couldn't stop looking at Wayne's body and the flow of blood that was becoming thicker.

The wail grew louder.

He turned away from Wayne.

To his right, maybe ten feet away, sat Junie.

She was under a cottonwood. Her hair was tangled, one cheek smeared with mud. She was wearing what was left of her school uniform—a plaid skirt, saddle oxfords, and a white cotton blouse.

The buttons had been popped off the blouse, one sleeve torn away. The skirt was ripped. In the dirt a few feet away were what appeared to be her panties, a ball of white cotton.

After a few moments the disjointed events snapped together like Legos, and Raul relived what happened as if a grainy piece of film were unspooling in his mind's eye.

Five minutes ago.

He arrived at the ranch in the old pickup, returning from the feed store with a couple of salt licks. Part of the chores he helped with around the ranch.

He parked by the barn. Got out.

Bobby was on duty for another hour. Junie was still at school. Or so he thought.

He saw Wayne's Camaro behind the barn, out of sight from the house and driveway.

The T-tops were off. Inside there was an overflowing ashtray and two cans left over from a six-pack of Coors, the metal sweating in the heat. The upholstery had the faint tang of marijuana.

Raul was contemplating why Wayne's Camaro was hidden when the screaming started.

Down by the water.

Junie's voice. Scared.

A shriek that pierced something deep inside Raul.

He ran toward the sound, ran like his life depended on the speed of his feet.

Junie was Bobby's child. He must protect her.

The screaming grew louder as Raul slid down the creek bank, the brush clawing at his skin and clothes.

A flash of white.

Wayne's bare ass on top of Junie, his stupid mullet hair dangling over her terrified face.

The Explorers taught a one-afternoon lesson on hand-to-hand combat, how to wrestle a suspect to the ground and make an arrest.

The only thing Raul remembered from the lesson was that feet were very powerful, resting at the end of the largest group of muscles in the human body.

Raul used this information, deciding in an instant that he most definitely wanted to be powerful at this particular point.

So he kicked Wayne in the ribs with the toe of his cowboy boots, putting everything into the swing of his leg.

Wayne squealed like a hog about to be butchered. He rolled off Junie.

Raul kicked him again. In the stomach.

Wayne tumbled a few feet toward the water.

Junie was screaming and crying.

Raul jumped on top of Wayne and pounded him in the face and throat.

Again and again.

And again.

Blood flew everywhere as Wayne's face assumed the texture of ground meat, and a gurgling sound emerged from his larynx.

After a minute or so, Raul stopped, breathing ragged.

He stood. Kicked Wayne in the side again, rolling him onto what was left of his face.

Raul stared at the unconscious figure until he heard the wail. Then he looked over at Junie.

She was huddled in a ball, shaking.

He took off his bloody shirt, put it around her shoulders. He was not wearing an undershirt. His bare skin was slick with sweat.

"Are you okay?"

She didn't reply. Her face was pale.

He saw no obvious injuries like broken bones or bleeding wounds, so he said, "Don't move. I'll be right back."

He ran to the house, a good seventy-five yards away. He dashed into the kitchen and called Bobby's beeper, entering the ranch's phone number followed by the family code for an urgent situation: 911.

He grabbed a first-aid kit and sprinted back to the creek.

Everything was more or less as he left it. Wayne hadn't moved. Junie, however, appeared to have gotten smaller, crawled into herself somehow, huddling, wrapped in Raul's shirt, eyes wide.

He knelt beside her, touched her arm. "Are you hurt?"

First Aid 101, again courtesy of the Dallas Police Explorers: evaluate the situation.

She slapped at his hand, tears streaming down her cheeks. She was angry, getting close to hysterical. Her face had turned red.

"I called your dad." He held up the first-aid kit. "Please, let me help you."

At the mention of her father, Junie's eyes opened wide.

"*Noooo.*"

In addition to being shaky with adrenaline and terrified by what he had seen and done, Raul was confused.

Why didn't she want her father here?

He would arrest Wayne, put him in prison where he belongs. Bobby took care of things like this. That was his job.

She shook her head frantically.

"Junie." Raul touched her shoulder. "It's okay. Everything will be all right."

She continued to shake, started to cry again. After a moment, she pointed to Wayne.

Raul tensed, thinking the man had regained consciousness. He jerked his head around.

Wayne hadn't moved. He was in the same position as when Raul left to call Bobby. The flow of blood seemed to have stopped, however.

Raul stared at the limp figure lying facedown in the mud.

The realization that Wayne was dead hit him like a brick to the gut.

Raul Delgado had killed a man. Another human being was no longer living because of his actions. Because of his swollen hands.

He remembered the horror and sense of doom he felt in the back of the squad car nearly six years ago when his brother was murdered. The feeling came over him again, but this time in a strange way, almost comforting, an old friend come to visit.

He looked at Junie. "I had to stop him. He was hurting you."

She gulped, caught her breath. Quit crying for a moment. A barely perceptible nod.

Raul sat beside her. He put an arm around her shoulder, hugged her close.

He tried not to think about her body under the torn school uniform and his bloodstained shirt.

The curve of her thighs. The firmness of her breasts.

He tried again to summon an image of his brother, but Carlos's memory had left him. So he sat there, holding on to Junie, staring at the body of Wayne.

He sat and waited and eventually Bobby arrived.

# - CHAPTER SEVENTEEN -

My hair ruffled as a strong wind blew across the fortieth-floor balcony of Raul Delgado's condo. The air felt cool and smog-free.

The building was perched on the north side of downtown in an area of upscale restaurants and shops. His outdoor terrace overlooked Klyde Warren Park, a popular green space constructed over the freeway that served as the northern boundary of the central business district.

I watched the sun set. Fort Worth's skyline was faintly visible in the distance, shrouded in a summer haze. The stench of jail permeated my clothes—sweat, cheap bleach cleaner, grease.

The balcony was chrome and glass. Hard angles, smooth surfaces.

Piper and Raul were in the living room having a discussion. Every so often their voices would get louder.

I chuckled to myself and stayed outside, admiring the scenery.

A few minutes later, I heard the swish of the sliding glass door, and Raul Delgado appeared by my side.

"These are yours." He handed me my key ring. "The Lincoln's in the visitor section downstairs."

He'd sent a pair of uniformed officers to retrieve my vehicle. Deputy Chief Raul Delgado was full service.

"Let's go inside." He pointed to the door.

"The view's nice from here. So's the breeze."

"Not trying to sound paranoid, but a parabolic mic from the place across the street could pick up every word we say." He turned and entered the apartment.

I sighed, took one last look at the city, and did the same.

Artwork decorated the interior, abstract paintings and hard-to-decipher collages made from old photographs. Iron statuary and a neon-pink rendition of Che Guevara over the fireplace. Everything appeared very expensive.

The furniture was black leather, low-slung, only a foot off the floor.

Raul was sprawled on a sofa by the fireplace.

I sat on the opposite couch, my knees rising higher than my waist, back at an awkward angle.

The furniture was like a stripper. Looked great but totally impractical.

"I bought Piper some new clothes for tonight," Raul said. "That was a mistake."

I tried not to laugh. Piper's idea of dressy was her least-ragged jeans and a retro concert T-shirt—her favorite being from the Sex Pistols' 1979 tour, a few years before she'd been born.

"When you were on the force," he said, "did you ever hear them talk about me?"

"Talk about you, like what?"

"Like why is a guy who's so damaged working for the people who did the damage?"

The two cops who'd been in the squad car when Raul Delgado's brother had been killed went to prison. One died there, the man who'd pulled the trigger. The second was released after a number of years and disappeared from public view. He'd died several years ago.

"Death is never pretty. I can't imagine what it's like seeing your brother . . . that way."

"You don't understand." Anger flashed in his eyes. "I'm not damaged in the least. I'm stronger for my experiences."

If I'd watched my brother's head get blown off, I'm pretty sure I'd be massively screwed up. I decided not to point that out.

There had been rumblings about him during my time with the Dallas police, of course, but I hadn't paid much attention. Too many problems of my own.

"People blamed me and my family for what happened," he said. "They thought we brought it on ourselves somehow."

"People are stupid. You should know that. You're a cop. That's the first lesson they teach at the academy."

"Last month, someone spray-painted the word 'pinko' on my personal vehicle. It was parked at Jack Evans at the time."

Jack Evans was Dallas police headquarters, just south of downtown. The brass had access to a secure lot, which meant that whoever vandalized his car was most likely a fellow cop.

"Didn't I read somewhere that you're on the board of the local ACLU chapter?" I said. "That doesn't exactly endear you to the rank-and-file redneck at the Dallas Police Department."

"The rank and file needs to change," he said. "A shift in the culture at the DPD."

"Good luck with that." I chuckled. "What's all this got to do with Tremont Washington?"

His eyes clouded for a moment, a memory that wouldn't stay forgotten or an emotion that couldn't be repressed. He took several deep breaths and retrieved a slim leather briefcase from the floor. He opened the case and withdrew a stack of manila folders.

"Somebody's killing bad guys." He tossed the files on the coffee table. "Take a look."

I picked up the documents, remembering a few vague mentions about this from a source a couple of weeks ago.

The first file was an open murder investigation into the death of a serial arsonist. The man had been killed by a nine-millimeter hollow-point to the head, fired by a Glock. He'd been in his garage in North Dallas at the time.

I skimmed the rest, seven more files, each an unsolved murder. The only thing they had in common was the killer or killers used the same weapon, a nine-millimeter, and the fact that in each case the victim was a lowlife of the highest order.

Murderers and rapists, an arsonist. A pimp from just the day before.

There were no witnesses. No leads either except for a few seconds of grainy footage from a video monitoring system at one of the crime scenes.

The image on the video, reproduced in the file as a series of still photographs, showed a man in what appeared to be a black or dark tracksuit. The man's age and ethnicity couldn't be determined because of the ball cap he wore low on his face.

"Not exactly pillars of society, were they?" I closed the last folder.

"They didn't deserve to die, not in that manner anyway."

"People like these, they tend to accumulate a lot of enemies," I said. "My guess is you dig enough you'll find the shooter in each case was somebody close to the victim."

"Who will be in charge of the digging?"

I didn't reply. That was a good point. The homicide squad would expend minimal effort to solve the murders of people like this.

"The pimp last night," Delgado said. "Tink-Tink Monroe. They took out most of his crew. Five dead bodies."

I nodded but didn't point out that each of them had a long record of violence, at least in Dallas County, according to the paperwork he'd just given me.

He pointed to the files. "Only a matter of time before a civilian gets hurt."

I struggled out of the uncomfortable seating, walked to the window overlooking the concrete and glass canyons that formed the central part of the city. "I go back to the same question," I said. "What's any of this got to do with your missing kid?"

"What if Tremont Washington overheard something," Raul said. "Somebody he believed was a police officer, talking about hurting someone."

"And then he disappeared," I said. This seemed possible, but then, so did almost anything.

Raul lumbered to his feet, joined me at the window. He pointed to the American Airlines Center off to our right, home to the Dallas Stars and the Mavericks. The sports arena served as the anchor for a large conglomeration of buildings—hotels, high-rise apartments, restaurants, expensive boutiques.

"You know what used to be there?"

I shook my head.

"The old Dallas Power and Light electrical plant." He paused. "That's where they took me and my brother. But only one of us came home."

The arena complex was majestic, a modern-day coliseum flanked by temples to wealth and prosperity. The edifices gleamed in the sun, solid and strong, representative of all that was good about Dallas and America. The land of opportunity.

"I try to help people like Tremont," he said. "The ones that don't appear on the radar." I turned around, surveyed the artwork and expensive condo.

In the inevitable lawsuit that followed the death of his brother, Raul Delgado had been awarded a sizable sum by the city. The money had been placed in a trust, out of reach of his parents. When he'd come of age he'd invested wisely. Real estate, blue-chip stocks. Google and Apple before they reached the stratosphere.

"There's more to life than just living on the fortieth floor." He tracked my eyes. "Don't you think?"

From the hallway, heels clicked on marble, and a moment later Piper appeared.

She wore a red dress that clung to her body, accentuating every curve. The hemline came to mid-thigh, the cleavage plunging. She'd fixed her hair and makeup. She was as beautiful as I'd ever seen her.

Then I noticed her eyes.

They were full of anger.

In her hand, she held a stack of photographs.

"You threw away my pictures," she said. "You threw away my kids."

# - CHAPTER EIGHTEEN -

I watched Piper walk into the living room of Raul Delgado's apartment. She cradled the photos in one hand. The sun highlighted her eyes and the lushness of the red dress she wore.

Only the three of us, standing in awkward silence.

"What are you talking about?" Raul said.

"My pictures," Piper said. "You threw them away."

"You left them here, remember?" He paused. "When you left me."

"They're my children."

"They're pictures of orphans scattered halfway across the world."

She didn't speak. Her lips were tight.

Raul looked at me, a confused expression on his face, clearly trying to figure out what the big deal was. "They were taped to one side of the TV in the master closet." He shrugged. "It didn't seem like she was coming back."

"You have a TV in the master closet?" I said.

"And I didn't throw them away either," Delgado said. "I just took them down."

"And put them by the trash can."

"*By* the trash. Not *in*."

"I was going to come get them." Piper's voice was low and cold.

"Oh yes. The next chapter in our little saga," he said. "The breakup, followed by getting back together."

Silence. Then:

"So, what, you use those pictures to mark your territory?" Raul said. "I mean, have you ever met any of them?"

Piper looked at me for an instant.

That had been the plan a couple of years ago. When it became apparent we weren't to die in some West Texas ditch or go to the federal penitentiary, we decided to visit some of the children.

But the best-made plans have a way of derailing themselves, and this was no exception.

I often wondered if we did it to ourselves somehow, if Piper had been afraid to meet the children she euphemistically called her own, and if I'd abetted her.

Did we place ourselves into positions where it appeared we had no choices? Do the fates just happen or are they the sum total of all our mistakes and lies?

Instead of locating the children, we'd drifted across the western section of the United States, living in motels and one-room apartments, trying to find a purpose to our lives.

Then the money ran out, as did our patience for each other, and we'd returned to the arid plains of North Texas.

"I'm sorry," Raul said. "I, uh, shouldn't have taken them down."

Piper strode to the granite bar that separated the kitchen from the rest of the living space. By the phone, she found a manila envelope.

"We need to leave." Raul looked at his watch. "We're going to be late."

With great care Piper slipped the photos into the envelope. After closing the flap, she looked around the apartment.

Nobody spoke.

Piper walked across the room. She handed me the envelope.

"Keep this safe for me, will ya?" she said. "I'll pick it up later."

Raul squinted at us like he was trying to decode a message, the meaning of which should be obvious but was muddled at present.

I tucked the envelope under my arm. "Shall we ride down together?"

Raul nodded, a blank look on his face.

The three of us left his apartment, boarded the elevator.

On the trip to the lobby, Raul stared at the door. Piper stood in the corner, her arms crossed, expression frosty.

Raul looked my way. "Do you know a man on the force named Mason Burnett? He's a captain."

"Heard the name before." I shrugged. "That's about it."

"He and I go way back. If he finds out you're working for me, he's likely as not to come after you. Just for sport if nothing else."

The floors flew by.

Raul said, "What I mean is, you can quit if you want to."

I didn't reply.

"Your arrest today. I can't guarantee your safety."

I said, "I'm still in."

One of the last times I'd seen Tremont Washington's father bubbled up to the top of my consciousness.

A dice game in the back of a barbecue joint in Waco.

The guy who owned the game was a bohunk mobster who the Texas Rangers suspected was running a child prostitution ring at a nearby truck stop.

Guns drawn, badges out, and zero probable cause, Washington and I barged into a room full of rednecks. And one barely clothed eleven-year-old girl in the corner. Washington, the only black guy there, had proceeded to break three of the bohunk's ribs with his pistol barrel, while I called for backup and put my coat over the shoulders of the girl. I'd like to think that my presence had kept the situation from escalating, but it was the ferocity of Washington's actions that caused everyone to fall silent and back away.

He was a hell of a man, Washington, and I'd be damned if I just let his kid disappear into the ether.

I didn't mention any of this or the fact that neither Theo Goldberg nor I were very fond of quitting.

A few more floors went by.

Piper said, "I got your back, Jon."

Before either Raul or I could reply, the elevator door opened and she darted out.

# - CHAPTER NINETEEN -

## THE SOUTH DALLAS ACTIVIST

The rush-hour traffic has started to wane when Demarcus Harris exits the interstate and heads west, past a strip center that houses a Burger King, a cell phone store, and a yogurt shop.

DeSoto, at the southern edge of the county, is a bedroom community, predominately home to well-to-do African Americans. Downtown Dallas lies fifteen miles to the north.

Demarcus, the young man in the red beret who'd been at the press conference the day before and asked about Tremont Washington, lives in DeSoto.

Demarcus Harris isn't wearing his beret today. He has on a skinny gray suit and a dark-green bowtie, his Louis Farrakhan look. He's been at Dallas City Hall, a council meeting, dressed up for the occasion.

His clothing choices are conscious decisions. The Dallas police with their soldiers and weapons are a military organization. Therefore, he'd worn military-style clothing for their press conference.

City hall is a civilian organization. So Demarcus wore civilian clothes there.

A person's appearance is important, something his father, a petroleum engineer currently working in Saudi Arabia on a six-month contract, drilled into his head.

Get your ass out of those saggy jeans, he'd say. Nobody's gonna take you seriously with your boxers showing.

His dad is establishment all the way, plaid shirts and no-iron Dockers, but Demarcus understands he does have a point.

Demarcus lives alone in his father's three-bedroom tract home built in the 1980s. The residence is on a street lined with other similar houses, solidly middle class, blandly suburban. All are one story. Brick on the front, wood siding everywhere else. Each home has a curbside mailbox made from matching brick.

Demarcus hates the street and the house.

So vanilla. Whitebread.

But the rent is free, and with his father out of the country for long periods, Demarcus can pursue his long-term goal as a web journalist without having to hear about how he needs to get a real job.

He has a busy afternoon planned. He wants to start his article about Tremont Washington, the child missing from the West Dallas housing project. Prior to the city council meeting, he'd done a little street work, reconnaissance of a certain North Dallas charity that is allegedly tied to Tremont Washington.

He doesn't have all the answers yet, but that's never stopped him from publishing an article, especially when he finds a juicy connection between the charity and one or more high-ranking Dallas police officials.

One slight problem is that he can't quite figure out exactly what the connection is or how juicy it might be.

But, like the old saying goes, never let the truth get in the way of a good story. What matters is the difference the story can make.

It's midafternoon. The street is pretty busy. Moms pushing kids in strollers, yard crews mowing lawns. A couple of repair trucks down the block.

Demarcus parks the Chrysler PT that his father lets him use in front of his house.

Across the street is an old Crown Victoria that appears out of place.

Demarcus slings his backpack on his shoulder and gets a bag of groceries from the rear of the car. He wonders who belongs to the vehicle. This is minivan territory, not old cop cars.

He walks up the sidewalk to his front door.

———

The man in the black tracksuit flexes his fingers. The latex gloves are getting hot.

He's in the family room of Demarcus Harris's house, a cavernous area with brown carpeting and an old-style big-screen TV, a huge, five-foot box.

The kitchen is off to one side. It is clean but unused, smelling faintly of cooked onions.

He's already inspected the rest of the home.

Sheets cover the furniture in two of the three bedrooms.

The third is clearly where Demarcus Harris spends most of his time.

Dirty shag carpeting, a picture of Malcolm X over an unmade waterbed. A flat-screen TV and several computer monitors. Stacks of books and files.

He's scanned the files. Notes on upcoming stories for Demarcus's website. Conspiracies are a favorite theme. Is the CIA poisoning the water in Dallas schools? Does the governor of Texas secretly belong to the KKK?

Nothing on Tremont Washington, which is good.

Even better, he's learned that the People's Blog is a one-man operation.

So he's returned everything to where it belongs, walked back to the family room, and is sitting in a La-Z-Boy recliner in front of the oversized TV.

A few minutes later, right on time, he hears the front door open and then shut.

Footsteps. Whistling.

The sounds of a man who thinks he's alone.

Demarcus Harris strolls into the family room, a stack of mail in one hand, a bag of groceries in the other. He looks younger than he had at city hall, barely out of high school even though he is in his early twenties. His gray suit is ridiculous-looking, too tight, pants not long enough to cover his white socks.

Several seconds pass before the young man realizes someone else is present.

"What the—" He drops the mail, sets the groceries down.

"Hello, Demarcus." The man in the black tracksuit remains sitting with his legs crossed.

"Who the—how—" Demarcus's mouth goes slack. "I know you. You were at the press conference."

"Nice place you have here. Your father, I bet he works really hard to provide this home for you."

Demarcus blinks several times.

"You've had an easy life, haven't you?" Black Tracksuit says.

Demarcus clenches his fists, angry.

"Everything's been handed to you on a silver platter." Black Tracksuit sighs.

"Silver platter, my ass." Demarcus cocks his head. "You ever actually known any black people?"

Black Tracksuit stands.

Demarcus takes a step back. "Get out of my house, you fascist cracker."

"Or what?" The man opens the messenger bag he's brought with him. "You'll call the police?"

Demarcus holds up his hands, ready for a fight, breathing heavily.

"Relax. I'm not going to hurt you," Black Tracksuit says. "I just want to ask you some questions."

Demarcus's eyes narrow. He nods slightly, clearly wanting to believe.

From the bag, the man pulls a metal object about the size of a large cigar. The item is an ASP baton, a retractable steel impact device, sort of like the switchblade of billy clubs. In its unopened state, it appears fairly innocuous.

"What's that?" Demarcus points to the baton.

"This?" The man holds up the ASP. "This is just a tool. I'm not gonna hurt you. I already told you that."

Demarcus nods, the politeness of his middle-class upbringing evident.

"So tell me what you know about Tremont Washington," Black Tracksuit says.

Demarcus doesn't respond. He keeps staring at the baton, mind clearly churning.

"I'm trying to find Tremont, too," the man says. "I want to help him."

The stupidity of the average civilian was amazing. A guy breaks into your house, starts asking questions, and you stick around? The man in the black tracksuit sighs. Rule one when somebody is in your crib who shouldn't be: get the hell out.

"I was, uh, working on a story about substandard housing at the Iris Apartments," Demarcus says. "I talked to his grandmother."

"Tremont's grandmother. Alice, that's her name. Right?"

Demarcus nods, eyes narrowing.

"And what did his grandmother, Alice, say?"

Silence for a few moments.

"You shouldn't be here." Demarcus licks his lips. "You should leave now."

"We're almost done," the man says. "Then you can go back to blogging or tweeting or whatever you kids do."

Demarcus's eyes are slits. The expression on his face indicates he understands he should have run in the first instant he realized his home had been invaded.

"What did the grandmother say?" Black Tracksuit asks. "Did she have any idea where her grandson is?"

"H-how do you know about this? Any of it?"

"Demarcus." The man extends the baton with a flick of his wrist. "You don't get to ask questions."

"She didn't know anything." Demarcus takes a step back. "Neither do I."

Black Tracksuit darts across the room, already swinging the metal baton at the younger man's knee. The steel slams into the flesh with a satisfying squish.

Demarcus screams and tumbles backward, arms flailing. His head hits the corner of an end table as he falls to the floor.

"You really thought I wasn't going to hurt you, didn't you?" Black Tracksuit kneels beside him.

Demarcus doesn't respond.

A thin stream of blood trickles from underneath his head, staining the carpet.

Black Tracksuit sighs and shakes his head. He feels for a pulse.

A faint heartbeat.

Fading, fading, fading—

Gone.

"Shit, Demarcus." He stands. "Why'd you have to go and die on me?"

He moves to the entryway windows, peers outside.

Two women, each with a stroller, stand in front of the house, chatting.

He intended to bring Demarcus with him to the Crown Vic under his own power, transport him to the dump site. Now he's going to have to go out the back, loop around, and get the Crown Vic. Then come back down the alley to retrieve the body.

This makes him angry. He has meetings scheduled for later this evening, business that needs his attention.

His vision goes red and a moment later he realizes he has been kicking Demarcus Harris's corpse.

He regains control and leaves by the back door.

# - CHAPTER TWENTY -

Early the next morning someone broke into my neighbor's townhome.

The neighbor was away on business, and the alarm was so loud it sounded like the end of time.

I lived in a new complex in the Oak Lawn section of town, across the street from a nightclub that catered to the gay demographic, and a Starbucks.

Quite a few homeless people spent their time in the alleys, so I figured one of them was probably a little too loaded on Boone's Farm and was looking for a place to crash for a while.

I stumbled outside at the same time as the neighbor on the other side did, a woman in her thirties who I was pretty sure worked as a call girl.

The alarm stopped, replaced by screaming. Furniture thrown against the walls. More screaming. The sounds one would expect from a homeless guy suffering a psychotic breakdown, a not-uncommon occurrence in this part of town.

"What the hell is going on?" The call girl rubbed her eyes.

"Beats me." I yawned. "Sounds like one of the local bums drank too much crazy."

"Well, would you shut it up?" She cocked her head.

"I missed the part where this got to be my problem."

"All afternoon I got appointments," she said. "I need some sack time."

The screaming grew louder, like a hyena stuck in a blender.

"This part of town is whacked." She shook her head. "It's either homos or winos. I swear I'm gonna move."

A police car squealed to a stop in front of our neighbor's and a uniformed Dallas officer got out. He strode up the steps and knocked on the door where the screaming was coming from.

No answer, just more yelling and furniture slamming.

"A bum got stabbed in the alley last week." The call girl looked at the cop. "Took you dipwads an hour to respond. This, you show up for?"

The cop looked back and forth between the two of us. "Either of you got a key?"

The call girl sighed loudly and went back inside.

"Call the management company," I said.

A black Suburban rolled up behind the squad car. Two men got out, one white, the other black. Each individual had close-cropped hair and was built like a weight lifter, barrel chest, broad shoulders, exaggerated gait from thighs that were as thick as tree trunks.

They wore matching black tracksuits with yellow stripping down the sleeves. They stood by their vehicle, amused looks on their faces, chatting with each other like they hadn't a care in the world.

One of them held a walkie-talkie in his hand.

The uniformed cop looked at them. Then he shook his head.

"What's with the Arnie Schwarzeneggers?" I said.

"You used to be on the force, didn't you?" the cop said.

I nodded. "A lifetime ago."

"The chief's new anti-crime initiative. Put SWAT guys on the street corners."

"They look like juicers," I said.

"They are. Probably sweat steroids." He headed toward his car.

"Where are you going?"

"I got real police work to do." He looked over his shoulder. "Don't piss 'em off."

He left without speaking to either of the new arrivals.

The officers in the tracksuits strode over. They stopped in front of my neighbor's door.

The black guy looked at me, hands on his hips, a belligerent expression on his face.

"Who are you?" he said.

"The neighbor." I smiled. "Joe Citizen."

The white guy reared back his leg and kicked in the door.

The black guy said, "Go back to your place, Joe. We got this covered."

———

By the time I left an hour later, the SWAT officers were gone and no more screaming was coming from my neighbor's place.

I called Piper to ask if she'd had any luck finding out who had been arrested at the Iris Apartments a week before. The call went straight to voice mail. I thought about driving by her house but I didn't want to know if she was there or not.

So I did what any self-respecting ex-cop would do. I went to IHOP for breakfast. Then I drove to the Uptown section of Dallas, just north of the central business district.

152

Raul Delgado's high-rise was on the fringes of the neighborhood. That was not my destination.

There were a lot of other skyscrapers in the area, intermixed with turn-of-the-century homes that had been converted into commercial uses—law offices, art galleries, small companies that had "investments" somewhere in their title.

The organization that employed Tremont Washington was located near McKinney Avenue, just past the trolley stop, according to the card Tremont's grandmother had given me.

The Helping Place occupied an old Victorian home that was painted the color of fresh lemons, a soft yellow that perfectly accented the immaculate lawn as well as the velvety blur of red and blue flowers in the beds that surrounded the house.

I parked on the street, behind a BMW with a leasing company license plate frame. I got out, left my sport coat in the back. I was wearing jeans and a black T-shirt.

A wide porch ran around the entire structure. Expensive patio furnishings formed a sitting area to one side of the front door.

On the outdoor sofa sat a young man in his midteens. He wore thick glasses, which did nothing to hide the too-broad distance between his eyes, or the unnatural slope of his forehead, both the result of Down syndrome.

He was playing with a Game Boy, lips pressed together in concentration.

I climbed the steps to the porch. The elderly wood creaked.

He looked up, smiled. "Hello, sir." He stood. Placed the Game Boy carefully on the sofa.

"Hi." I smiled. "How are you doing?"

"My name is Toby."

"Nice to meet you, Toby. My name is Jon."

"I am ready to go to work, Jon."

"Sorry, Toby. That's not why I'm here today."

He nodded, a stoic look on his face.

"I'm sure you're going to make someone a fine employee." I reached for the front door.

He picked up a wad of clothing from the sofa and approached me with it.

"I don't need my jacket, Jon."

I stopped, hand on the knob.

"It's not cold." He held up the garment to me. "Would you please take it back inside?"

I took a step closer, eyeing the clothing in his hand. It appeared to be a warm-up jacket made from similar material as the outfits worn by the two SWAT officers at my apartment this morning.

"Sure, Toby." I took the garment. "I'll take it inside."

He smiled and sat down.

I stepped into the office.

The foyer of the old home had been remodeled into a reception area. A hardwood floor refinished and polished to a high gloss. Stark white walls decorated with pictures of young adults who appeared to have mental faculties similar to Toby. They were all smiling and appeared to be in work environments.

In one corner of the reception area sat a glass and chrome desk with a Mac computer on one side and a phone on the other. Offices were to the left and right, the old parlor and dining room. More high-end, modern furniture, stark decor.

The entire place appeared to be empty.

I took this as an opportunity to examine the item Toby had given me.

A thin yellow pinstripe ran along each sleeve. In the collar was a tag that read "Property Dallas Police Department."

For the heck of it, I slipped the warm-up jacket on.

Not quite like having the badge, but not a bad feeling.

Noise from the rear of the house, a voice on the phone.

I sauntered down the hallway.

The rear of the refurbished home was one big office, the back wall glass, overlooking a yard with a fountain and several pieces of expensive art.

A large, ornately carved pine table dominated one side of the room, serving as a desk. Behind the table sat a woman in her early forties. She wore a cream-colored blouse and navy blazer that matched her skirt.

She was on the phone when I entered, staring at the fountain outside, a pen in her mouth. She looked up, motioned for me to sit in the leather chair in front of her desk.

I did as requested. Crossed my legs. Waited.

She stared at me as she talked on the phone. The conversation concerned an upcoming event, a fund-raiser of some sort. Her face was blank. Not the typical sheepish smile as if to say, *Sorry to keep you waiting; I'll be off in a second.*

After about half a minute, she ended the call.

Her expression changed. A glint of fear came into her eyes as she crossed her arms.

I thought about introducing myself and telling her why I was here, but I didn't.

Silence. Sometimes the best interview technique.

After a moment, she sighed, a nervous little gulp of her throat, and said, "Have you found Tremont yet?"

# - CHAPTER TWENTY-ONE -

Mason Burnett pushed the steel bar off its perch, three hundred pounds of dead weight.

He was lying on the bench-press in the workout room at his SWAT team's headquarters.

Sweat dotted his face. His muscles felt flush.

He took shallow breaths. *Onetwothree-onetwothree.*

The bar bent slightly as he eased it down to his nipples, then back up.

Ten reps, the final set of three. With the last rep, his pecs and arms burned like lava was flowing through his blood vessels.

He stopped, sat up. Caught his breath, face slick with perspiration, hair damp.

The Dallas SWAT team made their base of operations in a nondescript building located on a street that dead-ends underneath a freeway. The neighborhood was a no-man's land between the nightclubs of Deep Ellum, the crack houses around Fair Park, and Baylor Hospital.

The building was between a streets-and-sewers maintenance yard and the DPD property division, a massive warehouse that most people in the city couldn't find even with GPS.

Mason was wearing a black tracksuit, the unofficial uniform of the Dallas SWAT team.

It was midmorning and the weight room was empty.

Mason wiped his face with a towel and headed to the locker room.

He opened his locker, popped a Xanax.

He leaned against the cool metal, closed his eyes.

And the fist was there.

———

From the darkness.

His father's clenched hand strikes him in the chest.

The summer of 1978.

Cockrell Hill, a tiny blue-collar town deep in the southwest corner of the county, surrounded on all sides by the least prosperous sections of Dallas.

Potholed streets, knife fights at the bars on Saturday nights. Cheap Mexican speed sold at the truck stops. Food stamps and foster parents.

Crime and violence, everywhere. Suffering you can never seem to get away from, even when you're a nine-year-old boy.

Mason falls to the ground, the dirt that makes up the lawn in front of their wooden shack.

"Where's your bike?" Daddy says. The still air between them stinks of Marlboros and Budweiser.

Shirley, Mason's stepmother, is not around, so that makes what's coming even worse.

"I locked it up."

Daddy strolls over to the rotten railing around the front porch. One picket has been broken.

"They stole your bike," he says. "You let some nigger come into our yard and steal your bike."

"I locked it up, Daddy. Like you told me to."

"Honest folks can't even make it in this world." He shakes his head. "And then I got you to contend with."

Mason struggles to hold back the tears as he gets to his feet. He'd locked the Schwinn up, but they'd broken the wooden railing. It wasn't his fault. But that didn't matter.

"You know how hard I had to work to get the money for that bike?"

Mason's daddy is a deputy constable, an occupation that doesn't pay well but offers a certain amount of respect for a man without much in the way of education or family connections.

"Real hard, Daddy," Mason says. "You work real hard."

"Damn straight." His father sticks a cigarette in his mouth, flicks a lighter.

Mason flinches.

"Where's Shirley?" Daddy lets a trickle of smoke escape his nostrils.

"Please, Daddy, no."

"Where is she?"

Mason shakes his head, eyes welling with tears.

"That fellow from the tire store?" Daddy moves closer. "He come around, didn't he?"

Mason shakes his head harder, blinking back the tears.

Shirley is a fine-looking woman, feathered hair like Farrah Fawcett-Majors's, and a tight little body with big boobs. She's the kind of woman that makes men stop and stare, and a boy like Mason Burnett wonder what strange power she possesses.

The man who'd come by earlier had been a new one, Larry, according to the nametag sewn on the front of his shirt. Larry worked on the lube rack at Sears and had him some righteous weed, according to Shirley, as she got into his El Camino.

Mason can't tell any of this to Daddy. That would make what is coming all the worse.

"Who'd she leave with?" Daddy is next to Mason now. The cigarette smoke tickles Mason's nose, makes him want to sneeze.

"Please. No." Mason shakes his head.

"Won't tell me, will ya?" Daddy takes the cigarette from his mouth.

Mason vows he won't cry or make a sound. He'll be a man.

But, like everything else, he's wrong about that, too.

———

Mason came awake, breath caught in his throat. He was on the floor of the locker room, cold concrete pressed against his face.

He sat up, looked around, making sure no one had seen him.

The attacks, whatever they were—panic, some weird form of PTSD—were getting worse, something he hadn't told that bull dyke of a shrink about.

He had enough trouble already. That hug-a-thug libtard Raul Delgado was making waves about the gangbanger who'd fallen out of the window of the boardinghouse in Oak Cliff.

He got to his feet, stumbled into the shower, letting the cold water run over his head for a long time. Then he dressed in civilian clothes—khaki pants, an untucked golf shirt, tan tactical boots. A pistol in his waistband.

As an afterthought, he grabbed a change of clothes, a fresh black tracksuit, and strode out to his Suburban.

Ten minutes later, he parked in the rear lot of the Iris Apartments.

# - CHAPTER TWENTY-TWO -

I let the silence drag on.

*Why had this woman asked me about Tremont Washington?*

We were in the rear office of the Helping Place, in the expensively remodeled Victorian house just north of downtown.

The woman was attractive. She had a fashionable hairstyle. Layered, shoulder length. Colored to a shimmering brown that seemed to change in hue each time she moved her head. One moment it was henna-red, the next it was the color of chestnuts.

The nameplate on the desk identified her as "Hannah J. McKee."

"A reporter called yesterday," she said.

Her voice had no accent or emotion, bland like a newscaster's.

"About Tremont?" I said.

"Of course about Tremont." She slapped the desk.

A touch of twang crept into her inflection, no doubt unbidden, something she worked hard at erasing from her speech.

I noticed her hands. They were big. Thick knuckles, calloused fingers, at odds with the rest of her appearance. I imagined a childhood in one of the blue-collar suburbs, Garland or Mesquite. High school weekends at the 4-H show or rodeo, personal factoids she didn't bring up very much on the cock-tail-party circuit.

She said, "I told you people that someone would come ask-ing about him."

I nodded, one hand touching the hem of the black jacket. She thought I was a cop.

"Have you heard anything else about him?" I asked.

Wrong question.

She stared at me. Her gaze took in the black warm-up jacket and then traveled down to my jeans.

"What's your name?" The woman's eyes were slits, voice back to being smooth like a TV announcer's.

"Jon Cantrell."

"Show me your badge, Officer Cantrell."

"I don't have one. Because I'm not a police officer."

She sucked in a mouthful of air, eyes fearful. She stared at the black jacket.

"Toby, the guy outside. He gave me the jacket." I paused. "Is he gonna disappear, too?"

The fear vanished from her eyes, replaced by anger. "Screw you, Jon Cantrell." She pointed to the door. "Get out."

I didn't move.

"Funny you should mention Tremont Washington," I said. "That's why I came here. To find out what happened to him."

The fear returned.

"Tremont was a good kid." She looked at her nails.

"Was?"

"Is. Whatever."

"You think he's dead?"

She didn't respond.

"Why do you say he's a good kid?"

"He never missed a day of work. Always on time."

Based on what I had gleaned so far, the Helping Place functioned as a way to arrange employment for people who suffered from some sort of intellectual disability. The pictures in the hallway had been of young adults handling files or bagging groceries, semi-repetitive tasks that required little mental horsepower.

"Where did Tremont work?"

She didn't reply. Instead, she crossed her arms and stared outside.

"I'm assuming you want him found, too," I said.

"You like to piss people off, don't you?" She didn't turn her head.

I shrugged.

"Tremont worked here," she said. "In this office."

"Was that usual?"

"We have strict confidentiality policies, Mr. Cantrell. I've told you too much already."

"Did I mention I'm working for his grandmother?"

Not exactly true, but who's going to quibble at this point?

Hannah McKee ran a hand through her perfectly trimmed and colored hair. She unplugged an electronic cigarette from a USB cord, twisted the filter end, and stuck it in her mouth.

"Do those things really work?" I asked.

She blew a plume of water vapor toward the ceiling. The mist looked exactly like cigarette smoke but was completely odorless.

"Do you know how many charitable organizations there are in Dallas?" she said.

I didn't reply.

"Cancer this. Heart disease that. They get all the cash." She took a long pull on the e-cig. "Raising money for organizations like the Helping Place is brutal."

"So what do you think happened to Tremont?"

She didn't reply. She put the fake cigarette in her mouth but didn't puff.

"His grandmother told me she got him to the bus stop in front of the Iris Apartments on the day he disappeared," I said. "That would be eight days ago."

She plugged her fake cigarette back in. Shuffled some papers.

I took off the black jacket, dropped it on her desk.

"Just leave, okay." She looked up. "I've got a lot of work to do."

"There are some powerful people in DC who want Tremont found."

Again, not strictly true, but I didn't think she'd argue the point.

Theo Goldberg, my employer, wanted his hooks in Raul Delgado. Delgado wanted Tremont found, as did I. Interconnected goals.

"Tremont's dad and I were friends. Back when I had a badge." I paused. "He was good police."

A squad car pulled into the back parking area visible from where we sat.

"Who's that?" I asked.

No one got out of the vehicle. Exhaust spooled from the muffler.

"I have friends on the force," she said. "DPD likes what we do here."

I looked at the black jacket.

"Do you have children, Mr. Cantrell?"

I shook my head, envisioning Piper's herd of adoptees, far-flung across several hemispheres.

"I thought I'd have kids by now." Hannah McKee spoke softly. A wistful look came over her. "I'd be going to charity events with my husband, instead of doing the grunt work putting them together."

Still no movement from the squad car.

"Who was the reporter that called?"

"What?" She blinked, looked up at me.

"You said a reporter called asking about Tremont." I stood. "Who was it?"

She scribbled on a notepad, handed me a slip of paper. "You need to leave."

The driver's door opened and a uniformed officer got out.

I slipped the information in my pocket and headed to the front door.

# - CHAPTER TWENTY-THREE -

Mason Burnett parked in a handicap spot in front of the manager's office at the Iris Apartments. He got out of the Suburban, clipped his badge on his belt by the duty-issue Glock.

The complex seemed pretty quiet at the moment.

Mason remembered the departmental e-mail from yesterday. There'd been a shooting and several arrests, a small quantity of narcotics confiscated—a kilo or so of cocaine packaged in individual doses.

In the entire complex, on any given day, there were probably a hundred kilos of contraband. So yesterday, the Dallas police managed to confiscate one percent.

He shook his head. Burn the whole place down. Solve a lot of problems.

The grandmother lived toward the back. Mason headed that way.

After the building that housed the manager's office, he entered a bare dirt area that served as a courtyard.

Several groups of young men were there, standing around, watching him. Saggy jeans, wifebeater shirts, quart cans of beers.

Mason watched back, eyes unwavering.

The leader, a black guy in his late twenties with his hair in long dreadlocks, sauntered toward Mason, a cigarillo clamped in his mouth. As he got closer, the sunlight glinted off the diamond grill on his teeth.

He stopped in front of Mason, blocking his path. When he spoke, he affected an English accent and phrasing.

"I say, good chap, whatever brings you to our corner of the globe?"

"Move your ass, Prince Charles." Mason snapped his fingers. "You're in my way."

The man slowly stepped back. After a few feet, he swept his arm toward the rear of the property, a welcoming gesture.

"Until we meet again, good sir."

Mason strode toward the next building but stopped. He looked at the man with the strange accent.

"If we come across each other again, Prince Charles, you're gonna be picking that grill out of your ass."

The man with the dreadlocks squinted at Mason like he was trying to commit his face to memory, but he didn't speak.

Mason continued on his way. For the rest of the walk no one approached him. A minute later, he climbed the stairs of the rear building and knocked on the door to apartment 6225.

Timid footsteps.

The door opened a sliver, the crack filled with an old woman's wary face.

Mason badged her. "Are you Alice Simpson?"

The woman nodded.

"I'm here about your grandson, Tremont."

No response.

Mason said, "I'd like to talk to you about the day he disappeared."

"Did that Mexican fellow send you?"

"Who?"

She frowned. "Why's everybody so interested all of a sudden?"

Mason's turn to frown.

"Two white men in two days." She shook her head. "The Mexican, he quit coming around, though."

For no reason, Mason wondered if the Mexican could be Raul Delgado. If it was, he wondered how he could use this information. But who was the other person?

"I think it was two days ago." She shook her head.

"When did you last see the Mexican?"

"Was that you that came around?" She squinted at Mason's face. "Wait a minute. Don't you work at CVS down the street?"

He couldn't tell if her eyesight was bad or if she was suffering from some sort of dementia.

"These people that have been asking about your grandson," Mason said. "You remember anybody's name?"

Alice Simpson nodded. "I got his business card, the one from yesterday."

Mason put his hand on the door. "Perhaps I could come inside and we could talk about this a little more?"

The old woman remained wary. After a moment, she nodded, then removed the chain and opened the door.

## - CHAPTER TWENTY-FOUR -

I left the renovated house that served as the headquarters of the Helping Place, shutting the front door softly.

Toby was gone from the porch.

I jogged to the Navigator, jumped in, and sped away.

Instead of heading downtown to arrange for the pickup of Tommy Joe Culpepper's misplaced shipment, I drove north on Central Expressway. Traffic in this direction was light, and about ten minutes later I exited at Lovers Lane and headed east.

A few blocks after the apartments and shopping centers clustered around Greenville Avenue, I turned south on an interior street called Rexton Lane and found myself in a neighborhood of low-slung brick homes, snug little places built in the 1950s and '60s. Most had tiny front porches with painted wrought-iron railings, picture windows overlooking the street.

I stopped midblock in front of a house with two towering sycamore trees in the front yard. Piper's domicile du jour, a rental she kept on a six-month lease, her version of commitment.

From the console, I grabbed the manila envelope that contained her pictures. I got out, strode across the lawn, and knocked on her door.

She answered a moment later, out of breath, hair damp. One arm was behind her back.

"What do you want?" She slowly eased her hand down, fingers grasping a pistol.

"Here." I held out the envelope.

She was barefoot, wearing a pair of yoga pants and a T-shirt from the Broken Spoke in Austin, the fabric so worn it had the consistency of cheesecloth.

She took the package. "Thanks."

Neither of us spoke.

After a moment, she stepped away from the door. "You want to come in?"

I shrugged, entered her home.

The living room was decorated in early Pier 1. Wicker and bamboo, veneer woods that had been stained mahogany. Brass-plated knickknacks.

The coffee table had been moved to one side and a yoga mat set in its place. Candles and incense peppered the flat surfaces, making the air smell like vanilla-scented patchouli.

"You're doing . . . yoga." I tried not to sound incredulous.

"Keeps me centered." She shrugged. "Good for my chi, too."

"Your, uh, chi?" I paused. "It needs to be centered?"

Piper's idea of self-improvement was to read the Sunday papers. Yoga was a sign of maturity, or some damn thing. I wasn't sure what to make of it.

She cocked her head to one side. "What do you want, Jon?"

"The pictures."

She shut the door behind me.

"You said to take care of them. So I did."

She did a couple of stretching exercises, bending at the waist, palms flat on the floor. Then she stood up straight and exhaled slowly.

I clenched my hamstrings, aching just from watching her.

"Did I tell you my sergeant asked me out?" She picked up a bottle of water from a side table.

I didn't reply.

"Guy's got the IQ of a speed bump," she said. "And his mustache, jeez, it makes him look like a walrus."

On the wall opposite the front door were a half dozen pictures of children, eight-by-tens, framed in black. For some reason their presence filled me with a sadness that was hard to describe. Roads not taken, holidays spent alone, opportunities missed.

"My life is complicated enough, so of course I said no." She sighed.

"Of course."

"What's that supposed to mean?"

"Nothing. I was agreeing with you."

She drained the water bottle. "So, long story short, he goes all puppy-love on me. Starts talking about how he can help me get my life back on track."

I nodded, a nonjudgmental expression on my face. Hopefully.

"Am I a fix-it project, Jon?" She sat on the couch. "Do people look at me that way?"

"You can't run your life based on what people think," I said. "You are what you are."

Corinne, our DOJ-mandated counselor, would be so proud. It was almost like I'd been paying attention.

"Maybe it's because I grew up an orphan." She shook her head. "People want to save me or something."

"I need to get back to the office."

"The thing you asked me about," she said. "The pedophile busted last week at the Iris. The guy that Lysol Alvarez told you about."

"Yeah?"

"The arrest records were unavailable for a two-day period that week, including when your guy got popped."

"What does that mean?"

"No access," she said. "They're blaming it on a computer glitch."

The computer system at the Dallas County jail was legendary for its inefficiencies and abrupt shutdowns. Inmates got lost in plain sight for weeks at a time because of the jail computer. The company that had designed the system was run by people who knew nothing about computers but were experts in graft and kickbacks.

"Could be a coincidence," I said.

"It's not and we both know it."

I nodded.

"Shutting down access for a specified period," she said. "That's the kind of thing only somebody with a lot of juice could pull off."

"A deputy chief, perhaps?"

"Going right for the jugular, straightaway."

"I still can't figure out why he's so interested in one kid from West Dallas."

"He cries in his sleep sometimes," she said. "Calls out for his brother. And somebody named Junie."

"Delgado?"

"He's the only guy I've slept with lately."

"Not counting me."

"Right." She nodded. "Which we agreed was a mistake."

"What else does Raul Delgado do that I might need to know about?"

A long pause.

"I dunno." She shrugged, a wistful look on her face. "He's got as many snakes in his head as you and me."

I debated my next question. Decisions had been made. My life was on a different path than before.

"He wants to change me," she said. "Make me into some do-gooder socialite."

"Do you have a gun I can borrow?"

She raised both eyebrows, a look of mild astonishment.

"Things are heating up," I said.

"You told me no more guns. After the last time."

We were silent for a few moments.

"You never wanted me different," she said. "I always liked that about you."

Outside, a lawn mower started up. Inside, the smell from the incense and candles began to be cloying.

"So you need a gun. Welcome to Piper's Firearm Emporium. If we can't kill it, it's not from this planet."

I smiled. The tension between us had disappeared, replaced by a sense of comfort and familiarity.

"I've got a friend in records," she said. "He can track down everybody arrested that day."

"Thanks."

"My weapons inventory is in the bedroom." She smiled innocently. "The good stuff anyway."

I waited for her next move.

She took my hand. "Come with me."

———

*Ellis County, Texas*
*1986*

In the aftermath of the assault on Junie, Raul pieced everything together and realized how it must have looked when Bobby arrived at the creek thirty minutes later.

Bobby skidded to a stop, feet slipping in the mud. He was breathing hard, standing in the shade of the cottonwood tree as the cicadas screeched and a cow bellowed in the side pasture. He saw his daughter, barely clothed, being held by a shirtless Raul.

He stared at Junie's tear-stained face and bare legs and Raul Delgado's sweaty torso.

Raul and Bobby locked eyes, and Raul glimpsed the depth of a parent's love.

Bobby's expression was no longer kind.

The older man's face was cold and deadly, a gray bullet looking for something to kill.

Without speaking, Raul pointed to Wayne's body to the left of Bobby's line of vision.

Bobby turned.

Flies were buzzing around the dead man's bloody head. His bare ass was pale like ice cream against the muddy creek bank.

Junie pushed Raul's arm away. She stood, clutched his Explorer shirt tight around her chest.

"D-daddy. I'm s-sorry."

Bobby knelt beside Wayne, touched his neck. He stood, looked at his daughter.

"Are you hurt? Do you need an ambulance?"

She didn't reply. After a moment she shook her head.

Bobby's vision zeroed in on Raul's swollen hands. "What happened?"

Raul told him, a dry recital of the facts, just like they talked about at the Explorers. He began with his return to the ranch from the feed store. Then, seeing Wayne's Camaro and hearing Junie's scream, which led him to believe that an assault was in progress.

He ended his little speech, voice shaky, by saying, "I attempted to control the suspect and end the threat."

"*Control the suspect*." Bobby's voice was flat. "Is that what you said?"

After a moment of hesitation, Raul nodded.

Bobby looked at his daughter. Then he jabbed a finger at Wayne's body.

"I told you last week," he said to her. "Stay away from him. He's a suspect in a rape case out of Hillsboro."

Junie's eyes filled with tears.

"Go to the house," Bobby said. "Get yourself cleaned up."

Junie didn't move.

"Girl, are your legs broke?" Bobby's voice was angry. "*Vámonos*. Now."

Junie scampered up the creek bank and disappeared.

Bobby turned to Raul. "You did this?"

No reply. The answer was obvious.

Bobby paced, looking at Wayne's body and the muddy area by the creek, which was littered with footprints, blood, and Junie's underwear.

Raul cleared his throat. "I didn't mean for it to happen. For him to die."

Bobby glanced up, almost like he was surprised to find someone else there. He said, "Shut up, Raul. Don't talk until I tell you to."

Raul's breathing was shallow, skin cold even though the air along the creek was hot and still. He nodded, fearful of the tone in the older man's voice.

Bobby resumed his examination of what in most cases would be called a crime scene. After a few minutes he looked up and said, "The front gate."

Raul frowned, confused.

Bobby pointed in the direction of the highway. "Take the pickup. Go to the front gate and lock it."

"But—"

"Don't 'but' me, Raul. Just do what I fucking say."

Raul gulped. Then nodded. Bobby rarely swore.

"After you lock the gate, meet me at the barn. We're gonna need the tractor."

"I—I don't understand."

"The back part of the ranch," Bobby said. "Farthest from the road."

Raul tilted his head to one side, not getting the significance of what he was being told.

Bobby scratched his chin. "Then I've got to figure out what to do with the Camaro."

Raul did the ciphering in his head, comprehended what Bobby had planned. The tractor had a backhoe attached, a large implement capable of digging a big hole very quickly.

"No—you can't—" He shook his head. "We have to call the sheriff."

"And tell him what, Raul? That you beat a piece of trailer scum to death with your fists?"

"But—but—" Raul took a step back. "This is wrong."

"You want to go to prison? You're not a minor anymore."

Raul didn't speak.

"This isn't something I can sweep under the rug either."

Raul stared at Wayne's body.

"Let me explain it to you," Bobby said. "You're a Mexican, and you just killed a white guy in a county where the sheriff and all the judges are white."

High overhead a jet streaked across the sky, contrails flaring. Raul imagined himself on that plane, headed somewhere far, far away.

"This problem has to disappear," Bobby said. "That's the only way out of the situation we've got here."

Raul imagined Junie sitting beside him on the jet.

"Now, go lock the front gate," Bobby said.

"I didn't mean to kill him." Raul wiped his eyes. "I just wanted him to stop hurting Junie."

No one spoke for a moment.

"And that's what you did," Bobby said softly. "You stopped him from hurting my little girl."

Raul fought the emotion building in his throat.

"You did the right thing, son." Bobby smiled for the first time. "Hard for you to understand that now."

Raul nodded.

Bobby wrapped his arms around Raul's shoulders, hugged him close. Whispered in his ear, "We get this cleaned up today. And we'll never, ever talk about it again. To anybody."

Raul smelled the man who'd become a father to him. Old Spice cologne and gun leather and sweat. He tried not to cry.

Bobby released him. Gave a gentle shove toward the front gate.

Raul scampered up the creek bank.

Bobby called out to him, "One more thing."

At the top of the bank, Raul stopped, looked back.

Bobby stared at him for a long moment and then said, "Thank you."

# - CHAPTER TWENTY-FIVE -

You walk a path enough, you'll wear a groove in it. The groove gets too deep, metaphorically speaking, it becomes difficult to walk anywhere else. Maybe that path is the one you're meant to travel, and that's why the groove is there in the first place.

What am I, a philosopher?

I got dressed in Piper's bedroom, buttoned my shirt, found my shoes. I slid a heavy leather belt around my waist and attached a holster to the right side. Piper, wearing a bathrobe, opened a safe in her closet and handed me a .40 caliber Glock, a standard police sidearm. She loaded some magazines while I ran my fingers over the pistol.

"I feel like I'm in that gay cowboy movie," she said. "I wish I knew how to quit you."

"That such a bad thing? Us being together?"

"We'll get in a fight here in a few minutes." She handed me the mags. "We always do."

I didn't reply. She was right. Conflict was our way. Neither of us had the ability to take the high road, to let the feathers become unruffled on their own. Our nature was to stir things up, which made us good at certain activities but bad at others, like, say, being in a relationship.

"Are you familiar with an organization called the Helping Place?" I loaded the Glock. "It's a charity of some sort."

"You trying to change me, too, all of a sudden? Make me into some kind of socialite?"

I sighed. "It's just a question, Piper."

She didn't say anything. I slipped on my sport coat, looked at myself in the mirror. The bulge from the pistol wasn't too noticeable. As a federal agent, I used to carry openly or while wearing an oversized Windbreaker. This felt different.

"I don't know what's gonna happen to my job." She crossed her arms.

I paused at the door to the bedroom.

"It's the only job I got." Her voice was soft, choked with emotion. "And it was damn hard to come by."

"Here's a tip—don't sleep with a deputy chief. Shit rolls downhill."

"You're all heart, Jon." She sneered in my direction. "Thanks for not wiping your junk on the drapes after we had sex."

"What do you want me to say?" I walked down the hall to the living room. "I'm not the one who cut and ran."

"We weren't even talking about that." She padded after me.

"Whatever." I paused at the front door. "It always comes back to that."

"No, it doesn't." She stood across the room. "You always bring it back to that."

She was right but I wasn't going to concede the point.

I opened the door.

"The charity," she said. "The Helping Place."

"Yeah?"

"I've heard of it before."

I raised one eyebrow.

"Raul was involved with them. Helped raise money."

Another tidbit that Deputy Chief Delgado forgot to mention.

———

It was almost noon when I pulled into Judge Clark's driveway. The nurse's Toyota was in the same spot. Behind her car sat a white Suburban with exempt plates.

I parked to one side of the Suburban, got out, and rang the bell.

A uniformed Dallas police officer answered. He was in his midthirties, built like a Navy SEAL. The nurse hovered in the background.

"Come in," she said.

The cop moved aside after a moment of staring at my eyes, a quick attempt at establishing dominance, a technique I'd used before on numerous occasions.

"Who are you?" he said.

"An associate of the judge's." I stepped inside. "I work at Goldberg, Finkelman, and Clark."

The cop pointed to the living room. "They're in there."

I brushed past him.

Judge Clark was in his wheelchair by the window overlooking the lake. Another uniformed officer stood next to him, admiring the view. The man was about forty, lieutenant bars on his shoulders. He was bland like hospital food, colorless.

"You must be the facilitator." He looked at me with eyes the color of sword steel, a cold gray.

"Who are you?" I said.

"Hopper. The chief sent me."

"The chief of what?"

"They told me stories about you." Hopper chuckled. "This guy Cantrell, he's an Olympic-level smart-ass, that's what they said."

"The chief of police, Jonathan." Clark spoke for the first time. "Lieutenant Hopper is his assistant."

I nodded. "What brings you out on this fine day, Lieutenant Hopper?"

"Jonathan has a law-enforcement background, as you've alluded to," Clark said. "He handles issues in the field that relate to our law practice."

"*Issues in the field.*" Hopper stroked his chin. "That's precious. Does that include breaking the law?"

"You here to make an arrest?" I asked.

"The chief got a call from an old golfing buddy," Hopper said. "An attorney, on retainer to Tommy Joe Culpepper's daddy."

"I can't stand golf." I looked at Clark and then at Hopper. "Apropos of nothing."

Clark rubbed his eyes and sighed.

"You just walk around and hit a little teeny ball." I shook my head. "What's fun about that?"

Hopper was looking at me again. "Did you really need to rough him up?"

"Who? Tommy Joe?"

"You tune up so many guys this week you forget which one we're talking about?"

"Tommy Joe's a tweak-head and he's twice my size," I said. "Who's roughing who up?"

"Everything Jonathan did was perfectly legal," Clark said. "However, due to client confidentiality we can't disclose any specifics."

"Let's talk about your arrest then." Hopper pointed one finger at me like it was a gun. "You got out of the lockup pretty quick. Maybe next time you won't be so lucky."

"Perhaps I should call one of our criminal-defense specialists." Clark held up a cordless phone.

"Hey, we're cool." Hopper waved a hand dismissively. "I'm just busting your boy's chops."

"What is it you want?" I said. "Catch me up. I came in late."

Hopper cracked his knuckles. "You're asking questions about a missing person named Tremont Washington."

I looked at Clark. He looked back. We both shrugged.

"Yeah," I said. "What of it?"

"A bigger problem is the fact that you've aligned yourself with a certain deputy chief."

"Raul Delgado," I said, the obvious. "Let's go over the basics. I'm a private citizen working on a confidential matter. I'm not *aligned* with anyone."

"You guys are part of some East Coast law firm," Hopper said. "And you make nice-nice with a guy who's one psych evaluation away from being bounced off the force."

He spoke the words "East Coast" like they were a mild obscenity.

"Deputy Chief Delgado's health records are private," Clark said. "As HIPAA rules dictate."

"You've got to admire the balls on Delgado, though." Hopper nodded thoughtfully. "He's managed to get close to the brass ring."

"What are you telling us?" I asked.

"Delgado's not going to be chief of police or mayor," Hopper said. "The people who decide these things think he's wrapped too tight."

Neither Clark nor I spoke.

Hopper continued. "Which means he won't get to move into the governor's crib down in Austin."

The room was silent.

"That's what you guys do, right?" Hopper looked at each of us. "You suck up to politicos so you can keep the contracts flowing and going."

"Well, aren't you mister insightful," I said. "How come he won't make governor? You got pictures of him diddling a goat or something?"

Hopper smiled, a look of deep satisfaction on his face. He opened a briefcase on the desk and pulled out a stack of files.

I recognized them but didn't say anything.

He handed them to Judge Clark. Clark scanned them in short order. Hopper stared at me the whole time.

"Murder investigations," Clark said. "Somebody appears to be killing certain members of the criminal element in Dallas."

I walked across the room and stared out the window. The lake was beautiful. A light breeze ruffled the trees surrounding the water.

Hopper meandered over, stood by my side. "Want to guess who we like for the murders?"

I shook my head.

"I'll give you a couple of hints." He chuckled. "The perp is Mexican. He started his life of crime when he was eleven years old and stole some money from a convenience store along with his brother."

"I think you should leave now," Clark said.

"Lordy, I love fucking with lawyers." Hopper shook his head. "You should see the expression on your face."

"What proof do you have?" I asked.

"None. But that's the best part." He paused. "See, you're gonna get it for me, the proof."

Clark dialed a number.

"Do you have any idea how connected the law firm is to the feds?" I asked. "You really want to go down that road?"

"I'm not after you or Ironside here." He pointed to Clark, who was speaking on the phone in hushed tones. "Yet."

His gray eyes darkened to the color of a thundercloud in summer. A sheen of sweat coated his forehead even though the room was cool, and he gave off a sense of stridency that was out of line with the current situation.

"I'm after Delgado," Hopper said. "And you're gonna get me the evidence to put him away."

"Is this the part where I'm supposed to say, 'Or what?'" I asked.

Hopper smiled. "Or the chief is going to put your girl Piper under the fucking jail."

# - CHAPTER TWENTY-SIX -

Mason Burnett held the business card the old woman had given him in one hand, tilting the surface so the raised lettering glistened in the sun.

Jonathan Cantrell. The name was familiar. A cop at one time, tainted by some sort of scandal, details long forgotten.

Mason was in his Suburban in the parking lot of the Iris Apartments. He entered Jonathan Cantrell into the laptop mounted on the transmission hump of his SUV.

His DOB and last known address appeared, a townhome in the Oak Lawn section of Dallas. No arrest record.

Mason smiled at that. Somebody had done a little remodeling to Cantrell's records, if the stories he'd heard were even half true.

Employment history was next.

A Dallas police officer, terminated nearly eight years before. No mention why.

Cantrell's next position was with a private company, Red Talon Industries, a military contractor that had been swallowed up by a larger competitor.

Cantrell's position: a contract DEA agent.

Employment at Red Talon ended about two years before.

A gap of a year before his latest job—a non-attorney employee of a DC law firm.

So why was a DC law firm interested in a missing kid in West Dallas?

Mason closed his eyes and tried to think, to visualize the solution, a technique described to him by his dyke of a therapist, Corinne.

But the darkness didn't bring answers. The only thing he saw was his father, drunk and mad at the world. Then the hitting began and he became afraid and filled with rage.

# - CHAPTER TWENTY-SEVEN -

I called Piper as I drove south on Interstate 35.

No answer, straight to voice mail.

I left her a short message: "New intel. Get off the grid, ASAP."

She was a child of the streets, foster homes and social workers and running from the system. She could disappear into a crack in a sidewalk and be quite comfortable. One might even say she was more comfortable living on the lam.

Then I called Theo Goldberg's cell. He answered after a long time.

"What?" he said. "I'm busy."

"Getting a little hot down here."

"Isaac," he said, talking to his kid. He was at home, clearly not a scene of domestic bliss at the moment. "*Isaac*. Seriously. No." Then, to me, "The mess Clark e-mailed me about?"

"The powers that be aren't imagining Delgado's future quite the same way as you."

A female's voice, a girl in her teens, in the background, talking about her douchebag of a brother and how come the Internet was so slow today.

"His gerbil," Theo said—to me, I guessed. "Isaac keeps trying to put it in the microwave."

I gripped the steering wheel tighter, tried to control my frustration.

"Theo. We've got a situation here. Let's talk about Isaac later."

"His mother thinks it was that one glass of wine she had before she knew she was pregnant."

I veered around a slow-moving pickup. The Dallas skyline grew smaller in the rearview mirror.

"I'm gonna track down this missing kid, but I think you need to cut Delgado loose." I explained briefly about the meeting at Judge Clark's house a few minutes ago even though he'd heard most of it already from his brief conversation with Clark.

"I told her it couldn't have anything to do with all the dope she smoked in college when she was on the road with Bon Jovi."

"What the hell are you talking about?"

"My wife. She used to be a Bon Jovi groupie. Didn't I ever tell you that?"

"You're killing me, Theo." I slowed down as the exit I needed approached. "I'm dying a little more every second we stay on the phone and talk about your family."

Neither of us spoke for a moment.

"You want me to die, Theo? Is that what you want?"

He sighed loudly. "You think Delgado is whacking bad guys?"

I didn't reply.

"You think a high-ranking police officer is out there taking potshots at street scum?"

"No," I said. "Doesn't make sense."

"Never seen a cop who wasn't on the take in some way." He paused. "Except for Delgado. Guy's got his own money. Makes him close to squeaky clean."

"Any way you can call off the chief then?"

He rustled some papers. "We're gonna have to put Isaac in a, um, place for a while."

"I'm not much use to you if the top cop in Dallas has me in his crosshairs."

Silence.

"What? Oh, the chief." He chuckled. "You know he's on the payroll of the largest bookie in North Texas?"

"What an interesting bit of trivia. So can you shut him down?"

"I can try." Theo's voice was pensive. "We don't like to make too many waves in the provinces."

Theo Goldberg, a Yale and Harvard alum, was like most easterners in positions of power. He had a paternalistic view of the fly-over states. The action was on the East and West Coasts, not in the vast heartland where the majority of the population lived.

"I have faith in you, Jonathan."

The call ended.

I tried Piper again but there was no answer.

———

The guidebooks don't mention DeSoto, Texas, very much. A cookie-cutter suburb on the south of town. Street after street of homes that looked alike, the similarity comforting in one way, maddening in another.

According to the nifty, law-enforcement-only app on my phone that was plugged into the several different databases, Demarcus Harris, a journalist, lived in DeSoto.

His name had been given to me by the woman at the Helping Place.

I exited the interstate and followed the directions from my GPS. A few minutes later, I drove past the front of Demarcus's one-story brick home, a nice-looking slice of suburbia with a matching mailbox mounted curbside.

It was the middle of the day and there weren't many people out in the neighborhood.

A gray Chrysler PT was parked in front of Demarcus's house. On the rear, a single bumper sticker: "I ❤ the Smell of Black Power."

I kept driving, headed down the alley.

Behind Demarcus's house, the gate leading to his backyard was open, the only one in that condition on the entire block.

I parked at the end of the alley, snugged up against a backyard fence. Using a disposable cell phone, I called the number associated with Demarcus Harris's house. No answer. I hung up when voice mail clicked on.

From the rear of the Navigator I retrieved an empty clipboard and a lanyard with a laminated ID badge that indicated I was a supervisor with a nonexistent telecommunications company.

I strode down the alley with the clipboard in hand, ID around my neck, acting like I was examining the rear of each place as I went. In most neighborhoods, a well-dressed, clean-shaven white guy can do just about anything he wants if he walks with purpose and carries a clipboard.

At Demarcus's house, I entered the backyard. The area had a pool and several pieces of outdoor furniture. The attached garage appeared empty.

The pool was clean and clear, blue as the sky. The only blemish was a piece of newspaper floating in the middle.

One of the patio chairs lay on its side.

Probably innocent reasons for both the debris in the water and the knocked-over chair.

But I'd learned a long time ago to pay attention to my Spidey-sense, that extra layer of perception that people who've been in combat develop, the invisible feeling that oftentimes keeps you alive.

I slipped on a pair of latex gloves, tossed the clipboard over the fence into the alley, and pulled the Glock from its holster.

The sliding rear door of the house was open.

I eased inside, stood to one side, let my senses attune to the place.

The kitchen/breakfast room. Scuff marks on the white vinyl-tile floor. Scattered drops of something dark, the color of burgundy wine.

Another chair lay askew.

In the family room, the beige carpet made the maroon discoloration stand out, a large patch of what appeared to be dried blood about the size of a hardback book.

I knelt beside the blood, stared at the carpet, trying to put the pieces together.

Demarcus Harris had been attacked and then dragged out the back. There wasn't a car in the rear driveway or in the garage. So he probably came in the front and his assailant was waiting for him.

I strode to the front door, peered out the window. The Chrysler PT was parked directly in front of the house.

There was a covered area by the entrance, a small patio partially hidden from the street.

The door was unlocked.

I opened it.

Keys were in the dead bolt.

A black messenger bag was leaning against one wall of the covered area, out of view from the street.

So Demarcus came home, unlocked the front door. Maybe he had something in his hand and needed to put down his bag. The mail or a package of some sort. Groceries.

He opened the door, stepped inside.

Something caused him to leave his keys in the lock and his bag on the porch.

His own Spidey-sense?

I grabbed the messenger bag at the same time as a Hispanic woman in a maid's uniform began walking up the front sidewalk. We locked eyeballs. She stopped, put her hand to her mouth.

I ran back through the house.

In the distance, I could hear her yelling.

Out the back. I grabbed the clipboard, jogged down the alley, the messenger bag in hand.

I jumped in the Navigator and sped away.

At the first stoplight, I opened the bag.

It was empty.

# - CHAPTER TWENTY-EIGHT -

Mason Burnett wondered what it would feel like to punch Raul Delgado, a quick blow to the larynx. He imagined Delgado struggling for oxygen, hands grasping his throat, trying to clear his airway, life slowly disappearing from his eyes.

The image gave Burnett a quick smile.

That beaner Delgado had everything handed to him on a silver taco platter. Always playing the sympathy card about his brother being killed. A deputy chief while Burnett languished in the ranks as a mere captain.

Burnett was in the sitting area of the chief's expansive office at Jack Evans Police Headquarters, two sofas on either side of a large coffee table. He was there with Delgado and Hopper, the chief's bloodless right-hand man.

Instead of punching Delgado, Burnett turned his attention to the guy with a Mohawk haircut.

Mohawk wore skintight white jeans and a sleeveless shirt the color of ripe peaches. He was so flamboyantly gay that he made Liberace look like John Wayne.

Mohawk, a manicurist by trade, was across the room, polishing the chief's nails.

The head of the Dallas Police Department was leaning back in his leather desk chair, a cucumber emollient compress over his eyes.

Mason and Delgado stared at their boss until Hopper snapped his fingers.

"Let's get back to the business at hand."

Both men turned away and gave their attention to Hopper.

On the coffee table sat a stack of files, the recent murders of upper-echelon Dallas lowlifes. The so-called vigilante killings.

Hopper tapped the files. "Where are we on this?"

Mason pointed to the chief. "He gets a manicure every week?"

Hopper rolled his eyes. "What's it to you?"

"It's a little weird." Mason kept his voice low. "You have to admit."

"The chief has an image to maintain." Hopper picked up one of the files.

Mason nodded. "So what's with the vegetables on his eyes thing—"

Hopper cut him off. "I don't think you're in a position to be asking questions right now."

Delgado stared at the floor. After a moment, he stood and walked to the window overlooking Lamar Street.

The police headquarters had been built about fifteen years before, in a neighborhood just south of the central business district, an area devoid of people and buildings except for a few ramshackle industrial structures, end-of-the-line bars, and crack dealers.

Now the street bustled; the DPD headquarters serving as an anchor for new development, an oasis in what was otherwise an urban wasteland.

"How are the counseling sessions going, Captain Burnett?" Hopper grinned.

Mason Burnett felt his face get tight. He rubbed the knuckles of one hand with the fingers of the other.

From across the room the chief chuckled while Mohawk continued to buff his nails.

"The business at hand." Mason regained his composure. "We're making progress on finding the vigilante killer."

"What exactly does that mean?" Hopper said.

Mason didn't reply. There'd been no progress made. What cop wanted to stop someone who was killing the bad guys?

Hopper looked across the room to Delgado. "Hey, Raul. What's he talking about?"

"I don't know." Delgado spoke without turning around. "I'm not in charge of the investigation."

A long pause.

Hopper stared at Delgado's back like he was waiting for a dam to break. After an uncomfortably long stretch of time he said, "You pulled the files, though. Every murder case involving the vigilante."

Delgado didn't speak.

"You think we wouldn't find out?" Hopper asked.

Delgado crossed his arms, continued to stare outside.

Hopper stood, sauntered over to the window. "You trying to rat-fuck your boss, Deputy Chief Delgado?"

Delgado's shoulders hunched, but he didn't say anything.

"Maybe you were gonna take the info about the vigilante to the media?" Hopper said. "Try to further your own career?"

No one spoke for a few moments.

Mason broke the silence. "What is it you want, Lieutenant?"

Hopper returned to the sofa, swaggering like a bully, smiling as if he'd won some sort of schoolyard victory.

"I was doing police work." Delgado returned to the sitting area, too. "That's why I pulled the files. I was the one who put it together first."

"Aw, good for you." Hopper clapped softly. "Let's give you an affirmative-action gold star."

Delgado's face turned red; his breath quickened.

Mason said, "I've instructed my men to employ all legal methods to discover the killer."

"*Legal methods*. That's a nice term." Hopper picked up another file. "You want to talk about the banger that fell out of the window in Oak Cliff?"

Silence.

Delgado, eyes filled with loathing, stared at Mason Burnett.

"The banger was dusted, thought he could fly." Mason shrugged, seething on the inside. He imagined his fingers wrapped around Raul Delgado's throat.

"Deputy Chief Delgado insisted the hospital rush the blood tests," Hopper said. "The perp had marijuana and Valium in his system but no angel dust."

"Guy fessed up to hitting that *botánica*," Mason said.

"He's also lawyered up." Hopper put the file down. "We're gonna try and make the problem with the window go away since the banger had a record as thick as a phone book."

Mason nodded.

"That's the last freebie you're gonna get, Captain Burnett." Hopper rearranged the stack of files. "You understand what I'm saying?"

After a moment, Mason nodded.

"Let's move on to a different topic." Hopper pulled another file from his briefcase. "There's a missing kid from West Dallas."

Mason looked at Delgado, who returned the glance, face blank.

Hopper rattled off the basics of the case and then said, "A reporter was nosing around, a punk from some website."

"The People's Blog of Southern Dallas County," Mason said.

"Right." Hopper nodded. "He was at the presser for the chief's new anti-crime initiative."

"He wore camo," Mason said. "And a red beret."

"You're so observant." Hopper smiled. "You should consider a career in law enforcement."

The anger was a white-hot poker in the pit of Mason's belly. Mother-fucking, smug-ass Raul Delgado and the gray-eyed weasel Hopper, both out to get him. Mason's gun felt heavy on his belt. The walls of the room seemed to get closer, the air hotter.

Hopper appeared to be enjoying himself.

Mason leaned forward, whispered, "Go fuck yourself, Lieutenant."

Hopper laughed like a kindergartener watching the *Three Stooges*. Then he dropped the new file on the coffee table.

"Somebody took out the reporter. There's no body, but the DeSoto police think he's been killed. Signs of a struggle. Blood at the scene."

Neither Mason nor Delgado spoke.

Hopper continued. "So the question on the table is, what's so important about Tremont Washington?"

"You think Tremont and the vigilante killer are related?" Delgado said.

"The string theory of physics—everything's connected." Hopper crossed his legs. "I saw that on the Discovery Channel."

Across the room, the chief and Mohawk held a whispered conversation.

Hopper said, "What's the name of that fuck-stain who runs West Dallas?"

"Alvarez." Mason willed the anger away. "Lysol Alvarez."

"Who the hell names their child Lysol?"

Mason shrugged.

Hopper said, "Take a swing at Alvarez. See what he knows about this Tremont kid."

Across the room the chief reached into his pocket and pulled out a note card. He gave the slip of paper to Mohawk. The manicurist sashayed over to Lieutenant Hopper. He handed him the card.

Hopper read it. Then he tore the paper into shreds.

"The chief has a lead on the vigilante," he said. "A person of interest."

Mason didn't reply. The chief didn't come up with leads. To have a lead meant you would have to do police work. The proper way to phrase what was happening was to say the chief had someone he wanted to screw.

"An ex-cop," Hopper said.

Delgado leaned forward. To Mason he appeared eager to hear what Hopper would say next. Eager or afraid.

"Guy got shit-canned a few years back," Hopper said. "Worked for the feds for a while."

"What's his name?" Mason asked.

"Jonathan Cantrell." Hopper looked at both men. "That name mean anything to either of you?"

A sharp intake of breath from Delgado.

Mason smiled, remembering the business card he'd gotten from Tremont's grandmother.

"I've never heard of him," he said. "But I'll be happy to take the point on tracking him down."

Hopper nodded.

# - CHAPTER TWENTY-NINE -

## The West Dallas Gang Leader

Lysol Alvarez rubs a lemon rind around the edge of the demitasse cup.

He's in the kitchen of his house on Vilbig. At his request, the guards are outside. Pavarotti plays overhead, an aria from *La Bohème*.

The room is spotless, cleaned every morning by an Ecuadorian woman who speaks no English.

Except for the hardwood floor, most of the kitchen is either shiny metal or black marble.

The stainless-steel coffeemaker, a complicated affair with a number of nozzles and dials, gleams in the halogen lights mounted in the ceiling.

Two things Lysol Alvarez really likes: good coffee and righteous weed.

Pressing business has required his attention, so he's not smoked it up for the past couple of days.

But he's really looking forward to some coffee, especially after the morning's activities.

So he fusses over the controls and makes a cup of espresso. He's showered and changed, discarded the soiled coveralls. He's now wearing a gray linen suit over a silk T-shirt that is pale green.

The coffee is superb, one cube of sugar and just the right hint of lemon. He finishes the drink, puts the cup in the sink.

One thing Lysol Alvarez cannot stand. A single item he detests.

Cocaine.

Some might say this position is just a tad ironic, since Lysol's made so much money selling cocaine and her nasty sibling, crack.

Lysol doesn't see it that way. Peddling blow, well that's just good business. Give the customers what they want.

What Lysol doesn't like is for people around him to be in possession of or under the influence of cocaine. Everyone associated with Lysol Alvarez knows the rule: don't be using what the customers are abusing.

The girl Sawyer is huddled in the corner of the kitchen, hugging herself, sitting on the floor.

Lysol kneels beside her.

Her eyes are scared, face red from crying, one cheek purple from a blow she received at the Iris Apartments the day before.

Lysol clucks his tongue. The crew that controls the Iris, they're animals.

He's tried countless times to negotiate a treaty, reach a peace accord that would allow everyone to profit.

But his efforts were always rebuffed.

The leader of the Iris, a dreadlock-wearing piece of slime who insisted on speaking with a British accent, even insinuated that he was coming to take over Lysol's turf.

Now this.

He purses his lips, looks at Sawyer.

To think that they would dare touch something of his in this way.

"It's okay." He brushes back her hair. "Don't cry."

She flinches but doesn't speak.

He's taken aback. "Have I ever hurt you, Sawyer?"

She hesitates, shakes her head.

"Ever laid a finger on you?"

"N-n-no." Her voice is weak.

They're silent for a moment. No sound in the room except the hum of the refrigerator and the opera music.

"But what's the rule, Sawyer?"

She hyperventilates, eyes wide.

He caresses her cheek, and she flinches again.

"Don't. Use. Blow." The words slip from his tongue, almost a whisper.

Sawyer clutches her stomach, face pale.

Lysol shuffles back. "You gonna be sick?"

Her cheeks puff. She puts a hand to her mouth, leans to one side, vomits all over the floor.

He stands, waits for it to be over. He turns on the faucet and wets a cloth, hands it to her.

She wipes her face and inches away from him.

"You've put me in an awkward position," he says.

She hugs her knees.

"The men at the Iris, they've disrespected you." He pauses. "Which means I have to take action. Make a statement."

"I-I-I'm s-s-sorry."

"And I owe Jon Cantrell."

"I—I didn't ask him for h-help," she says.

"No, of course you didn't. But Jon's a man of honor and he saw a lady in distress. What was he supposed to do?"

They stare at each other.

Sawyer's face is a portrait of fear. Eyes wide, nostrils flaring, mouth a thin line.

"But the worst part is, you bought cocaine." Pause. "With my money." Lysol shakes his head. "From my competitors."

Sawyer begins to cry again.

Lysol strolls across the kitchen and opens the refrigerator door.

The interior has been emptied except for a large platter in the middle of the lowest shelf.

In the center of the platter sits a considerable puddle of blood and a severed head, dreadlocks swirling around the neck stump like so many greasy black snakes.

The leader of the crew at the Iris.

"Look what you made me do." Lysol points to the dead man's face.

Sawyer clutches her sides like she might vomit some more.

"Now I gotta send somebody to Home Depot," Lysol says. "Need to buy a pole we can stick in front of the Iris with this bitch's head on it."

Sawyer retches again. Nothing but a gooey string of bile comes out.

"A message has to be sent. Surely, you understand that?"

She nods timidly.

"All because *you* broke the rules." Lysol shuts the refrigerator.

"Wh-wh-what are you g-g-gonna do to me?" Sawyer says.

Lysol kneels again. He's careful to avoid the pool of vomit. "What should I do?"

Sawyer takes a deep breath, brushes the hair from her eyes. She starts to speak—

The kitchen door is flung open, and one of Lysol's guards staggers in.

Lysol arches an eyebrow, trying to keep his anger directed at Sawyer, not the sudden intrusion. He left specific instructions: do not come inside while he handles Sawyer's disciplinary infraction.

The guard opens his mouth. Blood gushes over his chin.

Lysol notices the damp spot on the man's chest.

The man falls to the floor, dead.

# - CHAPTER THIRTY -

I parked in front of a house across the street from Piper's, two lots down.

My beeper beeped again. I turned it off, dropped the device in the console next to my battery-less cell phone.

Theo Goldberg was calling about the shipment, wanting to arrange a pickup.

That was my job. Help Theo and the law firm with tasks like misdelivered packages and recalcitrant government contractors.

Screw the job.

I got out, chirped the locks on the Lincoln.

It was the middle of the afternoon. Four hours since I'd left her here. I'd called several more times. Her cell was now disconnected.

I walked across the street like I belonged, a hard-looking guy in a black sport coat and jeans.

Piper's SUV was not in the driveway. I strode to the front porch, peered through the window in the door. The glass was frosted, hard to see through.

I tried the knob. Unlocked.

The door swung open into the living room, Piper's meager furnishings still in place.

The couch and rug were still there. So were side tables and chairs. But the pictures of the children were gone.

The movement of the door disturbed the air. Bits of dust drifted across the hardwood like tumbleweeds on the desert floor.

Even the smell of incense was no longer there.

I headed toward the bedroom.

Bed and nightstand still there. Clothing and personal items gone, as were the rest of her pictures.

I sat on the bed.

Piper could be anywhere. An hour to pack her stuff, grab a bug-out bag and weapons. Three hours to get off the grid.

A lump of emotion swelled in my throat.

At least she'd gotten my message.

She was a survivor. She'd be okay. She'd always been in the past.

From the front of the house came the sound of hinges squeaking. Footsteps on hardwood.

I stood, pulled the Glock from my waistband. Eased toward the bedroom door.

Waited.

Seconds ticked by, each one extended into something longer, tiny slivers of eternity, the result of adrenaline and fear.

Movement in the hallway. Someone trying to be as quiet as I was.

A faint creak of wood, the rustle of clothing.

I stepped to one side of the entrance to the room, made myself as still and small as possible.

The door eased open.

A black shoe, toes only, slid across the threshold.

I held my breath, waited.

The muzzle of a gun, chest-high, breached the airspace.

An arm followed the gun. The index finger of the hand holding the weapon pressed against the frame, not the trigger, the habit of someone professionally trained to handle firearms.

A cop.

I grabbed the wrist, yanked it down, pulled the person it belonged to into the room.

A grunt. A sharp intake of breath.

I swept the hand behind the back, kicked the feet to one side, and fell on top of Deputy Chief Raul Delgado. The gun dropped, clattered on the hardwood.

He did not appear amused. His face was pressed to the floor of Piper's bedroom, one arm bent between his shoulder blades to the point of breaking.

"What the hell's going on here?" he said.

I grabbed his other arm, cranked it behind his back, slipped a cuff tie on both wrists, then rolled off him.

"*You.*" He stared at me. "Of all people. I should have known."

I retrieved his gun, stuck it in my waistband.

"Where is she?"

I shook my head.

"What did you do to her?" His eyes were slits.

I didn't reply, remembering what had transpired in this very space only a few hours before.

"I'm gonna bury you," he said. "You'll need a court order just to see daylight."

"There was a threat. A credible source," I said. "I told her to get out of sight."

He didn't say anything.

"Are you the one killing lowlifes?" I asked.

He kicked the floor, growled. Anger flooded his face, eyes lit up with rage.

"You wouldn't be the first cop to crawl in that particular hole," I said.

"You think I'm a killer?" he asked. "That I'd hurt people without a cause?"

I didn't reply.

"Do you even know anything about me?" His voice was shrill. "You think I would take the law into my own hands?"

I looked at my watch, debated my next move.

Delgado said, "You ever wake up with the taste of your brother's brain in your mouth?"

I didn't speak.

"You know nothing." His lip curled in a snarl. *"Nothing."*

"I know you've never been straight with me, not from the get-go. You knew where Tremont worked. You're involved with the Helping Place."

His eyes narrowed. "You've been busy."

"What'd you think I was gonna do?" I opened the closet again, hoping there was something there, a piece of clothing, anything.

It was still empty.

"She's gone, isn't she?" His face appeared sad now. "She used to brag about being able to disappear."

"One of her many talents." I shut the door.

"She could really get under your skin."

"They're coming after you," I said. "The chief wants to pin the murders on you."

His eyes closed, mouth moving as if in a silent prayer.

"I don't really give a damn about who's killing who," I said. "I just want to find the kid."

He opened his eyes. "You're not doing a very good job, now are you?"

"You got a smart mouth on you for somebody who's not in the driver's seat."

"I never should have hired you," he said. "You're a match in a gunpowder store."

"The feeling's mutual. Trust me."

We were both silent for a few moments.

"Piper." He took several deep breaths. "Do you love her?"

"Tell me you're not the guy killing these people."

"Tell me if you love her or not."

"What's it to you?"

"Everything seems to get taken away from me." Raul stared at my eyes. "Why should she be any different?"

I glanced around the room, debating my next move.

"I didn't kill anybody," Raul said.

"You know what? I don't really care if you did or not."

"I don't have the guts. That's a hell of a thing to say, isn't it?"

I didn't reply. Instead, I left the room and strode to the kitchen. In a drawer by the sink was a mismatched jumble of utensils—forks and spoons, a spatula.

And a paring knife.

I grabbed the knife, went back to the bedroom, dropped it in the corner. "Killing people doesn't take guts." I shook my head. "It requires blind fear and poor impulse control. Maybe a big dose of stupid."

"You just gonna leave me here?"

"You can get to the knife. It'll take a while, but you'll be able to free yourself."

I put his gun in the closet and then headed toward the door. Once there, I stopped.

"Why'd you hire me?" I asked. "Really."

No response.

"Do you think there's a connection between Tremont's disappearance and the vigilante killings?"

After another moment, he shook his head. "I knew they'd try to pin the murders on me, though."

I didn't speak.

"That's what they do," he said. "Find the weakest one in the herd and go for the kill."

An unfortunate choice of words, given that the topic was a string of murders, but certainly accurate on a metaphorical level.

"Piper's most likely somewhere in the city," I said. "She's prone to keep a safe house or two handy."

He nodded. "Then I'll find her."

"No you won't," I said. "Not if she doesn't want you to."

"What is it that you have that I don't?"

I could hear the emotion in his voice, hidden under a layer of gruffness. The subtext to his question was, why hasn't as much been taken from you as it has from me? Why did I get dealt this hand?

For this I had no answer. We are all damaged. We are all missing something, slivers of what we think happiness should be, broken parts from our emotional well-being.

"See you around, Deputy Chief." I walked out of Piper's bedroom.

From behind came the sound of thrashing, feet kicking the floor, heavy breathing.

"*Cantrell*," Delgado said. "*Stop.*"

I kept going.

His voice, fainter: "I need to talk to you."

I strode through the living room, slung open the front door.

"*Cantrell—*"

I slammed the door shut on Deputy Chief Raul Delgado.

# - CHAPTER THIRTY-ONE -

The West Dallas Gang Leader—Part II

Lysol Alvarez grabs a submachine gun from the utility closet, just off the kitchen.

His guard lies on the floor, blood pooling underneath his still-warm corpse.

Sawyer is behind him, crying, huddled in a corner.

The subgun has a silencer, three mags taped to each other. A SIG Sauer nine-millimeter is tucked in a holster in the small of his back. Lysol doesn't even go to the bathroom without the SIG.

A brick wall topped with broken glass surrounds the backyard.

Against the back of the property, at the end of the driveway where the garage should be, sits a gray Escalade, the front pointing toward the street. The keys are in the ignition.

Lysol eases out the rear door. He stands completely still on the back stoop, letting his senses get used to the ambient noise.

The yard is empty. Minimal landscaping, nothing for anybody to hide behind.

No sign of his guards anywhere.

From the front, around the driveway side of the house where he can't see, comes a whistle, a high-low trill. Soft, like a signal to a dog or a child.

Lysol clutches the subgun, wonders where in the hell his guards are.

The whistle again. The same volume, but longer, more insistent.

Lysol pulls his cell out, sends a text to his man in the house across the street: *911 where ru*

A few seconds pass.

No reply.

The first whisper of fear creeps up Lysol's spine, an icy caress that makes his stomach clench.

The whistle once more.

Lysol resists the urge to lash out, start firing, to let the fear take hold.

That's what the whistle is about, an effort to provoke. Lysol's been to the river a time or two. He's not going to fall for something like that.

A sound like a balloon popping. A silenced handgun firing. The noise comes from the driveway, followed an instant later by the clatter of the Escalade's front grill shattering. Coolant dribbles to the ground, green and oily, rendering the vehicle undrivable.

Lysol hops off the stoop and heads toward the other side of the house, opposite the driveway.

At the corner of the house, he turns, crouches low, and creeps toward the street, using the narrow area between his place and the one next door, which he owns, as cover.

Halfway down the length of the house he finds his man from across the street and two soldiers.

They've been shot in the head, dragged here, and dumped.

That's a ballsy move, a much bigger play than anybody from the Iris could even contemplate.

Lysol takes a deep breath, palms sweaty. His teeth chatter even though it's not cold.

The whistle again. Hard to tell where it's coming from.

Lysol kneels by the bodies. He glances at the side of his house, comes to the realization that this place is no longer his. It's dead to him, in a very real sense.

A moment of melancholy passes over him, followed by acceptance.

This is the life he's chosen. This is the price you pay to be something more than a half-breed piece of street trash from West Dallas. This is the price of respect.

He reaches into his pocket and removes a tiny electronic device that looks like an alarm remote for a car. The device is attached to a lanyard. He ponders the item for a moment before slipping the lanyard around his neck.

From the front of the house comes the whistle again, followed by a low voice: *"Lysol, where are you?"*

The exterior of the home next to his has an inset, a small piece of cover formed where the living room meets the dining area.

In a loud whisper, Lysol says, "Help me. I'm hurt."

Then he jumps across the gap and nestles against the inset, aiming the subgun toward the front.

Laughter.

Lysol waits. Sweat stings his eyes.

Thirty seconds drag by.

Lysol blinks. Once.

A dash of movement from the front.

Lysol fires a short burst from the subgun.

More laughter.

Lysol tries not to hyperventilate, struggles to maintain control.

Another thirty seconds go by. A car door slams.

Then:

*RAP-RAP-RAP-RAP-RAP.*

Gunshots, a high-caliber rifle, fired as fast as the trigger could be pulled. No silencer.

Glass shatters. Wood shreds. The shooter is firing into the front of his house. No longer worried about being stealthy. No longer caring if the police know.

Sawyer screams, her voice muffled.

Lysol swears. He retreats. Runs toward the rear, the way he just came.

He rounds the corner, sees one of his guards standing in the backyard.

The scene is wrong. The man appears unarmed but he's holding something close to his stomach, a bewildered expression on his face.

"What the—" Lysol hesitates, confused.

The item the guard is holding is a length of intestine he's trying to stuff back into his abdominal cavity.

Lysol tries to control his shock. That's his man, his possession. Who would dare disrespect him in this way? He swallows the outrage and sprints by the injured soldier, heading toward the alley.

From the driveway a figure appears, a white guy in a black tracksuit.

An AR-15 is in his hand.

Lysol fires on the run, a long burst from the subgun. Spits of flame and the rattle of the bolt.

The man in the tracksuit disappears around the corner of the house.

Lysol ignores the damaged Escalade. Instead he kicks open the gate that leads to the alley.

The AR-15 opens up. Chunks of brick wall fly everywhere.

Lysol keeps running.

Ten feet. Then twenty.

At about forty feet down the alley, nearing the back of the second house past his headquarters, he decides he can't wait any longer.

So he punches the button on the remote around his neck.

A nanosecond later, the bundle of C-4 plastic explosive in the hall closet of his house explodes, a blast of thunder like something from the hand of the Devil himself.

———

*Dallas, Texas*
*1991*

Raul Delgado was twenty-one years old. He sat in the back row of the auditorium, stiff and awkward in his new Dallas police uniform.

He was no longer an Explorer. Not a Boy Scout anymore. He was a duly licensed peace officer.

The badge on his chest seemed heavy, tugging at his shirt. The weight felt good, however, a silent reminder that he was doing something with his life that mattered.

That was a lesson that Bobby had drilled into his head over the years: make your time on earth count for something.

In a holster on his hip sat a brand-new Smith & Wesson Model 4006, the semiautomatic pistol that was slowly replacing the revolvers most police used to carry. The gun was heavy, too, another symbol of the direction his life was taking.

A rookie, two weeks out of the DPD academy. He worked in the southeast division, which included the Fair Park area, the roughest part of Dallas.

Trial by fire, they called it. If you could make it in the war zone south of Fair Park, you could make it anywhere.

The auditorium where he was sitting was part of the Dallas Baptist High School campus, a private institution near downtown.

Tonight was graduation.

Junie's night.

In a little while, she was going to walk across the stage and receive her diploma. In the fall, she would be a freshman at Baylor University, her tuition paid by a scholarship that benefits the children of police officers.

The college was in Waco, a little more than an hour south of Dallas, a straight shot down I-35. An easy drive.

He planned to see her as often as possible.

Her personality—kind and caring one minute, mischievous the next—seemed to fill a void inside Raul, the dark place where he didn't like to let his thoughts dwell too long.

Junie had just turned eighteen. Her hair had darkened to a light chestnut, the color accentuating the green of her eyes. Her legs were still long, but the swell of her hips and the slenderness of her waist made everything perfectly in proportion, at least in Raul's mind.

Tonight, in her culture, she left childhood behind, like girls in his old neighborhood do with the *quinceañera* on their fifteenth birthday.

Raul didn't know any girls from his old neighborhood. Lately, he hadn't spent much time in that part of Dallas.

The last four years had been busy.

Ride-alongs with Bobby. Studying his way to a criminal justice degree at UT Arlington, just a few miles from Dallas. Weekend chores at the ranch. Keeping an eye on Junie when Bobby was working.

The people he knew from childhood had scattered as the homes in Little Mexico fell to the bulldozers preparing the ground for new buildings.

His *abuela* moved back to Brownsville. His cousins were uncomfortable when he came around, disdainful of his new way of speaking and his college degree, openly hostile to his career choice.

He wished they could understand.

Police work offered a chance for order, a way for Raul to control things and make a difference.

Who wouldn't want that?

Tonight, as a gesture of respect, Raul planned to ask Bobby for permission to date Junie.

He and Junie were close—friends but more. Physically attracted to one another, emotionally bound by what happened one summer afternoon almost five years before.

Raul was craning his neck, looking toward the front, when the seat next to him creaked. He turned to see Bobby sitting there.

The older man was wearing a navy-blue suit and black cowboy boots. The suit looked dusty, like it had been in the closet for years. The boots were polished to a high gloss.

In his midfifties now, Bobby had worked for the Dallas police for more than thirty years, and he would be retiring soon.

"You didn't have to come." Bobby shook his hand. "But we appreciate you being here."

"You've always been there for me. You and Junie."

Birthdays and graduations and holidays too numerous to mention, Bobby and Junie had both been welcoming to a young man who for reasons beyond his control found himself with no real family.

"How's your partner?" Bobby said. "I told him to take good care of you."

Raul's partner was a crusty ex-Marine with twenty years on the force, almost all of it behind the wheel of a squad car. Two weeks with the man had taught Raul more than the entire three-month course at the Dallas police academy.

More people had entered the auditorium. Toddlers and school-age children, mothers and fathers in their forties, grandparents.

Raul told him everything was going well. Then he said, "Where is the family sitting?"

Bobby's people were blue-collar. They would not be at the ceremony. His brother worked on an oil rig in Louisiana. His sister lived in West Texas with her husband, a prison guard. There was a nephew in New Mexico, punching cows on a ranch by the border.

Junie's deceased mother, however, came from a well-to-do family in North Dallas. Her people were lawyers and bankers and such.

High society, Bobby called it. Raul wasn't too sure what that meant. Debutante balls and tennis tournaments, maybe. Old guys with white hair, dressed in tacky clothes like in the movie *Caddyshack*.

For a moment, Bobby didn't reply to the question about where everyone was sitting. He watched people walk down the aisle. Finally he said, "The family. Yeah, they're, uh, at the front."

They sat in silence for a while.

"Junie will be happy they're here," Raul said finally.

The older man didn't reply.

A woman in her forties, wearing a peach-colored silk blouse and a gold necklace, approached Bobby. He stood and they embraced. Bobby introduced the woman, Junie's aunt.

"Hello, Rah-ool." The aunt pronounced his name with twang in her voice and a smirk on her face. She made no move to shake hands. "Don't you look nice in your uniform. Like a bus driver or something."

Bobby stared at the ground while the aunt prattled on.

Her words and attitude indicated she regarded Raul in the same way she would the guy who mowed her lawn, a lesser human, not worthy of her time.

Raul was used to that attitude. Growing up, he'd learned about racism firsthand, and then had the concept explained to him in minute detail by the radical Latinos who came around after his brother was killed. The radicals were wrong about many things, of course, but a lot of what they said made sense. The white man had kept people of color impoverished by his actions and economic tools.

Raul didn't concern himself with politics, though. He just wanted to be a good cop, an officer that Bobby could be proud of, and go out with Junie.

A buzzing sound. The aunt pulled a mobile phone, a bulky Motorola, from her expensive-looking purse. She talked loudly about Junie's graduation and the party later at the country club. Then she hung up and told Bobby she'd see him at the party.

Bobby nodded but didn't say anything.

The aunt said good-bye and walked down the aisle toward the front. She managed all this without looking at or speaking to Raul again.

"Don't mind her." Bobby shook his head. "That branch of the family thinks they're better than us mortals."

"There's a party for Junie?"

Raul wondered why he didn't know about the celebration. He had always been included before, at least when Bobby was in charge.

"Junie's aunt." Bobby stared at the floor. "She does things different."

The crowd had gotten larger. The ceremony was supposed to start in a few minutes.

"You had fun in college, didn't you?" Bobby fiddled with the knot of his tie.

The question came from nowhere. Raul was confused. He nodded after a moment.

"Junie's aunt and her people, they're real big on college."

While he was in school, Raul worked two jobs and spent whatever extra time he had at the ranch. He didn't have a lot of free hours for the traditional college pursuits—beer drinking, chasing girls.

He wasn't much of a drinker and, truth be told, there was only one girl he wanted to chase, and she was still in high school.

"Not having a mama around," Bobby said. "That's not a great way to raise a young lady like Junie, you know what I mean?"

Raul shrugged, not understanding at all where the conversation was going.

"Living on a ranch out in the country." Bobby smoothed a wrinkle from his pants. "Looking back, that might not a been the best move for her to meet people."

The memory of one of the people she did meet near the ranch hung between them. Neither man acknowledged Wayne or what they'd done.

"She seems happy," Raul said.

"College is gonna be good for Junie," Bobby said. "Her aunt'll make sure she gets into a sorority and everything. You know, to meet the right kinda people."

"The right kind of people?" Raul said. "What does that mean?"

Silence.

"I've seen the way you look at her, son." Bobby's voice was hard to hear. "She's an attractive young woman."

Raul's breath caught in his throat.

"I've always taken a shine to you. You know that, don't you?"

Raul nodded.

"First time we met in that interview room, I knew somebody oughta be looking out for you."

Raul's badge seemed heavier.

"My wife had just died. I suppose I needed somebody who needed me back. Me and Junie both did."

"What are you trying to say, Bobby?"

"Junie. She's gonna go to college. And she's gonna meet her a boy there." Bobby's voice was soft. "She's gonna have a different kind of life than what you're offering."

Both men were silent for a long few moments.

Raul tried not to sound indignant when he finally said, "So you don't want your daughter to be with someone like you?"

Bobby's face was blank.

"You don't want her to end up with a cop?" Raul said.

"A cop?" Bobby shook his head. "That's only half of it. You saw the way her aunt is."

Raul sat there for a moment, numb. With Bobby and Junie, he'd never been conscious of their different ethnicities.

"I'm sorry, son," Bobby said. "I had her for eighteen years. Now her mother's people want to get more involved."

"But you're her father."

"They're her flesh and blood, too," he said. "Hell, they don't even like to call her Junie anymore. Not sure there's much I can do to stop it."

Raul didn't reply. Instead, he got up and left the auditorium.

# - CHAPTER THIRTY-TWO -

I strode past a Suburban parked in Piper's driveway. The SUV had exempt plates, the mark of a law-enforcement vehicle. It was empty, locked.

The official transport of Deputy Chief Raul Delgado, currently fighting his way across Piper's bedroom floor.

A woman in running shorts and a tank top watched me as she power walked down the street.

I nodded hello and then jogged to the Lincoln.

The beeper was rattling in the console when I got in.

Theo Goldberg's number.

I put the phone together, called.

He answered after the first ring. "Why don't you carry a cell like everybody else?"

"Because the people we work for are listening in."

"The No Such Agency?" he said. "We haven't done anything for them in a couple of years."

No Such Agency was a euphemism for the NSA, the National Security Agency.

"That was a rhetorical statement, Theo. I meant that in general someone is listening to most everything we do electronically."

"Their in-house counsel, the one in charge of our account, he was such a putz. Every invoice he wanted to audit. Thought we were padding the bill."

"An ethical government employee. What's this world coming to?" I started the Lincoln. "Why are you calling me, Theo?"

"Why are you *not* calling me? I've beeped you like ten times."

"I've been busy."

"I'm your supervisor, Jonathan." He sounded huffy. "I should be accorded a certain amount of respect."

I pulled away from the curb. "The mess you got me into with the deputy chief. I've been busy with that."

I checked the rearview. Still no sign of Raul Delgado.

"Your performance review is coming up." Theo made a tsk sound. "I'd hate to give you a less-than-stellar evaluation."

I stepped on the brakes, and the Lincoln stopped in the middle of the street, neighbors and bystanders be damned.

"Am I the kinda guy you give a bad performance review to?"

No response.

"Think that one through, Theo." I lowered my voice. "Carefully."

He cleared his throat several times, a sure indication he was agitated. And nervous.

"The Culpepper shipment," he said. "Our client needs to take possession as soon as possible."

"Transport taken care of?"

"That's all been arranged. They're waiting on your call."

I accelerated away. "You really stepped in it this time, Theo. The Delgado mess."

No response.

"Did you hear me?" I turned onto Lovers Lane.

"I, um, don't think we should be talking about that on an open line."

I started to reply, but the phone went dead.

———

Mason Burnett tried to control his breathing.

Anger filled him, swelling up inside like water from a bitter well. The feeling battered against his chest, threatened to overwhelm him.

He watched Jonathan Cantrell hustle across the street after exiting a one-story house with two large trees in the front yard. Mason was parked at the end of the block, maybe a hundred yards away.

His ears rang, palms were sweaty. The stench of booze and cigarettes from the breath of his long-dead father filled his nostrils.

He slid the transmission into drive as Cantrell got into the Lincoln.

Daddy's face filled his vision, indistinct like a mirage but close enough to touch, almost like a mirror. Father and son, one and the same, two sides to the same battered coin.

The Lincoln pulled away from the curb.

Mason waited a couple of seconds and did the same.

The Lincoln stopped after only a few feet, right in the middle of the road.

Mason took his foot off the gas.

After a long moment, the Lincoln slowly headed toward Lovers Lane.

Mason gently accelerated. When he was even with the house where Jon Cantrell came from, he saw the most extraordinary thing—Deputy Chief Raul Delgado staggering outside, tic askew, shirt dirty and untucked.

The Lincoln turned the corner.

Mason slowed, his attention torn between Cantrell's vehicle and Delgado.

He made his decision and sped up to follow the Lincoln.

The anger lessened just a bit.

# - CHAPTER THIRTY-THREE -

I removed the battery from my phone as I drove.

The Dallas North Tollway formed the backbone of the northern part of Dallas, a concrete ribbon running from downtown up to the suburbs, the ever-growing ring of farming towns turned bedroom communities, which were fast encroaching on the Oklahoma border.

Seemed like a large chunk of my life had been spent on the oil-stained surface of the Dallas Tollway, chasing dopeheads and drug dealers and other lowlifes, or women who should have known better than to ever give somebody like me their digits.

The Lincoln barreled through the traffic like a bull charging through swamp grass, and twenty minutes after leaving Piper's place I pulled into the parking lot of the building next to the address where the misdirected shipment of weapons and supplies were to have been delivered.

The lot was empty. The building appeared undisturbed since my previous visit.

I parked on the other side of the first building, completely out of sight from the target structure. Then I ran to the rear boundary, where a single Dumpster sat roughly on the dividing line between the two properties.

Several trees grew around the Dumpster, so I found a spot that was out of sight from both parking areas but afforded me an unobstructed view of the target building.

The pickup crew was a group of ex–Army Rangers. They worked for a private contracting firm that specialized in the transport and safekeeping of items that your traditional moving companies shied away from.

Two years ago, at the behest of one of Saddam Hussein's daughters, they'd moved ninety kilos of gold bullion from Tikrit, Iraq, to a villa in the South of France. That operation had involved a truck convoy, a plane, and a Liberian freighter. This would be a stroll in the park in comparison.

My disposable cell chirped with a text from the transport team leader.

*ETA about 1 min.*

I texted back that everything was a go.

As my phone dinged that the message had been sent, a black Suburban pulled into the parking area of the target building.

The SUV drove slowly across the parking area, making a circuit around the empty office.

I swore under my breath, tapped out another message.

*Hang tight. Go on my OK only.*

My finger hovered over the Send button. The Suburban could be nothing. Could be a real estate broker looking for some real estate.

The SUV stopped by the rear entrance to the building. At this angle, the exempt plates were visible.

The driver's door opened, and a man in his late forties got out.

I hit Send.

Too late. A nanosecond later a large panel van pulled into the parking area.

The pickup team had arrived.

The guy from the Suburban couldn't see them.

The van stopped immediately, clearly receiving my message.

The guy from the SUV looked around the parking lot and then tried the back door. It didn't open.

He walked back to his Suburban, leaned inside, and came out with a pistol.

A suppressor was attached to the end of the weapon.

He shot the dead bolt on the door at the same time as a police helicopter flew overhead.

# - CHAPTER THIRTY-FOUR -

Mason Burnett fired a second round into the lock and kicked the door open.

Metal fragments from the dead bolt scattered on the concrete sidewalk, pinged the side of his Suburban.

The Lincoln Navigator he'd been following had pulled into this driveway thirty seconds before but was nowhere to be seen.

He realized he should be looking for the Lincoln, but there was something about the empty building that stopped him.

He was a cop. He'd seen too many supposedly vacant structures in the city, full of too much stuff they shouldn't contain.

The week before, he'd been in an unoccupied warehouse near Love Field with a lieutenant from auto theft. The warehouse had contained nearly a thousand third-row seats from various GM vehicles—Tahoes, Yukons, and Suburbans. It was an easy-to-steal item but one that brought top dollar on the street.

There was nothing unique about this building on the Dallas North Tollway. There were a million like it. But something about the situation didn't feel right. An ex-contractor pulling in here. The connection to the East Coast law firm.

And now the crate that was barely visible through the tinted glass.

A shipping container marked on one side: "Border Patrol—Forward Operating Base. Do Not Open Unless Authorized."

Almost surely what Cantrell was after.

The container was by the rear cargo door, out of view from most of the building, except the back.

Mason took a quick stroll through the place and determined it was in fact empty except for dust, rat crap, and the strange box. Then he approached the shipping crate at an angle, wary.

The container was made from a plastic material of some sort, a polymer that appeared to be indestructible.

Two side-by-side doors on the front, secured by a heavy-duty padlock.

A stenciled warning above the lock:

No Unauthorized Entry!

—

May Contain Hazardous Material!

Mason examined each side of the container. He ran a finger down the corners, touched the exterior walls. The material felt cool and slick, except for the rear, which was slightly warm. Mason wondered if the warmth could be his imagination. He rapped the surface with a knuckle, got a solid sound back.

Then he returned to the front, to the doors. He shrugged once and shot the padlock with the silenced pistol.

The lock shattered.

Mason stared at the still-unopened doors. He wondered what a fix-it man for a fancy-pants bunch of lawyers would be doing with a government-issued shipping container in an empty building in North Dallas.

A helicopter buzzed overhead. DPD air support he'd arranged. Because you never could tell what a deserted building might bring.

Only one way to find out what was inside.

He yanked open the doors.

On the ceiling of the shipping container, a battery-operated light flicked on, illuminating the interior.

What he saw took a moment to process. The longer he stared at the contents, the more his brain refused to believe what his eyes were seeing.

It wasn't the row of M-4 carbines lining one wall. Maybe twenty of them, standard US Army issue.

Nor was it the crates of ammo underneath the rifles, full-metal-jacket 5.56 millimeter rounds. It wasn't the other stuff either—the medical supplies, communications equipment, several boxes of what appeared to be Border Patrol jackets.

None of that mattered to Mason Burnett.

What made his pulse quicken and palms sweaty was a large metal box that took up the rear third of the shipping container.

The metal box had a series of dials and gauges on the front, each the size of a pie pan. There were also a half dozen throw switches like the kind you find at a power plant or an electrical substation.

Mason lowered his silenced weapon as he stared at the contraption.

"What the hell—" He took a half step back.

In the middle of the metal box, right at eye level, was a yellow-and-black trefoil, the three-prong emblem that was the international warning for radioactivity.

# - CHAPTER THIRTY-FIVE -

I dashed across the parking lot.

The guy from the Suburban had maybe a ten-second lead on me.

At the rear of the building, the door was open.

I paused at the entrance.

Footsteps echoed inside. The lack of furnishings and interior walls made them loud and easy to track.

My cell phone vibrated, a text from the leader of the pickup team.

*Status?*

I could smell their adrenaline. Rangers were notorious for being proactive, juiced for action. This guy and his crew were armed with enough automatic weapons to invade a midtier Central Asian republic, itching to use them.

I didn't text back.

The team had a mission window, a predetermined amount of time to accomplish the pickup. Unless it was a Code One transport, which this certainly didn't qualify for, they would abort after the window closed, leaving the shipment in place.

That would not make Theo happy. He'd probably rupture a spleen or get impacted hair follicles or whatever health malady befell neurotic attorneys when a crisis loomed.

But I didn't want the team in the building until I figured out who the guy in the Suburban was and what he represented.

I stepped inside, using the interior walls that surrounded the restrooms as cover.

*Pfft.* A silenced weapon fired. Then, the tinkle of metal bits landing on concrete.

I stepped away from the wall.

The man from the Suburban stood by the front of the shipping crate, staring inside, a look of astonishment on his face. The crate was positioned so that I couldn't see its contents.

He lowered the gun. Took a step back.

I drew my Glock, aimed at his chest. "Drop the weapon. Put your hands on your head."

He looked up, startled. The pistol slid from his fingers but his arms remained by his sides.

"You're Cantrell, aren't you?" His face was white.

"Hands on your head, now."

The man from the SUV didn't move. He blinked several times like he was trying to think about too many things at one time.

"Do you know about this?" He pointed to the shipping crate.

"That's not your concern." I eased closer.

"What?"

"Last time I'll tell you." I found a zip tie in my pocket. "Put your hands on your head and get on your knees."

"Not my *concern*?"

The helicopter overhead got louder, a new wrinkle that had a 101 percent chance of making the pickup team extra nervous.

Nervous Rangers: not a good situation. They'd probably fire up a surface-to-air missile, and we'd end up with chopper parts scattered over half of North Dallas.

"Who the hell are you people?" The man who would not put his hands where I told him to shook his head.

I kicked away the silenced Glock. It skidded across the floor.

"You have any idea what they're gonna charge you with?" he said.

I holstered my weapon, reached for his hand, zip tie at the ready.

"I'm a cop, asshole." The man from the SUV yanked his hand away from me. "Don't even think about touching me."

He was six or eight years older than me. We were about the same size and fitness level. Getting him cuffed would be messy, and I'd had enough of that for one day.

"We're taking the crate," I said. "You do not want to interfere with that."

He shook his head again, slowly.

I moved behind him, at an angle so I could keep distance between us but have a glimpse inside the container.

The helicopter buzzed closer.

"Need you to call your dogs off." I pointed upward. "My guys will be in and out before you can write up the overtime request."

"How long has it been since you've worn a uniform, Cantrell?"

I didn't say anything.

"Homeland Security," he said. "I'll need to contact them." He slumped his shoulders. "Then there's the hazmat teams. The media liaison office."

"Consider Homeland notified." I took another step and looked inside the container.

The radioactive sign was stark yellow, like a beacon in the night.

"Crap," I said. "They sent a nuke with a regular shipment? Again?"

Portable fusion reactors, made by a Japanese company with deep ties to the American military-industrial community. Maintenance-free, not much bigger than a refrigerator, strong enough to power a town of ten thousand.

"You know about this?" He sounded incredulous.

A portable reactor meant this was a Code One pickup. No aborting the Rangers. No wonder Theo was so nervous.

"The Nuclear Regulatory Commission is gonna pitch a fit," I said. "Reactors are *supposed* to ship separately, but contractors are always looking to save money."

The gun in the man's hand seemed to materialize from the ether, another Glock, this one without a silencer, the muzzle pointed at my face.

"Put it down." I still had my weapon aimed at his torso. "You don't know what you're getting involved with here. Trust me."

With his free hand, he grabbed a walkie-talkie from his belt. He held the radio to his mouth.

"This is Captain Mason Burnett." He rattled off the address of the building. "Officer needs assistance. All available units."

I shuffled toward the back door, keeping the gun aimed at him.

"Don't move." Burnett tracked me with his weapon.

"You don't understand," I said. "Outside, there's six guys in a van. They make your best SWAT boys look like Barney Fife."

"You're the vigilante, aren't you?" His voice was a whisper. "Tell me why you're killing the lowlifes."

I didn't reply. Nothing I could say would make a difference.

"I want to be able to give the press a motive." He smiled. "And you're not gonna be in much condition to talk in a few minutes."

From outside came the sound of rubber soles squeaking on concrete.

I placed my gun on the floor. "Other than the chopper, do you have anybody with you?"

He frowned but didn't speak.

More noise from the back entrance. Nylon rifle slings rubbing against tactical vests. Gloved fingers patting automatic weapons.

"How far away are your people?" I asked.

He gave me a blank stare.

"Your backup," I said. "What's their ETA?"

The first red dot appeared on his chest, a laser sight.

He didn't appear to notice. "Another minute or so, tops."

"That's too long."

I dropped to the floor and covered my head as the Rangers burst into the room.

# - CHAPTER THIRTY-SIX -

Lysol Alvarez may be the king of West Dallas, but it's been a long time since he's mingled with his subjects, other than passing them by while riding in a tinted-window Escalade.

He's running down Navarro Street, headed south toward Singleton, the subgun in his hand.

Every few steps he looks behind him.

A column of smoke streams upward from where his house used to be.

The guy who started this all, the cat in the black tracksuit, is nowhere to be seen.

Lysol hopes the son of a bitch got blown up. But he knows deep in his bones that somehow the man has survived.

Quite a few people are in their yards, the noise from the blast having brought them outside from the comfort of their satellite TVs and window AC units. They're milling about, pointing toward the smoke.

They watch him run by with blank faces. No one says anything, no acknowledgment that a man in a linen suit and silk T-shirt is galloping down the street carrying a machine gun.

Lysol realizes the depth of his predicament.

Kings don't run.

Each step knocks another notch from his prestige in the neighborhood, a rip in the persona he's spent years developing.

Each step makes him angrier.

At the corner, he leans against a stop sign to catch his breath.

He owns more than one place in West Dallas, safe houses that have been set up for just such an occurrence as this.

The nearest location is several blocks on the other side of Singleton. If he can make it there in one piece, he can regroup and find out who is trying to destroy him. Then he can go on the offensive.

Because that's how a king operates.

*Ching.*

The pole vibrates like it's been struck by a rock.

Lysol glances up.

A bullet has punctured the stop sign, right in the middle of the *O*.

He drops to his knees, lungs heaving, fingers tight on the subgun.

Another hole appears a few inches from the first.

He looks in the direction he's just come.

The man in the black tracksuit is about seventy-five yards away, using a two-handed grip to steady the silenced pistol.

The rage builds until there's no stopping it. Lysol's arms tingle. Breath comes in snorts.

*"Aaayyh!"* He raises the subgun, empties a magazine at the tiny figure.

Spent brass clinks on the asphalt.

Black Tracksuit ducks behind a car, either taking cover or injured. Lysol can't tell which from this distance.

From a long way away comes the Klaxon sound of a fire-truck siren.

Lysol gets to his feet, staggers away from the stop sign, headed south. He reloads the subgun as he goes.

Another block and he reaches Singleton, a six-lane street, median in the middle. Traffic is heavy.

A break in the stream of cars appears as something that feels like a wasp nips him on the side of one thigh.

Lysol rushes across the street. He tries to ignore the liquid oozing down his leg.

Horns honk as he reaches the median.

He turns.

Black Tracksuit is dodging cars, the gun aimed.

Lysol fires a burst. He misses the man but hits a plumber's truck instead.

Tires screech.

More horns blare.

Metal rams into metal.

Vehicles on both sides of Singleton come to a stop. The bulk of a city bus separates Lysol from his pursuer.

Lysol's pants are bloody. His leg starts to hurt. He threads his way through the cars and a few moments later he is on the south side of Singleton. Once there, he crouches in the bushes in front of an abandoned service station and surveys the situation.

More cars have stopped. People have gotten out. They're pointing, talking on cell phones.

The man in the black tracksuit does not appear to be among them.

Lysol turns and heads south.

The streets that have served as home for his entire life are suddenly alien, no longer comforting, dangerous-feeling even in the bright light of day.

The wound in his leg, minor though it is, throbs, and he wonders if he'll make it to his safe house alive.

# - CHAPTER THIRTY-SEVEN -

I lay facedown on the floor of the empty office building, arms and legs splayed.

I did not move. Did not speak.

A good rule of thumb: do not get in the way of a team of Special Forces operatives on a Code One pickup.

After a few minutes one of the pickup team dragged me toward the far end of the building while his boss called in the situation to their home office.

Then shit got real, as the kids say.

In a nutshell, here's what happens when a private military contractor—a former Ranger and decorated veteran of the war in Iraq—puts three rounds into a Dallas police captain, in a room that contains a portable nuclear reactor that has been inadvertently shipped to the wrong location at the behest of the US government.

The nearest FBI hostage rescue team, the special forces of federal law enforcement, descended from the heavens, in the literal sense, rappelling from three Apache helicopters.

After disgorging the FBI agents, the helicopters continued to hover over the area at an altitude of five hundred feet.

The team from the Apaches, along with agents who arrived in a convoy of armored Suburbans and at least one half-track assault vehicle, secured the perimeter of the building.

The FAA had been notified, of course, and they'd declared a one-kilometer circle around the building a no-fly zone.

The local authorities—i.e., the Dallas police—were barred from the scene. This drastic action was based on several court rulings that said Homeland Security, in concert with the FBI, could establish temporary martial law anywhere it damn well pleased if an incident was deemed a threat to the security of the United States.

This point, I had to concede to the feds.

If an unsecured nuclear reactor wasn't a national security issue, then I didn't know what was.

It went without saying, of course, that a total media black-out was in effect. No public statement regarding the events at the empty office building had been made nor would one ever be released.

Twitter and Facebook, the ubiquitous social media services, were suffering from an unexplained outage that would later be traced to an offshore server controlled by the NSA.

Except for one aspect of the operation, everything was pro-gressing like a finely tuned mechanism. As slick as cat shit on linoleum.

The problem was the exclusion of the local authorities.

You see, the last message the Dallas police received was from one of their own, Captain Mason Burnett, a request for all available units to respond, officer needs assistance.

Now the captain was not responding to his cell or radio, and the men and women of the Dallas Police Department—all 4,200 of them, all of whom were armed—were a tad anxious to learn about his condition.

According to the FBI agent in charge of the cleanup operation, a man in his forties named Drake, about a hundred Dallas police officers had amassed on the access road in front of the building where the reactor sat.

After a while I was allowed to join Drake just inside the entrance of the vacant building. He offered me fresh-brewed Starbucks from the mobile command center that had been set up in the rear, a pod-like unit that contained a portable cell tower, radio repeater, and a coffeemaker, among other nifty gizmos.

I accepted and together we drank coffee and watched the sea of blue uniforms on the street in front of the building.

"They look angry," I said. "You sure your people have everything under control?"

Drake ignored my question. He added some stevia to his cup and said, "You been a contractor long?"

"I'm not a contractor. I work for a law firm." I glanced toward the rear of the building. "Shouldn't we be, oh, I dunno, doing something?"

An FBI medical team was in the rear, trying to save Captain Mason Burnett's life. A government medevac helicopter had just landed in the back parking lot. The recovery team was securing the doors of the container, preparing to load the shipment onto the forklift they'd brought with them.

"Your law firm." Drake took a sip of coffee. "Goldberg, Finkelman, and Clark. They have a contract to arrange pickups. That makes you a contractor."

"Makes me an employee of a law firm. Not a contractor."

"Tomayto, tomahto," he said.

I pointed to the captain. "You think he's gonna be all right?"

He shrugged. "What's it to you?"

"He's a cop."

Drake gave me a blank stare.

"One of the good guys." I arched an eyebrow. "You understand the concept, right?"

Drake frowned but didn't say anything. He took another sip.

"How about this?" I said. "I don't like seeing somebody wearing a badge get hurt."

Drake nodded knowingly. "So he's a friend of yours?"

"I didn't say that."

"You brought him here, though." He smiled innocently. "To the location of the pickup."

"He followed me."

"With your background." He pursed his lips. "You let a desk jockey trail you? To a Code One."

I tried not to sound exasperated. "It's not like I knew there was a nuke on-site."

"So you would have been more careful if you'd known?"

I didn't reply. I wasn't a big fan of "Have you stopped beating your wife?" questions.

"We're gonna need to debrief you. Won't take long." He paused. "If you cooperate."

I sighed and tossed my coffee on the ground, stomach sour.

"Let's assume you're willing to play ball." He smiled. "Makes everything easier."

A thought occurred to me.

"How'd you know the name of my law firm?" I said. "They keep the connection buried pretty deep."

He turned his attention to what was going on outside but didn't reply.

The Dallas cops were getting more and more unruly. An older officer was pointing his index finger in the face of an agent in his twenties, yelling.

An FBI agent like Drake wouldn't know that Goldberg, Finkelman, and Clark did legal work for contractors. He wouldn't even know the name. A field agent would know about the tactical issues—securing the shipment, maintaining order, keeping the media at bay.

I slapped my forehead, the obvious becoming clear.

"You're a contractor," I said. "And your company uses Goldberg, Finkelman, and Clark."

The expression on his face indicated I was correct. The law firm handled the paperwork for a number of companies who did business with the feds, oftentimes serving as a proxy signer of contracts.

"That makes me your equal." I smiled. "Maybe your superior."

A swell of angry voices from the police officers, followed by the crackle of radios in the empty building.

Drake crossed his arms. "I'm just trying to do my job."

I pointed outside. "Before you get to debriefing me, you might want to contain the situation."

A police officer was engaged in a shoving match with a pair of FBI agents.

Drake's shoulders twitched. He pulled a walkie-talkie from his belt and asked for a status report. A second later he received a slew of responses more appropriate to a war zone than suburban North Dallas—*situation critical, imminent threats, please advise ability to engage targets.*

Drake stared at the walkie-talkie and then looked at me.

"You think you've got a problem now?" I said. "What happens if those cops don't back down?"

The noise outside got louder.

"You used to be part of this department," he said. "How should we handle this?"

"What *we* are you talking about? Is there a mouse in your pocket?"

Before he could answer, the shouting outside increased exponentially, a roar of voices growing desperate.

Then a gunshot rang out and everything got quiet.

For a moment.

———

*Dallas, Texas*
*1999*

Raul Delgado, twenty-nine years old, parked his unmarked squad car in a gravel lot, underneath a billboard advertising Marlboro cigarettes.

One of the most popular watering holes for the Dallas PD was a concrete building a few blocks from the county jail. Sam Browne's sat between a strip joint and a bail bondsman's office on Industrial Boulevard just a few hundred yards from the Trinity River.

Raul picked up the mic and called in a ten-fifty, a food break.

The notification was a formality. Raul was a sergeant in the Crimes Against People Division, a rising star in the DPD hierarchy. A homicide detective, he had a clearance rate ten points above the state average.

His position was regarded as a stepping-stone for those who wanted to advance into the upper echelons of the department.

The position, along with a drive to succeed that was a marvel to his superiors, and his ethnicity, which was becoming more important as the city's demographics changed, had led various local politicos to approach Raul about running for office one day.

Not for a few years, they said. You need seasoning. But keep the idea in mind. Politics would be a great way to give back to the community. To do something with your life that matters. Surely, you don't want to be a cop forever?

Raul took the meetings. He was friendly but kept his comments noncommittal. Coy.

For the present, he concentrated on his police work. He was fluent in Spanish, of course, and worked the Latino neighborhoods, pockets of the city that continued to expand as the population shifted from white and black to brown.

It was midday, April.

Clouds, dark like charcoal, swelled the sky. The air was humid, smelling of ozone from the coming thunderstorm, and hamburger grease from the slatted windows of the kitchen attached to the rear of the bar.

Raul pushed open the door to Sam Browne's and stepped into a narrow room filled with cigarette smoke and neon beer signs.

Bobby presided over the bar at the back, a half-filled pitcher of beer in one hand, the other pressed against the handle of the tap.

Nearly a decade had passed since Bobby retired from the force and opened Sam Browne's, the name an homage to the traditional style of holster and belts that police wore.

Nobody called Bobby by his real name anymore. He was Sam to one and all, old friends from the force, rookies, day drunks who passed away the hours in the booths by the pool tables.

Raul sat at the end of the bar. Two vice officers greeted him and then drifted away. They understood that Raul and Sam/ Bobby had a special friendship. As a matter of courtesy, they gave the owner and the hard-eyed homicide cop some breathing room.

Without being asked, Bobby opened a Diet Coke and placed the can in front of Raul.

Raul took a sip and waited while the older man moved back to the beer taps, where he filled another pitcher and handed it to an Asian guy in a dress shirt and tie.

Bobby returned, drying his hands on a rag. "Thanks for coming."

"You told me it was urgent," Raul said.

"It's about Junie."

"What's happened now?" Raul hadn't seen Junie in months, maybe a year or more. He still thought about her often but not in the same way as when he was younger.

Bobby didn't say anything, as if words were hard to come by all of a sudden.

Junie was twenty-seven years old and on her second marriage.

The first had been to her college sweetheart, right after graduation.

The groom had been president of his fraternity and had taken a job offered by his pledge brother's family. The marriage lasted about a month, until Junie caught her husband in bed with the pledge brother.

The second marriage was a little over two years old. Junie's new husband was a stockbroker, a good provider except that he spent most of his money on strippers and cocaine.

Bobby said, "She miscarried."

Raul paused with the can halfway to his mouth.

"That son of a bitch she's married to." Bobby's voice choked with emotion. "He beats on her."

"Is that—" Raul's limbs tingled. "Did she lose the baby because he hit her?"

Sounds became sharper, lights brighter. The anger built in the pit of his stomach.

"I dunno." Bobby shook his head. "Sure as shit didn't help."

"I'm sorry." Raul took several deep breaths, tried to calm himself. "I didn't even know she was . . ."

"She didn't want to tell people yet."

Raul took a gulp of Diet Coke, something to keep his hands busy.

"She had trouble getting pregnant. Went to this specialist and everything."

"Where is she now?"

Bobby prepared a scotch and soda for a man Raul recognized as a district judge. The bar brought in a cross section of Dallas. Politicians and cops, journalists and sports figures. After chitchatting with the judge for a moment, Bobby returned.

"She's at home. She's scared."

Raul arched an eyebrow.

"Her husband's on a bender. He won't come out of the bedroom."

No one spoke.

"Call the police," Raul said. "The unis need to take care of this."

Bobby stared off into the distance, and in the dim light Raul thought he saw tears in the older man's eyes.

"If I reach out to the substation, then people who come in here will know," Bobby said. "You think I want that?"

Raul leaned close, lowered his voice. "The guy's hitting your daughter. Why don't you just give him a little tune up yourself?"

Bobby picked up an ashtray, dumped cigarette butts into the trash.

"What do you want me to say? I'm not as young as I used to be." The older man sighed. "I'd give anything to roll the clock back ten years. That guy wouldn't know what hit him."

Raul wanted to help Bobby and Junie. Especially Junie. Especially when somebody was causing her pain.

But he was not in a position to give somebody an off-the-books beatdown.

He was also busy. He was dating the niece of a city councilman and serving on the leadership committee of the Latino Law Enforcement Officers Association, slated to be the president of the local chapter next year.

Raul liked politics, which was why he took the meetings that the power brokers offered. He enjoyed the art of leadership. Turned out he had a knack for directing people toward a consensus, horse-trading favors and such.

From time to time, he imagined that this skill set was something supernatural, a gift from Carlos in the great beyond. He often wondered, however, if he had embellished Carlos's skills, burnished them in his memory.

Beating up Junie's husband was not a good idea for someone who eventually wanted to run for office.

Bobby had been wiping the same ashtray for a long time now. He was ignoring customers, too, letting one of his waitresses come behind the bar and fill the orders.

"What aren't you telling me?" Raul said.

Bobby put the ashtray down. Without looking up, he said, "She doesn't want me around anymore."

"Who . . . Junie?"

Raul could hardly believe this. He hadn't been close with Junie in a long time, as their lives had taken different courses. But Bobby was her father.

"Her aunt had to tell me about the miscarriage." Bobby paused. "And the other thing."

"Why wouldn't she talk to you? I don't understand."

"Her mother's people." Bobby shook his head. "They never much like that Junie's mom married somebody like me. A cop."

Raul remembered the aunt well. She was a symbol of everything that was bad about Dallas. Shallow and vain, concerned only about her money and the new fashions at Neiman's.

After Junie had graduated high school, the aunt had taken her niece under her wing, changed the way she dressed, the way she acted. The way she thought.

"What is it you want me to do, Bobby?"

"My little girl's in trouble. I—" He wiped his eyes. "We—we need your help."

Raul pushed the can of Diet Coke away. "You think I'm the family fix-it man?"

Bobby took a sharp breath, leaned close. "We made a pledge, remember? Not to talk about that ever again."

"Talk about what?" Raul headed toward the door.

# - CHAPTER THIRTY-EIGHT -

Lysol ties a bandana around his leg to stanch the flow of blood.

The wound is minor, little more than a nick, but it's dribbling like a Bourbon Street hooker with a month-old case of gonorrhea.

He's in an alley one block south of Singleton. The subgun is slung over his shoulder.

He hasn't heard much from the area where he last encountered the guy in the tracksuit. A few horns honking, some yelling, but that's it.

No sirens yet either, but they will come, of that he's sure. You don't have a ten-car pileup and two guys shooting at each other without the po-po at least putting in an appearance, even in this piss-hole section of town.

Lysol leans against a rack of trash cans behind a ramshackle old house. His breathing is labored. Too much hydro smoke, not enough exercise. Not enough time on the streets, battling the enemy one on one.

A tale as old as history—the king gets soft on the throne.

He pulls a cell phone from his pocket and starts calling people in his organization, the next layer down from those who were destroyed on Vilbig Road. But the calls go unanswered. Some slide straight to voice mail. Others just ring and ring.

Lysol struggles to control the fear pooling in his stomach, an electric glow that sends currents of shakiness throughout his body.

It's time to move. He clutches the subgun in one hand, pushes away from the rack of garbage cans.

A helicopter buzzes overhead, low and loud.

Lysol crouches instinctively, looks up. The blood begins to seep from his wound again.

A TV station, not the police.

Behind him, a shuffle of feet on cracked asphalt.

Lysol spins around. He brings the gun up, finger on the trigger, starts to squeeze.

A boy, maybe nine years old, wearing a pair of ragged denim shorts and a dirty Dallas Cowboys T-shirt. The child's hair is done in cornrows, his skin so dark it's the color of eggplant.

Lysol moves his finger from the trigger, terrified at what he'd almost done.

The child stares at him, head cocked.

Lysol says, "What's your name, boy?"

The child doesn't respond.

"I axed you a question." Lysol lets the street patois creep into his speech. Rulers need to relate to their subjects, the common people.

The child scratches his nose but doesn't say anything.

Lysol stands up. "You know who I am?"

After a moment the boy nods.

"Who your people?" Lysol limps closer. "Your daddy do business with me?"

The helicopter flies over again. In the distance, the sound of a single siren.

"The five-oh," the boy says. "They gonna fuck you up."

Lysol looks at his cell phone. Then he drops it on the ground and smashes it with his good leg.

"You are one funny-looking nigger." The boy shakes his head. "You're all uptown and shit. They give you that suit at the country club?"

"Got a mouth on you, boy. Your mama teach you to talk like that?"

"My mama dead." The youngster kicks an empty can of Schlitz. "Smoked that crack day and night."

The man and the child stare at each other for a few seconds, neither speaking.

"The five-oh," Lysol says. "They on your street right now?"

"Uptown Negro." The boy laughs. "Hiding out in the alley like a hobo."

Lysol realizes the child might be just a tad crazy about the same time it dawns on him that the mother died because of the product he sold.

"Your momma," Lysol says. "I'm sorry about her."

"What you sorry about?" Anger flashes in the boy's eyes. "You light the pipe for her?"

Neither of them speak for a moment.

"I got a crib three streets over," Lysol says. "I need to get there. You wanna be my scout?"

"You got nuthin', Negro." The boy shakes his head. "Fuck me running, you as dumb as a Pop-Tart."

The insolence is amazing. If it wasn't for the child's age, Lysol is pretty sure he'd put a cap in his ass right now and leave him to rot in the alley.

The boy rubs his crotch absentmindedly.

"Well then, I'll see you around, mister man." Lysol smiles, swallows his anger. He slings the gun on his shoulder and prepares to leave.

"You in my alley, Negro." The boy pulls a pistol from his shorts. "You owe me a toll."

The gun is a tiny thing, silver, maybe a .380 or a .32.

Despite the circumstances, Lysol can't help himself. He laughs.

"Put that thing down, 'fore you hurt yourself," he says. "I'll give you five dollars. Okay?"

From behind him comes the sound of feet, lots of them, scurrying down the alley.

Lysol turns.

More boys. Ten, maybe twelve of them. Around the same age as the youngster with the cornrows. Some are holding pistols, others have clubs. One carries what looks like a broken machete.

"You gonna give me whatever you got," the boy says. "You ain't no thing here. This is my territory."

# - CHAPTER THIRTY-NINE -

I watched a sea of blue run toward the empty North Dallas office building.

Dallas police officers. Angry. Breaking through the line of federal agents trying to maintain a secure perimeter.

I turned to Drake, the FBI contractor in charge of the operation, eager to see what he'd do.

His radio sounded like it was on meth.

*Agent needs assistance!*

*Shots fired! Shots fired! Please advise.*

*WHERE THE HELL IS OUR BACKUP?*

I grabbed his arm. "We need to get out of here."

"The shipment." Drake pointed to the container.

The pickup team had loaded the crate onto a forklift. They were securing it with canvas straps, nearly ready to drive the package out the back door.

The team leader, the ex-Ranger, looked at us.

"This is a Code One," he said. "Mission protocol authorizes deadly force."

"Who's your parent company?" I said.

The police were at the building now, banging on the door. The FBI agents who'd been in charge of the perimeter were pressed between them and the glass entrance.

The Ranger told me a name, one of the larger and less felonious multinational military contractors. The company in question used Goldberg, Finkelman, and Clark exclusively for all their legal work.

"Your orders have changed," I said. "Per your employee handbook, in the event of an emergency, legal counsel's instructions supersede those of the mission commander's."

The medical crew wheeled Captain Burnett out through the back door. At the front, more police officers had arrived, hitting the tinted windows.

I pointed to the shipping container. "Unless you can get that out of here in the next thirty seconds, you are hereby ordered to abort this mission."

The Ranger looked at the back exit, maybe a dozen meters away. The forklift traveled like a really fast tortoise. Right now he was probably trying to do the math in his head. Maybe he could make it, maybe not.

"One way or another, the police are going to be crawling everywhere before you know it," I said. "We need to fall back and let the DOJ work out the pickup when everybody's calmed down."

Drake stared at me, paralyzed.

A window at the front broke. The shouts of angry cops filled the room.

"What's plan B, fellows?" I asked no one in particular. "You gonna open fire on a bunch of police officers?"

"What's your name?" the Ranger said.

"Jon Cantrell."

"This is on you, then." He ordered his men to abandon the mission.

The pickup team stopped what they were doing and ran out the back, leaving the forklift and its contents.

The first cop entered the office building at the far end.

I grabbed Drake's arm, pulled him in the direction the Rangers had gone. "If we stay, it will only get worse."

He nodded and followed me out the back.

———

The medevac chopper was a Sikorsky, a big old workhorse with enough floor area to accommodate Captain Mason Burnett and his medical team as well as me and Drake.

By the time we lifted off, the Dallas police had overrun the entire building and spilled out into the rear parking lot where the chopper had been idling.

The FBI agents stood around, jabbering into their walk-ie-talkies, no doubt trying to be cooperative now.

The police were pointing to the chopper, shouting.

Drake and I sat on a bench seat on the back wall. We wore headsets with boom mics. We were both watching the mayhem unfold below us as the chopper slowly gained altitude.

"It's like the fall of Saigon," I said.

"What?" Drake looked up.

"Vietnam. The fall of Saigon. Last chopper off the roof of the embassy?"

"Was that a TV show?"

My mouth fell open. I didn't reply.

"No, no." Drake shook his head. "That was a musical. Broadway. *Miss Saigon*."

"Didn't you take any history classes?"

The Sikorsky banked right. North Dallas lay spread out below, a sea of green trees and gray concrete.

"Or watch *Apocalypse Now*?" I said.

The chopper made a loop around the three Apache helicopters and headed south.

"Boy, this is a mess." Drake rubbed his hands together. "The reports I've gotta fill out."

I didn't say anything, silently agreeing with him. I dreaded the call to Theo Goldberg. Still, this was better than having a bunch of Rangers open fire on the Dallas police.

"You were going to debrief me," I said.

Drake nodded. He pulled out a tablet computer from his backpack and then asked a series of questions centered around one central theme: did Captain Mason Burnett ever identify himself as a police officer?

I told him no each time he asked.

This seemed to satisfy him, as did the data from the shipment itself. The container had been outfitted with the latest in surveillance cameras—wireless, unobtrusive, equipped for sound and video, powered by batteries with a two-year life span.

Drake reviewed the footage on his tablet, showed me the relevant portion. Then he shut down the device and said, "I think we're in the clear. The captain never indicated to anybody he was a cop."

"I hope you tell him that," I said. "If he wakes up."

Drake changed channels on his headset and had a quick conversation with the medical team. Then he clicked back to me.

"He wants to see you."

"Who?"

"The captain."

"He can talk?" I raised an eyebrow. "He's alive?"

"Bulletproof vest." Drake tapped his sternum.

I took off my headset and staggered toward the front of the chopper.

The medical team, two EMTs and a field assistant, moved to one side when I approached.

Mason Burnett's face was pale, eyes dark-rimmed. They'd taken off his shirt and vest. His chest was muscular but bruised, skin the color of thunderclouds.

One bullet had punched through the fleshy part of his bicep. The wound had been bandaged but there was still a fair amount of blood everywhere.

I leaned close.

He pulled aside the oxygen mask with his good hand.

"Y-you're the vigilante." His voice was hoarse, weak.

"Not me." I shook my head. "I'm a lover, not a fighter."

"They're gonna pin it on you and Delgado's little split-tail."

"Piper. That's her name."

I tried not to think about where she was at the moment.

Burnett grimaced. One of the EMTs checked the injured man's pulse and then stepped back.

"Why were you following me?" I said.

"W-what's that kid to you?"

"Tremont?"

"He's dead by now. Has to be," he said. "Statistically, that kid would never have made his twenty-fifth birthday. A drive-by waiting to get popped."

I pondered the truth of his statement for a moment. Then I said, "Everybody needs at least one person who gives a damn about them."

I wondered what would have happened to Tremont if his father had not been killed.

Would he have been at the Iris Apartments? Almost certainly not. My friend Damon Washington would have gotten out of law enforcement at some point, maybe quit living on edge. There would have been a house in the suburbs, backyard cookouts.

Burnett shook his head. "You know what my life was like when I was that kid's age?"

"Don't take this the wrong way, but I don't really give a damn about your life."

I realized the fallacy of my thinking. Damon Washington couldn't have left law enforcement any more than I could have spent the last twenty years working an office job. We are what we are.

Burnett coughed. His face blanched, eyes wide. Then he licked his lips and said, "Did you find out where the kid worked?"

I didn't reply. He stared at my eyes.

"How did you know he had a job?" I said.

"You got any children?"

I shook my head.

"My old man. He was a piece of work."

"What does Tremont's job have to do with anything?"

He coughed again, and shivered once like he was cold.

"I never wanted children," he said. "I didn't want to keep the bad genes flowing, one generation to the next. Know what I'm saying?"

I nodded. The helicopter banked again. In the distance I could see the medical district, a row of hospitals along Harry Hines Boulevard.

"Delgado's a whackjob." Burnett's voice was weaker. "Guy joins the PD, then beats everybody over the head with the dead-brother thing. How does that make sense?"

The idea that I had been suppressing bubbled up to my consciousness.

"Do you think he's the vigilante?"

Burnett started to speak but no words emerged. Blood trickled from the corner of his mouth.

One of the EMTs approached. He listened to Burnett's chest with a stethoscope and then looked at his colleagues.

"We've got a punctured lung here." He then grabbed my arm. "Sir, you need to step away from the patient."

I pushed the EMT's hand away, leaned back over Burnett.

"Make all this count for something," I said. "Tell me what you know about Tremont."

No response. His skin color had gotten paler.

A second EMT grabbed my arm.

Burnett looked at me and smiled.

The first EMT fitted the oxygen mask back over his mouth and nose. Burnett said something that I couldn't hear because of the mask.

"What?" I strained against the EMT pushing me away.

"Sir, you need to give us room to work." The EMT grabbed my wrist.

This was an amateur move. The man was facing me. He had no leverage. Just an attempt to exert control. One that was destined to fail.

Instead of pulling back, as was expected, I pushed forward. The move caught the EMT off guard. His balance was wrong.

I kicked one foot out from under him, and he fell to the metal floor of the Sikorsky. I yanked my wrist free and leaned over Mason Burnett.

"What did you say?"

"McKee." His voice was hard to hear. "Talk to McKee."

The name was familiar. Before I could think about it or ask him who that was, Drake and the other EMT were all over me like a cheap suit.

I let them drag me away as the Sikorsky began its descent to the helipad on top of Parkland Hospital.

# - CHAPTER FORTY -

Lysol Alvarez is not a butcher or a sadist, despite what some of his enemies might say about him.

He's never inflicted pain without a reason or killed anyone whose passing didn't serve a larger purpose. Each death had been a business decision. Because, at the end of the day, that's what everything comes down to—business. Dollars and cents.

For example, he knows how many people he's killed. Would a butcher keep track?

Seventeen. Not a large number when you consider his line of work.

The first had been when he was a teenager, not much older than the boy with cornrows.

Nineteen ninety-one. A low-level thug in the organization that sold cocaine on the corners of West Dallas at that time. The man had stiffed Lysol's brother on some money he'd owed, a gambling debt.

Lysol told his brother he'd get the cash if he wouldn't ask any questions.

So he sat on the corner opposite from where the thug did business. He sat and waited.

The thug approached him about thirty minutes later, wanting to know what the fuck Lysol's skinny ass was doing on this particular corner.

Amazing the things you remember, a quarter of a century later.

It was summertime, the middle of the afternoon. A Tuesday. The sprinkler across the street sprayed water across a half-dead lawn.

Lysol didn't answer. The man got angry. Lysol waited until the thug knelt beside him and asked the question again.

Then he hit the thug in the head with a lead pipe, swinging like he was trying to knock a ball into the outfield, a solid blow that crushed the man's temple and sprayed blood along the gutter like the sprinkler across the street.

He'd taken the man's money and his product, left him lying in the gutter, another unsolved homicide the DPD didn't work too hard at figuring out.

From that humble but violent beginning, Lysol had begun his empire, a multilayered business that today generated nearly fifty thousand dollars a month in gross income.

But one thing Lysol has never done was harm a child.

Which makes this particular situation awkward.

He's counted thirteen of the little fuckers, and each one is armed. He doubts there is a single pubic hair among the lot of them.

A bunch of pissant kids. Telling Lysol Alvarez, the king of West Dallas, what to do.

They are now in the backyard of the house where Lysol stopped in the alley. The area behind the home looks like a junkyard. Rusted cars, a rotting storage shed, dirt instead of a lawn. Bits of metal and wood lying about.

"Where we going?" Lysol says.

The boys have formed a half circle, angling him toward the back door of the house.

Cornrows is the leader. He points to Lysol's subgun, still slung over his shoulder, and says, "Put that on the ground."

Lysol shakes his head slowly.

One of the kids in the semicircle steps forward and whacks him on the knee with the back of a broken machete.

Lysol manages not to scream. Or fall to the ground.

He grunts once and hyperventilates for a moment. Then he drops the subgun.

Machete Boy picks it up. Puts the sling on his shoulder. He's so short the barrel is only a few inches away from the dirt.

Cornrows points to the back door.

Lysol nods, tries to look defeated. In the small of his back, he can feel the SIG resting comfortably, covered by the gray linen coat.

Cornrows and his crew are deadly, of this he has no doubt, but they're still nothing more than a group of kids. Any street guy over the age of sixteen would know to check a prisoner, head to toe, before bringing him inside.

One of the boys opens the back door, motions him in.

Lysol steps into a kitchen that is completely at odds with the exterior.

The room is sparkly clean, the air smelling of pine disinfectant, bacon, and warm milk.

The appliances are new—an oven and burner across from a refrigerator that is still plastered with tags from the manufacturer.

The linoleum floor is old but freshly mopped, probably original to the wood-framed house, which appears to have been built sometime in the 1930s.

Cornrows and Machete Boy follow him in. The rest of their crew stays outside.

"What is this place?" Lysol says.

"Keep going, Negro." Cornrows points toward the dining room.

Lysol takes a last look around the kitchen, a nice, slow perusal. Time to start establishing himself as the boss, even in little ways. The age of the children and the fact that they haven't found the SIG gives him a wedge of confidence.

All that changes when he enters the main part of the home, one large room that was designed to serve as a combination dining and living area.

One side of the room contains a table and chairs, room for six or eight people to eat.

The other side is dominated by baby beds lined up in rows. Fifteen or twenty at least.

Most appear to contain sleeping infants. The soft mew of slumbering babies fills the air. One begins crying, the occupant of a crib at the far end.

Machete Boy strides over to the fussy infant. He rocks the cradle, makes a cooing sound to soothe the child.

"You running some kinda orphanage here?" Lysol says.

"Transportation tax, you owe me," Cornrows says. "Remember?"

"I think it's time you answer me, little man." Lysol makes no move to give the youngster any cash. "This place, all these babies, it ain't right."

Cornrows doesn't reply.

"Where'd these kids come from?"

"The street," Cornrows says. "Where you think?"

"And you boys take care of them yourself?"

"I need your money now, Negro."

"We'll get to that in a minute." Lysol surveys the room. "Where their parents be?"

In the far corner, on an end table, he sees a stack of foil rolls, Reynolds Wrap, next to several boxes of plastic sandwich bags. He realizes the boys are moving product. They've found a wholesaler willing to do business with them, and they are cutting the package in this very house. In his neighborhood.

He can't decide if what he feels is anger or admiration.

"If whitey finds out about these babies," Lysol says, "you boys are screwed like a two-legged dog."

"The Man don't know about us," Cornrows says. "And he ain't never gonna find out."

Lysol shakes his head. "Whitey always finds out."

"Your money." Cornrows raises the gun. "All of it. Now."

Lysol shakes his head, a gentle smile on his face. "That ain't the way this is gonna go. Let's you and me figure out something to both our benefits."

Cornrows squints real hard, trying to look tough. His arm is shaking.

"You've got some balls on you, little man, I'll give you that." Lysol shakes his head. "But you're a pup still. Let me help you."

Cornrows is breathing fast, cheeks bellowing. Tears well in his eyes.

"You gonna put me down?" Lysol says. "In here, with all these babies?"

From the hallway leading to the bedrooms comes the sound of footsteps, a woman walking.

The boy's attention wavers. He turns toward the noise.

Lysol slides a hand under his jacket and grabs the SIG.

A woman's voice, singing a nursery rhyme.

"Hush, little baby, don't you cry—"

A skinny white chick, on the bitchy side of forty, enters the room, cradling a newborn. She's pretty but her eyes are sad. A richy-rich lady, based on her clothes and expensive haircut.

She stops singing when she sees Lysol standing in the middle of the nursery, aiming a gun at Cornrows.

"Jamal?" She presses the baby to her chest. "What's going on?"

"That your name, little man?" Lysol says. "You Jamal?"

The boy with the cornrows nods. He's staring at Lysol's weapon like it's a snake.

"Drop your fucking gun, Jamal." Lysol raises his weapon. "I'd hate to wake all these kiddos."

The room is silent.

Jamal keeps staring, mouth open like he's trying to figure out how it all went to shit so fast.

Lysol looks at Machete Boy. "You. Put the blade down and come over here."

The woman says, "Do what he tells you, both of you."

Machete Boy drops the knife and scampers over to the woman.

Jamal keeps the gun aimed at Lysol, fingers on the grip, arm shaking even more than before.

"Listen to the debutante, Jamal." Lysol cocks the SIG's hammer. "You're too young to check out like this."

Jamal slumps his shoulders, defeated. He drops the gun on the carpeted floor.

Lysol scoops it up while keeping the SIG raised.

Then he turns his attention to the woman.

"Jamal and me, we were having a little visit about arranging transport to a place of mine a few blocks away."

The woman nods. "May I put the child down?"

"Where?" Lysol says.

She points to an empty crib. Lysol slides across the room and checks the bedding. No weapons.

"Go ahead."

She deposits the baby, arranges the covers, and then stands by Jamal and Machete Boy. In her hand is an electronic cigarette. She sticks the device in her mouth and exhales a plume of smoke that has no smell.

"You know who I am?" Lysol says.

She takes another puff. "Besides a man with a gun?"

Lysol stares at her, his mind awhirl, trying to figure out what in the hell is going on.

Jamal and Machete Boy nestle closer to the woman, looking like the children that they are, not the gangstas they want to be.

"I've seen you around, haven't I?" Lysol says.

The woman doesn't respond.

"Over at the Iris Apartments." Lysol nods. "You're one of them do-gooders from North Dallas. Come around thinking you're gonna make shit better."

"If that's how you see it." She crosses her arms. "At least I don't sell poison to my own people."

"What is it you're pushing then?" Lysol doesn't take offense. "Something that makes you feel better on the inside?"

The woman remains silent.

"I got some righteous ganja that'll do the same thing."

"You don't know anything about me." Her lips are pressed together.

"So what do you got going on here?" Lysol points to the stacks of foil. "Your North Dallas check writers know you're selling product down here?"

The woman puffs some more on the fake cigarette, a nervous expression on her face.

Lysol smiles and a moment of satisfaction envelops him, the feeling that always comes when he spots a business opportunity.

———

*Dallas, Texas*
*1998*

Raindrops pinged the hood of the squad car as Raul Delgado parked in Junie's driveway.

The storm was about to begin.

Bobby had asked Raul to help his daughter, and Raul couldn't say no.

Lightning jagged across the black sky. Thunder rumbled.

Junie's house was in northwest Dallas, near Inwood Road and Royal Lane, a well-to-do neighborhood a few blocks from a private girls' school.

Huge, sweeping live oaks in the front yard, flower beds bursting with color.

The home was one story, long and low, spread out over the half-acre lot like someone squashed a two-story structure to make it fit under the trees.

Raul called his lieutenant, told him he was going to be out of pocket for a while. Then, he requested a favor. He asked the lieutenant to beep him if a call came across from the northwest dispatch, anything with Junie's address.

He got out of the car. From the trunk he grabbed a baton.

Raul was wearing civilian clothes, a gray jacket, navy slacks, heavy rubber-soled boots. He clipped his badge to the breast pocket of the jacket as he strode up the sidewalk to the front door.

No answer when he knocked.

He tried the knob.

The door swung open.

A large entryway. Marble flooring, black like the clouds outside. The walls were stark white.

The entryway led to a family room that was decorated like a cross between a south Texas hunting camp and an English bordello.

Deer heads and leather chairs, a pool table. Walls painted olive drab.

The room smelled like stale cigars and air freshener, two competing odors, each worse because of the presence of the other.

Junie was sitting in a folding chair by a set of sliding glass doors, an unlit cigarette dangling between her lips. She was wearing a pink running suit, the jacket open over a white T-shirt.

The doors overlooked the patio and swimming pool. Drops of rain cratered the surface of the water.

"Junie?" Raul kept his back to the wall.

Every access point to the room was visible.

She looked up. Her eyes were red, hair disheveled.

"That's not my name." She seemed distracted.

He felt a bolt of fear that something had happened to Junie's mind, then recalled that she no longer went by her nickname.

"Are you okay?" he asked.

"What are you doing here?" Her voice was scratchy like she'd been crying.

"Where's your husband?"

Bobby had said he was locked in a room, coked-up, and wouldn't come out.

She lit the cigarette, then opened one of the patio doors.

"Tell me what happened."

"You shouldn't a come, Raul."

"Your father's worried about you."

She smirked.

"Talk to me, Junie."

"What do you want to hear?" She blew a plume of smoke outside.

"Bobby told me about the baby. I'm sorry."

No response.

"You want me to call an ambulance, get you checked out?"

She cocked her head. "Now, why would I want that?"

From the hallway leading to the bedrooms came a sound like furniture being moved.

Outside, a crack of thunder.

"Let's go for a ride then," Raul said. "Take a little break from here. What do you say?"

More furniture moving from the bedroom. Groaning.

"You really want me to tell you something?"

Raul nodded. "Yeah. Sure I do."

"I keep thinking I'm gonna make something out of nothing. But it never works out that way." She shook her head. "That's what I got to tell you."

Silence for a moment.

"You don't have to live like this," Raul said.

"What do you know about the way I live?" She wiped her eyes. "What do you even care?"

Banging on the bedroom wall.

Raul evaluated his choices.

High levels of cocaine made the user paranoid. The paranoia manifested itself in a desire to keep the world away. Based on what he'd seen before, Raul figured this was why the furniture was being moved in the bedroom. Her husband was blocking the door.

This meant Raul and Junie were safe for the moment, because the husband would stay put. So he stepped away from the wall and approached her. He needed to get her in the squad car.

"How come you never made a play for me?" Junie said.

Raul stopped, at a loss for what to do or say. Some of the best police training in the world, halted by a simple question.

"I always thought you were so good-looking." She flipped her cigarette outside. "Summers, you used to work in the pastures with your shirt off. Damn, you were fine."

"Junie. We need to leave."

"Didn't you think I was attractive?"

Raul tried to squelch the memories of the old days, when the three of them had spent so much time together.

But the memories came back, unbidden. They always did.

He remembered how Junie had looked dressed up for church. How beautiful she'd been. The way the dress clung to her body, demure yet suggestive at the same time. He remembered working on the fence line in the summer and Junie bringing him iced tea.

He shook his head, tried to clear the images from his mind.

"Maybe you thought I was damaged goods." Junie lit another cigarette. "After what happened."

One thing he never thought—that Junie was damaged in any way. She was about as perfect as a person could get.

"Let's don't talk about that now, okay?" He put a hand on her shoulder. "Let's just get out of here."

"That's what Daddy believed," she said. "After that day, he never looked at me the same."

"The past should stay in the past. We don't need to be talking about Wayne right now."

From the other side of the room, by the hallway, came a thumping sound.

Junie and Raul looked up at the same time.

A man in his thirties, wearing a sleeveless Dallas Cowboys T-shirt and plaid boxer shorts, stood where the hallway met the family room.

Junie's husband.

The flip side of cocaine abuse. The user became irrational, did the unexpected.

The man's face was as pale as buttermilk, except for the dark circles under his eyes.

"Who the hell is Wayne?" The husband's voice was ragged, like he'd been screaming.

Raul took stock of the situation.

The subject appeared to be unarmed but was under the influence of a narcotic. He needed to be subdued as quickly as possible so that he wouldn't be a danger to himself or anyone else.

"I know who you are." The husband walked toward Raul. "You're that Mex they're always talking about."

Raul raised the baton. "Sir. I need you to stop and place your hands on your head."

"What are you gonna do if I don't, taco man?"

Junie started to cry.

Raul kept his voice soft. "I'll have to take you down. And it's not gonna be much fun, on your end at least."

The husband rubbed his nose. "When did they start letting wetbacks be cops anyway?"

Raul didn't respond. He'd heard much worse on the street. And in the locker room at the substation.

"I called some real police," the husband said. "My cousin, he's a sergeant at the northwest substation."

"Last time," Raul said. "Put your hands on your head and turn around."

The husband smiled. He raised his arms, a gesture of surrender, then launched himself toward Raul like there was a rocket in his ass.

Raul had time to rear back the baton.

The husband was in midair, fingers aimed for Raul's eyes.

Backpedaling, Raul swung for the man's head with the baton. The wood connected with the husband's forearm, a meaty thunk followed by a cracking sound. Then the two men were as one, rolling around the floor, limbs entangled.

The husband had the advantage of the drugs in his system. He didn't feel or care about the broken arm.

Raul, however, was trained for such circumstances. He kneed the man in the crotch and then slid away, slamming the baton into the attacker's unprotected kidneys.

The husband yelped several times, the injuries burning through the drugs.

Raul grabbed his bracelets, yanked the damaged arm behind the man's back, and cuffed him.

The husband screamed.

Raul stood, pulled a radio from his belt, called the local substation. He gave the address and his badge number, and told the dispatcher that he needed a domestic abuse team and a supervisor.

Junie was outside on the patio, peering in, breathing heavily.

A wall of glass that might as well be an ocean separated them.

She spoke through the glass, her words muffled.

*"Is he okay?"*

Raul didn't reply.

A flash of lightning filled the sky. Thunder bellowed.

*"Why'd you hit him so hard?"*

Raul went outside, trying not to let the anger take hold. "You want me to uncuff him?"

She didn't say anything.

"I bet he's in good enough shape to punch you a couple of times."

She started to cry again.

"Is that what you want? Spend your life getting slapped around by a cokehead?"

She shoved Raul away, tears streaming down her face.

"You don't understand." She put her palm against his chest. "You just don't understand."

"Try me, Junie." He grasped her wrist gently. Pulled her close. "I bet I understand more than you think."

She wept against his chest. After a moment, she looked up and said, "Don't you get it? He's all I've got."

Raul knew at that point that despite their shared history, he understood nothing. About her or himself.

From the front of the house a group of uniformed police officers entered the family room. They were all young and white. The leader, a man with biceps that strained the material of his shirt and sergeant stripes on his shoulders, stepped onto the patio.

He took in the scene—Raul holding Junie. A bound man on the floor. He said, "How come my cousin's in handcuffs?"

Raul was weary. His limbs felt heavy. He disengaged from Junie. "Because I didn't feel like shooting him."

The sergeant chuckled. "Well, aren't you a spicy enchilada."

Raul didn't speak.

"What's your name?" the sergeant asked.

Raul told him. "Who are you?"

"Mason Burnett," the sergeant said. "And I bet we cross paths again real soon."

# - CHAPTER FORTY-ONE -

Parkland Hospital, where they brought Kennedy in 1963, was just a few blocks from Dallas Love Field.

The Sikorsky carrying Captain Mason Burnett landed on a helipad on the roof of the hospital.

I waited with Special Agent Drake while the EMTs offloaded the wounded man.

When the chopper was empty, I said good-bye to Drake and made my way to the aircraft's exit.

"Hey," Drake called after me. "What about the shipment?"

I turned. "What about it?"

"What's our plan now?"

"You're an FBI agent, for Pete's sake," I said. "I'm sure you and Homeland Security can figure something out."

Honestly, the quality of contractors these days was appalling. Where was the initiative?

By this time, a team of lawyers from the Dallas office of Goldberg, Finkelman, and Clark would have been dispatched to oversee the disposition of the misdelivered shipment. With the Dallas police no doubt aware of the contents of the crate, the shipment was no longer an operational issue but a legal matter.

Injunctions would be issued, temporary restraining orders filed. Lawyers in expensive suits firing paper bullets at each other in a crowded courtroom.

I made my way through the throngs of medical personnel on the roof and found a staircase. Four floors later I was on the street.

Taxis were everywhere, disgorging a cross section of the typical urban demographic in various states of distress. Construction workers missing fingers, women about to go into labor, a pair of drunk drag queens.

I hailed a cab that looked reasonably clean and not too infectious, and ten minutes later I was at the Hertz Gold counter at Love Field.

The law firm's AmEx card secured me a Chevrolet Suburban, white like a cop's vehicle. No reason not to blend in.

Thirty minutes after that, I parked in front of the restored Victorian house off of McKinney.

The brass plaque that read The Helping Place looked a little tarnished since my last visit. That could have been my imagination, though.

The front door was locked, lights off. The place appeared empty.

I strode around the side yard to the rear of the building. No cars were present in either the driveway or the garage.

Through the wall of glass that formed the rear of the house, I could see Hannah McKee's desk. Her computer was off.

I headed to the back door. It was flimsy, glass and wood, a century old if it was a day, secured by an inexpensive dead bolt.

I reared back one leg and slammed my heel just above the lockset.

The old wood splintered. The door swung open as an alarm panel beeped a warning tone from somewhere inside.

I entered the office, went to Hannah McKee's desk, counted to thirty.

At twenty-five, a siren sounded from the front.

I watched the desk phone.

At forty seconds it rang. Showtime.

I answered gruffly. "Yeah."

A woman's voice. "This is Ace Alarm Company. We've received an intruder alert from your location."

"I'll bet you have. This is Dallas po-lice."

"Uh . . . I'm going to need the password."

I held the phone away from my face and thumped the desk a couple of times while mumbling as if three or four people were in the room. Then I came back on the line.

"Look, lady. We've got a crime scene here. Pretty sure the person who's got whatever password you're looking for is bleeding out on the floor right now."

Silence. Then: "Oh dear. I've never had this happen before. What should I do?"

"Don't matter to me." I tried to give the impression of a weary cop at the end of his shift. "Homicide squad's on their way."

"Okay. That's, uh, good." Alarm Lady sounded relieved. "I'll clear the signal."

"That'll work. 'Preciate it." I hung up, amazed that the technique had worked.

A couple of seconds later the alarm stopped, and I turned my attention to Hannah McKee's work space.

The surface of the desk contained the usual stuff.

Office paraphernalia, pens and paper clips, and a coffee cup full of yellow highlighters. A box of vanilla-flavored nicotine cartridges for an electronic cigarette. Stacks of folders about upcoming projects and fund-raisers for the Helping Place, everything labeled and color-coordinated.

Underneath the perfectly organized folders was an unmarked one, secured by a binder clip.

I removed the clip, leafed through the papers, most of which were threatening letters from attorneys and past-due notices from various vendors.

Apparently the Helping Place did not manage its money well. One attorney's letter threatened criminal charges because "funds have clearly been transferred in a fraudulent manner."

I put the letters back in the file, clipped the folder shut, and returned everything to its original position.

Then I searched drawers.

Again, the usual stuff.

In the bottom file compartment, however, underneath a container of facial tissue, I found a stack of books on fertility and conceiving after the age of forty.

Underneath the books was a plain manila envelope, no markings or labels.

I opened the flap and slid the contents out onto the desk.

Two receipts. One from Target, the other for Walmart. Both stores were in the west part of town and listed the same purchases—twenty baby cribs, ten from each store.

Something made me look up from the desk in time to see a blur of motion in the yard.

I slid out of the chair, fell to the floor. Reached for the Glock.

Noise at the back door. Footsteps crunching on wood fragments.

The desk was between me and the intruder.

I crawled around the side farthest from the door as the footsteps came toward the desk.

No chance to escape. The intruder would be where I'd been sitting in a couple seconds.

I sprang up, pistol aimed in the direction I'd last heard movement.

Piper stood on the other side of the desk, a gun pointed at my head.

"Hey, Jon." She lowered her weapon. *"Qué pasa?"*

I let out a breath, eased my gun toward the floor. "What the hell are you doing here?"

"Should I ask you the same thing?" She frowned. "I never know how to handle these situations."

She was wearing faded jeans and an unzipped hoodie over a Rolling Stones concert T-shirt.

"You look like shit," she said.

"Been a rough day."

She looked spectacular—well rested, peaceful, supremely capable. Like I remembered her from when we first met. The underground life agreed with her.

"I did a little digging," she said. "Figured out where Tremont worked. And who should I find there but you. What a coinky-dink."

I didn't say anything.

"So?" she said. "What tripped your lights to this place?"

"You know who Mason Burnett is, right?"

"A whackjob with a badge." She nodded. "Burnett's been itching to give Raul the high, hard one for years."

"He knows something about Tremont." I explained briefly about my morning's activities. "Said McKee might be able to help."

"The thing in North Dallas?" Piper whistled. "That was you?"

"That was *not* me. A vendor delivered a shipment for a Border Patrol FOB to the wrong address. The law firm was handling the pickup."

"When are you gonna get out of the contractor game, Jon?"

I shrugged.

"Nothing but a bunch of politicians and lobbyists in five-thousand-dollar suits," she said. "Ass-fucking the Constitution."

"And what would I do for gainful employment?" I cocked my head. "Be a cop again like you?"

Silence.

"How's that working out, by the way?"

She didn't reply because there was no answer.

We were alike in this manner. We didn't really fit in anywhere.

Too rough for the regular world, the nine-to-five demographic. A few scruples too many for the gray market that was the federal contracting arena.

"So, did you miss me?" Piper asked.

"It's been, what, a day?"

She arched an eyebrow.

"I was worried about you," I said. "Is that what you want to hear?"

"I missed you, Jon." She picked up the receipts from the desk.

Her next words were soft, hard to understand. "But then I always do."

I smiled for an instant but decided not to comment.

Piper cleared her throat, held up the receipts. "These are all from the same part of town."

"West Dallas. Tremont's hood."

"And your old pal, Mr. Alvarez."

"Let's take a drive." I pointed to the door. "Have a powwow with Lysol."

She nodded as a Suburban pulled into the parking lot.

The SUV squealed to a stop and all four doors opened, disgorging a squad of officers in full combat regalia—black fatigues and flak jackets, helmets, assault rifles.

From the front came the sound of the door crashing, followed by heavy footsteps on the hardwood floors.

The officers from the back could see us through the glass wall. They advanced toward the rear door, rifles at the ready.

Piper held her Glock up, muzzle pointing toward the ceiling, and then made an exaggerated show of placing it on the desk.

I let mine slip from my fingers to the floor. Then I held my hands up as high as they would go.

The first person to enter the room came from the front, the butt of an M-4 carbine pressed to his shoulder.

Deputy Chief Raul Delgado.

———

*Dallas, Texas*
*2010*

Raul Delgado was forty years old, a captain with the criminal intelligence unit of the Dallas police.

Depending on who you talked to, his rise in the department was described in various ways.

Meteoric.

Well deserved.

The result of political correctness run amuck.

On this sunny October afternoon, he was at the State Fair of Texas, not far from where he'd gotten into a fistfight with the preppy all those years ago.

The fair brought tens of thousands of people to one place at one time. Not all of them were law-abiding citizens. Raul's idea had been to place intelligence officers at the event, wearing plain clothes. If needed, they would supplement the unis. Otherwise, their job was to observe and report potential problems.

The unofficial motto of the intelligence unit: nothing beats eyes and ears on the ground.

Other officers of his rank spent their time behind a desk.

Not Raul Delgado.

He liked the street, or in this case the esplanade, the sights and smells of a living city, the pulse of the inhabitants.

Officers on patrol nodded hello to him as he passed down the midway.

They were respectful, and for the first time in a long while Raul Delgado felt a sense of peace and contentment. This was not a bad life he'd made for himself. What would Carlos think if he could see him now?

How far he had come from the scared little boy with blood on his shirt and urine-soaked pants.

A decorated veteran of the Dallas Police Department. A civic leader whose public speaking skills had been compared to those of a young Barack Obama. He was a natural born orator, the larger the crowd the better. He had addressed congressional subcommittees, the 2008 Democratic National Convention, and too many local groups to remember.

Something about an audience brought out the best in him, the ability to breathe passion into his subject, his words and delivery nuanced, his demeanor humble yet forceful. He was good-looking, too, which didn't hurt. Fit, with a full head of wavy hair.

The politicos he continued to meet with no longer talked about his chances running for the city council or the mayor's job. Now they spoke about higher office.

In the shadow of the Ferris wheel that dominated the midway, Raul bought a corny dog as a horde of schoolchildren rushed by him, eager to get to the rides.

The children were a cross section of the area. Black and brown. White. More than a few Asians and subcontinent Indians.

The demographics in Texas were changing, the politicos said. The time was coming when a Mexican American would occupy the governor's mansion in Austin. As an aside, they mentioned his personal narrative, the great tragedy that he overcame, how that could be a plus in his run for office. Raul took more meetings, listening to their ideas. He was intrigued, of course. Their words were seductive; they were designed to be.

Only one slight problem, the politicos said, one area that needs to be addressed.

You need a wife, Captain Delgado. Someone to complete the image, a supportive spouse by your side.

Raul had had plenty of opportunities, of course. He'd dated cheerleaders and models, lawyers and bankers. One local magazine voted him the most eligible bachelor in Dallas.

But no one had captured his desire.

As the last of the children passed, Raul noticed one left behind.

An African American boy. Maybe eight or nine years old.

He kept an eye on the child for a moment, hoping to see a parent running to catch up.

No one appeared.

The child looked from side to side, apparently searching for someone. Then he sat on a bench. The bench was by a booth where you could win a stuffed animal by tossing rings on a bottle.

The carnies tried to entice him to play. He ignored them, and after a moment they did the same.

Raul watched for a few minutes. People came and went, dozens passing the boy like he wasn't there.

The child appeared off somehow. His eyes were intelligent but vacant, like he was thinking about things that no one else could fathom or would even want to.

After another couple minutes, Raul approached, sitting on the bench next to him.

"How you doing, little man?" Raul pointed to the badge clipped to his belt. "I'm a police officer. Anything I can help you with?"

The boy stared straight ahead. His lips moved silently like he was having a conversation with someone who wasn't there.

"What's your name?" A long pause. "Mine is Raul."

More silent mumbling. Then, the boy looked up. "Tremont. My name is Tremont Washington."

"Where're you from, Tremont?"

The boy hummed, eyes closed.

"You here with your family?"

Tremont opened his eyes. He stared at Raul's badge.

"My daddy. He was police."

"That so? What department?"

More humming.

Raul watched the crowd, looking for someone who might be a parent or guardian. Nothing. Just a river of people moving from one booth to the next, eating cotton candy.

No one paid any attention to a forty-year-old Latino man and a grade-school-age black kid.

Raul realized this is how child molesters operate. Find a target, alone, start talking to him. He hoped to locate the parents of this child and tell them the danger they were placing their son in.

"My daddy, he worked for the state po-po." Tremont rubbed his hands together. "But they kilt him."

"Who killed him?" Raul leaned forward. "Your daddy died on the job?"

"They didn't let me go to the cemetery. But they gave me a flag."

This kid was the survivor of a line-of-duty death?

Raul pulled his BlackBerry out, sent his assistant an e-mail. *Run a check on the name Tremont Washington. See if there are any ties to any LEOs.*

The boy sat up, alert, staring across the midway.

Raul followed his gaze, saw throngs of people no different from the crowd who'd been there a few moments earlier.

The boy gulped. He pointed to a woman wearing camo fatigues, a soldier. The woman was pushing a toddler in a stroller.

"Mama."

Raul stared at the woman. She was Caucasian with blond hair. She could have been a guardian or adoptive mother, but there was no biological connection between the two.

"Is that your mother?" Raul asked.

Silence.

"You want me to talk to her?" Raul pointed to the woman.

Tremont Washington shook his head. "Mama's gonna come home on furlough. We go to the fair then."

"Your mama's in the army?"

The boy didn't reply.

Raul checked his e-mail.

Tremont Washington's father had been working undercover for the Texas Department of Public Safety when he was killed by a suspect. His mother was deployed in Iraq. His legal guardian was his paternal grandmother, address in West Dallas, the projects.

"Where's your granny?" Raul said.

"I want some cotton candy." Tremont looked up. "Will you buy me some?"

"If you tell me where your granny is."

The boy frowned like he was trying to put a long string of words together.

"My grandma." He licked his lips. "She don't remember good."

Raul nodded as his BlackBerry dinged with a text from the number associated with Fair Park command center. The message was about a missing child named Tremont Washington. His grandmother was at the lost-child station, frantic.

Raul replied that he had the boy. He stood. "Let's get you some cotton candy. Then we'll find your grandma."

The boy smiled for the first time.

"You want to ride in a police car?" Raul patted his shoulder. "I'll let you work the siren."

The boy squealed with delight.

# - CHAPTER FORTY-TWO -

In the bathroom of the makeshift orphanage south of Singleton, Lysol Alvarez finds some gauze, tape, and a bottle of hydrogen peroxide. He cleans and bandages the wound on his leg.

The round fired by the man in the black tracksuit grazed the outside of his thigh, and the bleeding has mostly stopped, no major damage.

Jamal, the boy with the cornrows, stands in the doorway, watching.

"Don't that sting?"

"A little." Lysol picks up his SIG from the counter. "But it beats digging out a bullet with a pair of pliers."

"When you get shot," Jamal says. "Does it hurt right away?"

"You're full of questions, ain't you?" Lysol looks up. "You ever put a cap in anybody, little man?"

Jamal stares at the bandage and the blood on Lysol's pant leg. He doesn't say anything.

The rich bitch from North Dallas with the fake cigarette is in the living area, hands duct-taped behind her.

Lysol conducts a quick but thorough search of the bathroom, the cabinets, under the sink, behind the toilet. He finds nothing of value.

Jamal continues to watch him like he's a superhero come to life, eyes tracking his every move, fascinated.

Lysol says, "How old are you?"

"Eleven." Jamal crosses his arms.

Lysol arches an eyebrow.

Silence.

Then: "I mean ten."

"That so?"

"Yeah." Jamal sticks his chin out, trying for a little swagger. "In two months anyway."

Lysol chuckles and leaves the bathroom. In the hall, he ponders where a ten-year-old would hide his stash. Not a bedroom or the kitchen, too obvious. He could ask and force the answer, but he wants to make a point.

There's a narrow door by the entrance to the bathroom.

Lysol opens it. Jamal watches but doesn't react. The door reveals a closet containing several almost-empty boxes of diapers. And a small duffel bag in the corner.

"You live here, right?" Lysol pulls out the duffel. "In this house?"

Jamal nods.

Lysol opens the bag.

The herbal aroma of marijuana fills his nostrils. The bag is full of loose weed, maybe two or three kilos, a lot of product for a crew of ten-year-olds, but Lysol's seen stranger things in the dope biz, that's for damn sure.

"This your ganja?" He holds up the duffel.

Jamal nods again, a look of pride on his face.

Lysol drops the bag, shoves the youngster against the wall. "You don't ever, ever bring the product around where you stay." He looks into the child's eyes. "You feel me, boy?"

Jamal's lip quivers.

"Lesson one. You figure out who your stupidest guy is, the one you don't mind losing, and you hold the package at his crib."

Jamal nods, blinks away tears.

Lysol is immediately sorry he came down so hard on the youngster. The boy doesn't know his way around the game. That's what adults are supposed to do, teach the next generation.

"Don't worry, you'll learn." Lysol pats his cheek. "You're a smart kid."

The boy smiles for the first time, clearly eager for some form of adult approval other than what comes from the bitchy bleeding heart in the next room.

Lysol returns to the living area, carrying the duffel.

He's kicked Machete Boy out of the house and dead-bolted the doors, after taking his blade and telling him if he tried to get back in he'd cut his nuts off. Lysol figures he'll deal with the rest of the child gang in due time. Their leader, Jamal, seems to have lost a lot of toughness since Lysol pulled a gun on him.

The woman watches, face blank. The babies are all asleep.

Lysol drops the duffel in the middle of the floor and searches the rest of the house, Jamal trailing after him.

The first bedroom has two sets of bunk beds and children's clothing in the closet, age appropriate to Jamal and his crew. Several more handguns. Cheap Korean nine-millimeters.

Lysol sticks the pistols in the pockets of his suit coat, making the garment hang strangely on his body.

The second bedroom has an overnight bag full of a woman's things. Expensive clothing, toiletries from Nordstrom's, and an envelope full of cash, maybe three or four grand.

Lysol pockets the envelope and then searches the woman's purse, which is on the bed.

A Texas driver's license is in the wallet. Her name is Hannah June McKee, address an apartment or a condo near Northpark Mall.

Next he locates what he's looking for: a cell phone.

The cell is beside something he isn't expecting to see but is not all that surprised to find—a nickel-plated revolver, a .38 Smith & Wesson. The gun looks like something the five-oh on an old cop show might use.

Back in the living room, he kneels in front of the woman and holds up the revolver.

"Why you packing heat, Hannah McKee?"

"What are you going to do to me?"

"I'm the one asking the questions. That's how this situation works."

She doesn't say anything.

Lysol looks at Jamal. "You give her the piece?"

The boy shakes his head.

Lysol doesn't speak, letting the silence set the tone.

After a few moments, Hannah McKee says, "The children. They sell drugs because it's the only thing they know."

"And where do you come in?" Lysol says. "You and your *Adam-12* gun?

"The place where I work, we tried to establish a new project. An outreach to this part of the city."

"What do you call it?" Lysol looks around the room. "The West Dallas Baby Zoo?"

"It was supposed to be for prenatal care. Plus aid for new-borns and their mothers." Hannah pauses. "Girls who were too young to be in high school in some cases."

"So where're all the baby mamas?"

From the far side of the room, a child cries. Jamal goes to the crib, picks up the infant, rocks him on his shoulder.

"We, uh, misunderstood the receptiveness of the commu-nity," Hannah says.

Lysol stares at her, trying to figure if she's crazy or just stupid.

"They're precious, these babies." Her tone is edging toward belligerent now. "Each one a gift from God."

"White lady come down here and tell everyone how to raise their kids." Lysol chuckles. "What do you think this neighbor-hood is, a science project?"

"How many children have you fathered?" she asked. "And then never even seen?"

"How about none," Lysol says. "I take care of my babies."

He thinks about his oldest, a young woman now, though it's hard for her daddy to see her as anything but a toddler in his arms. She's going to college in a few months. She'll make some-thing of herself, something that doesn't involve spitting out welfare babies in West Dallas. Her father has worked damned hard to make sure of that.

Hannah McKee stares at him, eyes like slits, anger wafting off her in waves.

"These little ones here." Lysol points to the cribs. "What happened to their mamas?"

"Gone." She whispers the word like a curse.

"Mothers don't just leave their babies. Not this many."

She doesn't reply.

He pulls out the envelope of cash. "What's this about?"

Silence.

Lysol looks across the room at the boy with the cornrows, who's still holding the crying infant.

"Jamal, what's the cash for? This dope money?"

The boy turns to Hannah McKee, eyes pleading. But he doesn't speak.

"West Dallas," she says. "They say you can buy anything."

"You *bought* these kids?" Lysol's mouth hangs open.

She smiles proudly. "Half of them weren't even born in a hospital. I'm trying to save them."

"Shee-it, sister." Lysol stands. "Somebody done beat you with a crazy stick, didn't they?"

The room is silent. Lysol hears the whump-whump of a low-flying helicopter.

He walks to the window, peers outside.

A police car is driving slowly down the street. Several of the boys are sitting in the front yard, watching.

Lysol holds his breath. The car slows almost to a stop in front of the house and then continues on. He realizes the five-oh is going to flood the streets south of Singleton, the last direction he was seen. He's not going to make it to his place a few blocks away.

For better or worse, he's going to make his stand in a wood-framed shack full of unwanted babies and a crazy-ass white woman.

# - CHAPTER FORTY-THREE -

Here's a little factoid about my life.

This was not the first time I'd been caught by a jealous ex-boyfriend in a compromising position.

Fort Worth, 2001. The mayor's son had a thing for an ex–call girl who I'd met on Match.com. Note: I didn't know until later she'd been a working gal or that she was dating anybody else. Honestly.

Anyway, the son caught us in a hotel room in downtown Fort Worth and stuck a .357 in my face. Unfortunately for him, he was high on cocaine and didn't realize the gun was unloaded. I managed to take the weapon and leave him handcuffed to a maid's cart while the girl and I beat a hasty retreat.

The funny part of the story, what the movies would call an "ironic twist," was that the mayor's son and the ex–call girl eventually got married and moved to Dallas. They had a couple of kids and the woman ended up being a society bigwig, chair of the Bull Wranglers Ball, one of the bigger charitable fund-raisers in town.

I was pretty sure this current scenario wasn't going to play out as well.

For one thing, Raul Delgado wasn't high on coke.

Secondly, I was pretty sure his M-4 was loaded.

Thirdly, there were at least another five officers backing him up.

We were all in Hannah McKee's office in the Victorian house off of McKinney Avenue.

Nobody said anything. The other officers were waiting on Delgado's lead.

He aimed the muzzle of his rifle at my face. His eyes were wide, unblinking. Expression blank.

I smiled. Tried to look nonchalant. Said, "Well, this is awkward."

No response.

Piper said, "Lower your weapon, Raul. We're unarmed."

After a moment of hesitation, Delgado eased the rifle down. He looked at his men, said, "Everybody out. I got this."

The officers glanced at each other and shrugged, then exited the building.

After they left, there was an uneasy silence in the room. Then Delgado looked at me and said, "I should call the DA, file charges."

"I left the knife where you could get to it. You made it out all right," I said. "I wouldn't be complaining too much."

Delgado rammed the butt of his rifle into my stomach.

I fell to the floor, stars swimming in my vision, lungs searching for oxygen. I didn't remember much after that.

————

Sunlight on my face. The rocking of a vehicle. Steel biting into my wrists.

Piper's voice: "Where are we going?"

I opened my eyes.

I was in the backseat of Raul Delgado's Suburban on Woodall Rodgers Freeway, the short stretch of highway that formed the northern boundary of downtown Dallas.

Raul was driving, Piper next to him in the front.

To our left lay the gleaming skyscraper canyons of downtown and the Winspear Opera House, a futuristic building made from red metal panels and polished glass. To the right, a few blocks past the Dallas Federal Reserve building, was Raul's high-rise condo.

The Suburban kept driving, heading toward Stemmons Freeway and the county jail, the place where he'd picked me up only a few days before.

Piper looked in the back, a worried expression on her face. "You okay?"

I nodded.

Piper said, "Why'd you cuff him, Raul?"

"Ask your boyfriend." Delgado accelerated around a pickup.

"He's not my boyfriend. Neither are you." She shook her head. "And when did we time warp back to the seventh grade?"

"Raul and I had a little altercation at your house." I coughed, stomach aching like I had the flu. "After you decamped."

"Both of you? Stalking me?" she said. "Did anybody remember to bring a bunny to boil?"

Delgado took the north exit for Stemmons Freeway, the wrong direction for the jail.

"A lovely day for a drive," I said. "Perhaps you could give us a hint as to our destination."

"We need to talk," Delgado said. "The vigilante killer. I need to know what you've found out. Away from prying eyes and ears."

"Where's your cell phone?" I asked. "They can listen in that way, too."

He glanced at me in the rearview mirror.

Piper shook her head. "Did you two ever consider that I'm not some piece of property you can trade back and forth like a damn lawn mower?"

My beeper was sitting on the front console. It went off.

Raul Delgado rolled down the driver's window and threw it out.

"While you're tossing," I said. "Get rid of your cell, too."

"It's turned off."

"Doesn't matter."

"It's the property of the Dallas Police Department. No one is listening in."

"I'm not worried about the local heat," I said. "You need to—"

He pulled abruptly to the shoulder of the highway, just south of the Inwood Road exit. An abandoned bar and a tire store were just across the access road.

Traffic whizzed by, a torrent of cars headed north.

"Quit telling me what to do," he said. "I need the cell and I'm trying to help both of you out."

"Don't take this the wrong way." I leaned forward. "But we don't need your help. The way things are going, it's likely to be the other way around."

Silence. An eighteen-wheeler zoomed by, buffeting the SUV.

Delgado craned his neck, looking south. "You'd think there'd be a marker, wouldn't you?"

"What?" Piper glanced at me and then back to the front. "What are you talking about?"

"They built an arena there." He turned back around. "Where the silos used to be."

Neither Piper nor I spoke.

"That's where they took us. The old power plant. By the grain silos."

"Where your brother died," I said.

"Where they killed him."

I didn't reply.

Raul Delgado looked in the back like he was seeing me for the first time. He fished a key out of his pocket and handed it to Piper. "You can uncuff him."

Piper did so as he pulled a cell phone from his pocket.

"Why were you two in that office?"

"Tremont worked for Hannah McKee." I rubbed my wrists. "A fact you neglected to mention."

"She doesn't know anything about what happened to the boy."

"How can you be so sure?" Piper asked.

No response.

"Who is she to you?" I said.

Raul opened his door.

Wind gusted through the inside of the vehicle. Piper and I were silent.

He stepped outside, walked to the front of the SUV, then tapped some keys on his cell phone.

"He's having a breakdown of some sort," I said. "His eyes, did you see them?"

"He's been through a lot in his life."

"And we haven't?"

"This isn't about us, Jon."

"Then why are we here with him right now?"

She didn't reply.

Raul Delgado returned to the vehicle a few moments later.

"We should get off this highway." He slid the transmission into drive. "There's somebody you need to meet."

He drove down the shoulder until he reached the exit for Inwood. Then he took the off-ramp and headed south toward the river.

———

*Ellis County, Texas*
*2011*

Raul Delgado padded across the wood floor and peered outside. His unmarked squad car sat in the gravel driveway, gleaming in the summer sun.

He was at Bobby's ranch.

The rains had been good that year, so the pastures were green, dotted with cows that were fat and healthy-looking. The cattle kept their heads low, chewing on grass, tails swishing at flies.

Bobby, nearly seventy and with a heart condition, lived in Dallas in order to be close to his doctors and the bar he'd opened years before, Sam Browne's. The cattle operation was run by a neighbor, the house still furnished but unoccupied.

Raul was wearing a pair of boxer shorts, nothing else.

His suit and gun belt were on a chair. The chair sat underneath a Nirvana poster, the edges curling with age.

Junie lay on the bed. A tangled sheet covered her from the waist down, bare breasts exposed to the sunlight filtering into her childhood room.

On the bedside table was a nearly empty bottle of chardonnay and two glasses. Junie'd had most of it, Raul just a taste.

"Come back to bed," Junie said.

Raul stared at the endless horizon. No clouds in a pewter sky.

"You want some more wine?" Junie poured herself another slug.

"I have to go."

"Aw, really?" Her tone was pouty. "Don't you want to stay for a while longer?"

Raul didn't reply. But he made no move to put on his clothes either. Instead he turned and looked at her.

Junie was thirty-nine.

In the years since they'd met, she'd made a life that Raul would have never imagined.

Her fourth divorce was final a few months ago. Despite repeated attempts, she could never get pregnant again, not after the miscarriage during her second marriage.

She flitted around the peripheries of the North Dallas social swirl, an environment that she could ill afford. Charity fund-raisers and fashion galas, usually as the guest of her aunt, who was increasingly reluctant to pay. Girls' trips to places like Cabo and New Orleans, weekend getaways that she financed with MasterCard.

An artificial existence that left Raul bewildered. He donated his time and money to a variety of progressive causes—environmental charities, the ACLU, immigration reform. When he mentioned these organizations to Junie, she looked at him like he was speaking Korean.

They inhabited the same city but were worlds apart.

Despite her obsession with cosmetic surgery and the latest Botox treatments, neither of which she'd availed herself of as of yet, she was still beautiful, at least in Raul's view.

Her face was unlined, stomach taut, breasts firm. The eyes, however, showed her age. Not so much sad as they were weary. Except when she'd been drinking. Then they were animated like the old days, alive with the possibility that something marvelous lay ahead.

He turned away. Stared outside again.

A few moments passed.

From the other side of the room came the rustle of sheets, the creak of bedsprings. Then bare feet padding on the floor.

An instant later her breasts pressed against his back, arms around his stomach. Lips to his ears. Whispering.

*"Don't you want to fuck me again, Raul?"*

He could smell her—perfume, sweat, and wine.

*"I want to do it hard this time."* She ran a finger underneath the waistband of his boxers. *"Fuck me hard, Raul. Real hard."*

He closed his eyes as his body responded. "Please. Don't talk like that."

She chuckled, nipped his ear. *"Tough-guy cop doesn't like dirty words."*

They'd been meeting like this for two months. They weren't dating. They didn't have dinner together, no nights out at the movies.

Just the sex.

Fuck buddies, that's what Junie called them.

Raul had run into her at Parkland Hospital, the location of her Junior League volunteer placement. He'd been there with Tremont Washington, the boy he'd met at the state fair a few months before. Tremont had a twisted ankle.

The next night she'd showed up at his condo. Three minutes later, they'd been in the bedroom, tossing clothes every which way.

Lately, they'd taken to meeting at the ranch, away from prying eyes. Neither could say why they wanted to keep their relationship secret. Just that they did.

Perhaps it had something to do with Tremont Washington. Could it be that they didn't want him to know about their status as . . . fuck buddies? Or was it because they didn't want Bobby to know?

Raul had no idea; they never talked about it. He just knew that both of them had made a conscious but unspoken decision to keep their activities secret.

He looked at his watch. He would have to hurry if he wanted to get back to the office before he picked up Tremont for dinner.

He'd been spending a lot of time with the boy, taking him to school, buying him stuff, trying to make the child's passage in life a little easier.

Junie had been around for much of that, their only activity together that didn't involve getting naked.

She treated Tremont like an exotic piece of art. Fragile, likely to break. Interesting only in the abstract sense, like a vase in a museum. She was distant with the boy and Raul couldn't tell if it was because she was afraid of feeling something for him or if the maternal instinct had been forced out of her by the death of her own mother when she was a child.

A hawk flew across the horizon, alighting on one of the cottonwoods by the creek.

Junie licked his neck. Her fingers were still inside the waistband of his boxers. They caressed the sliver of flesh where leg joins torso.

His pulse quickened, body continued to react.

The kissing and the groping stopped.

He turned.

She stood at the foot of the bed, naked, his handcuffs dangling from her fingers.

"Put these on me, Raul. Then let's do it."

He shook his head.

"Really?" She snapped one side to her wrist. "You liked it before."

He didn't reply. He had liked it before, with the handcuffs and the dirty talk and the leather belt slapped against her ass just like she wanted.

Sex with Junie was raw and dangerous and unlike anything he'd ever experienced in his life. When they were together, he was exhilarated and more than a little fearful. When he was apart from her, he was consumed by the thought of their next time together.

She jingled the cuffs.

Raul was powerless. Her nakedness, this house, the way she gave herself over to him. He could not resist her.

So he went to her and did what she wanted. He handcuffed her, looping the metal around a bedpost so her arms were restrained above her head.

Then he mounted her, thrusting hard and fast like she wanted him to.

When they climaxed together, her chest flushed red and tears welled in her eyes, streaming down her face after a moment.

She always cried afterward, just a little.

At first Raul wondered why.

Now he just held on and tried to keep his mind from going to the dark places where images of his brother dwelled along with Wayne's crushed face.

He removed the cuffs, and they dozed for a while. When they awoke, the shadows were long. So much for going back to the office.

Junie drank the last of the wine. "I've got a new job."

"Yeah?" Raul moved across the room to his clothes.

Junie's work history, much like her love life, had been somewhat checkered. Lots of jobs for a year or so at a time. The titles of her positions had always been nebulous—office manager, sales consultant, director of web marketing.

"A nonprofit," she said. "They try to find work for people who are mentally challenged."

Raul pulled on his pants.

"They need someone to run the organization. Somebody with the right connections in town."

Raul pondered the idea. Working for a nonprofit might actually be a good fit for Junie. Because of her aunt, she knew a lot of well-to-do people, potential donors.

"That sounds like a great idea, Junie." Raul buttoned his shirt. "You've always liked to help—"

"I told you." Junie stared at him, eyes cold. She was half-dressed, skirt and bra. Blouse in one hand.

He realized his mistake. "Sorry."

"That's not my name. Not for years and years." Her tone was frosty. "That's my middle name. My kid name."

"I forgot."

"Talk to me like an adult. Call me by my real name, Raul." She slid her blouse on. "Call me Hannah."

# - CHAPTER FORTY-FOUR -

Lysol presses the End button on Hannah McKee's cell phone.

His people are still not answering. None of them.

He's on his own, without a lot of options.

The next step is to call his attorney and activate the escape plan.

That's the equivalent of going nuclear, however, and he's not real keen on treading down that particular road. The escape plan means never coming back to Dallas, probably never seeing his children again. Never watching his oldest even start college.

Hannah is sitting on the floor of the makeshift orphanage, hands duct-taped behind her. Jamal is running from crib to crib, trying to shush the ever-growing number of crying babies.

The noise is giving Lysol a headache. He looks at Jamal, says, "Can't you shut them fuck-trophies up?"

The boy doesn't reply. He glances at a clock on the wall and goes to the next crib with a bawling baby, rocking several others as he walks by.

"They're hungry," Hannah says. "He can't feed them all by himself."

"Maybe if their mamas were here, they could feed them." Lysol drops her cell phone on the dining room table. "Just a thought."

One infant shrieks. The sound, a piercing wail, seems to start at the base of Lysol's spine and shoot its way up to his brain.

"You have all the answers, don't you?" She smirks. "The gangster with the plan. The great Lysol Alvarez, king of West Dallas."

Her words bore a hole in his skull. They jangle around with the crying babies.

In all his forty-two years, Lysol has never craved anything so much as he does a single hit of ganja right now, just a taste to mellow everything out, to make the screaming infants and the bitchy white woman a little more tolerable.

Instead of sparking up some of Jamal's stash, however, he allows the anger and frustration to wash over him. He strides across the room, grabs the lapels of Hannah McKee's blazer and shirt, and yanks her to her feet.

"I got more options than you do, white girl." He gets in her face. "I can walk away anytime I damn well feel like, and leave your skinny ass here while I call CPS."

Her smirk deepens.

Anger turns Lysol's vision red on the edges.

He grabs her throat, squeezes.

She continues the infuriating smile. Then she cuts a look toward the table.

"There's the phone." Her voice is a croak. "Go on. Give CPS a ring."

He lets go. She's called his bluff.

Several more infants start to cry, increasing the overall noise level.

Lysol strides to the window, peers through the shades.

A police car has stopped across the street, headed in the opposite direction from the one a few minutes before.

A cop gets out. A white guy in his twenties. He leans against the hood of his vehicle and pulls out a cell phone. Not doing anything too threatening right now, but not going away either.

Several of Jamal's boys are milling around the front yard, playing and roughhousing with each other. Lysol's not worried that they'll say anything to the officer about his presence. No street kid would tell a cop, especially a white one, anything. It's ingrained in their DNA. Do not talk to the Man. Ever.

But what does worry him is if the cop starts doing a door-to-door, looking for a wounded guy in a gray linen suit who was shooting at a dude on Singleton.

If a cop comes to this house, knocks, and hears eleventy-seven babies crying when a ten-year-old answers, there's a high probability he's coming inside.

Therefore, Lysol has to shut the babies up.

Which means they need to be fed.

Hannah McKee is still standing where he left her, still sneering at him.

"Where's their food?" he asks.

"Their formula?" she says. "That's what infants consume. Not food."

Her tone is condescending.

"Yeah. Their *formula*. Where is it?"

"It's in the kitchen," Jamal says. "Needs to be heated up first."

"Can you do that?" Lysol asks.

The boy nods.

"You're my number-one man, Jamal." Lysol smiles. "Get to it."

The boy beams and scampers away.

Lysol turns to Hannah McKee. Pulls a knife from his pocket, a lock-back Spyderco. He flicks open the blade and approaches her.

Her smirk slowly disappears. She inches backward until she hits the wall.

He keeps walking. When he's about a foot away, he says, "Turn around."

She hesitates and then complies.

Lysol slices the duct tape away, frees her hands.

"Okay. You can turn back now."

She does as requested, rubbing adhesive off her wrists.

"Now take your clothes off."

She stops rubbing, eyes wide.

"You heard me. Strip."

"W-what?" Her voice is timid.

"You need to help Jamal feed these babies," he says. "And I don't want to worry about you running away or finding a weapon and hiding it somewhere."

She doesn't say anything.

"Naked white woman, cruising down the streets of West Dallas." He shakes his head. "I don't see that happening."

She gulps, face pale.

"It's real simple," he says. "You take your clothes off, you won't be a threat."

She crosses her arms like she's cold and then immediately uncrosses them.

He slides the knife under the top button of her blouse. Slices the threads.

The button drops to the floor. The fabric shifts open, exposing the tops of her breasts encased in a black bra.

"You can keep your panties on," Lysol says. "I'm not an animal."

Hannah McKee stares at him for a long moment. Then she slowly takes off her blazer and unbuttons her blouse, dropping both to the floor.

Lysol smiles.

Homegirl is in good shape, from the waist up at least, everything firm and tight.

She stares at him for another stretch of time and then removes her bra, dropping it on the floor with her other garments.

Her breasts are pale and firm, nipples the color of almonds.

The funny thing is, by the way she moves and her facial expressions, Lysol is pretty sure she's enjoying herself.

———

*Dallas, Texas*
*2013*

Raul Delgado didn't remember much about his father.

The breath of a drunk man and a violent temper. A calloused palm slapped against a boy's cheek.

Carlos, ever the rebel, had taken the brunt of their papa's rage. Beatings for talking back. For not cleaning their room. For not bringing a fresh beer from the kitchen fast enough.

In Raul's mind the memories of both father and brother were shadows, fading more and more as time passed. Events that seemed so important thirty-five years ago were just whispers now, snippets of time tucked in a closet, remembrances that might or might not be real.

Papa had been deported back to Tampico in 1983; he died soon after.

Raul wondered if his father and brother were together in the great beyond, if they acknowledged each other. If he still went to Mass, perhaps the priest could have told him.

Raul had always vowed that if he had children he would not treat them badly, the way he'd been treated. He'd be like Bobby. Kind but firm.

All of which made him very curious as to why he felt a burning desire to punch Tremont Washington in the mouth.

He was a nice kid, but whiny. Deficient, as the doctors say.

He fretted over the simplest things, opening and shutting a door a hundred times in a row, rearranging a stack of magazines in dozens of different combinations. Setting the table with a ruler so that all the utensils were equal distance from each other.

At the moment, they were alone in Junie's office, the large room at the back of the Victorian house in the Uptown section of Dallas.

Raul sat behind Junie's desk, going through the bills for the organization that employed her. More than a couple were past due.

Tremont was playing with a Nintendo, humming and talking to himself. The noise grated on Raul's nerves.

A Wednesday morning. Junie was in the front of the building, arranging for a job placement with a client.

Raul sighed and pulled some cash from his wallet, enough to cover the electric bill.

Tremont's game made a ringing sound, and he cackled with pleasure.

Raul, who'd never had children or a wife, didn't know how most people stood the banality of a family. And the noise.

His politico friends urged him to get a wife and/or a baby, preferably both, and soon.

Find a woman, any woman, and marry her. And if you played for the other team—you know, if you're gay—that's all right. Then find a man to be your partner. That narrative would work just as well as the traditional picket-fence scenario.

What didn't work, they said, was the loner bachelor who was a workaholic and, quite frankly, a little odd.

Voters didn't like odd, the politicos told him. They liked people they could have a beer with. And that's not you, Deputy Chief Delgado.

Raul wondered if he should ask Junie to marry him.

They no longer had sex together. He'd caught her in bed a few months ago with a man fifteen years her junior.

Strangely enough, the person most upset by the discovery was the young man. He was convinced that Raul was going to kill him.

Raul had shrugged and told him to leave. Then he and Junie sat in her darkened living room and stared at the wall. Not talking. Not fighting. Just sitting, both lost in their own thoughts.

He snapped back to her office, to Tremont on the couch. From the front came the sound of the door shutting. A few moments later Junie entered the room.

"What are you doing at my desk?"

"Keeping the lights on." He tossed the cash so that the currency fanned out across the top of her work space.

"You didn't need to do that." She took a puff from her e-cig.

The Nintendo made a losing sound and Tremont whined. Both Raul and Junie ignored him.

"Do what?"

"Throw your money around. You think I'm impressed by that?"

Raul didn't reply.

"I have everything under control." She hurriedly picked up the currency. Made no move to give it back.

Raul pondered the other women in his life. He was attractive and had a sizable net worth, thanks to the investments from his settlement with the city decades before.

So there was no shortage of female companionship. But most were, for lack of a better term, *whole people,* and Raul realized that he was not. Parts were missing from him. Feelings and emotions that didn't function in the same manner as in other people.

So perhaps he was not the marrying kind. Unless his spouse was someone like himself.

Like, say, Junie.

What would a marriage with her be like? He couldn't imagine.

She'd become withdrawn and morose, bitter about her life and the choices she'd made. She continued to surround herself with people of means, nominally as part of her work at the Helping Place. The proximity to wealth was like salt to a wound, however, leaving her full of envy and regret.

Then, there was Tremont.

The boy worked at the Helping Place, in the office. When he was not playing games, he sorted files, emptied the garbage cans, picked up trash from the lawn.

Junie (he could never get used to calling her Hannah) had warmed up to Tremont, taking an interest in him and his activities. She brought him along when she met with African American families who had disabled children. The boy was her passport into a world that would normally be shut off to a white woman from North Dallas.

"Tremont and I have some appointments in Oak Cliff this afternoon." She mentioned an address deep in gangbanger territory. "Will you give us a ride?"

"Where's all the money, Junie?" He pointed to the bills. "Why's everything past due?"

"Don't call me that." She held up her nameplate.

"Where's all the money, *Hannah*?"

"We're establishing a new program. Pre- and neonatal health care for low-income women."

"Your organization doesn't have the resources for any new programs."

"What do you know about this place?" She pointed at him with the e-cig. "What do you know about the needs of children in economically depressed areas?"

Her words sounded like they came from a brochure.

"How much do you need to keep the ship afloat?" He crossed his arms.

"I'm not dependent on your largesse."

"There's a fancy word. *Largesse*." Raul chuckled. "You fucking a college professor now?"

"Nice language." She nodded toward Tremont. "A great way to talk in front of a child."

"He's heard worse. Let's get back to the financial health of your organization."

They stared at each other. Raul imagined he was angry, but deep down he knew that was not the case. He was just tired. He wanted things to be normal. But therein lay the rub. What the hell was normal?

"The finances of the Helping Place are none of your concern," Junie said.

"Really?" He stood. "Whose money do you use to balance the books every month?"

She didn't reply.

"Does the board know how bad it is?"

The Helping Place was managed by a group of directors, all volunteers. Civic leaders and socially prominent individuals. People who would be aghast at the fiduciary mismanagement.

"I looked at the financials." Raul pointed to a file. "It's obvious there's money being used inappropriately. Last week, what was the cash withdrawal for?"

Tremont put the game down and stared at them, eyes wide. He always seemed to have a sense of when they were brewing up to have a big fight.

"I needed a new dress." Junie's voice was soft. "For the Crystal Charity Ball."

"Of course." Raul tried not to sound too sarcastic. "Everyone needs a new dress for the Crystal Charity Ball."

She shook her head, an angry expression on her face. From the desk she grabbed a nicotine cartridge and fiddled with her e-cig.

"Who'd you take to the ball?" Raul said.

"What's it to you?"

"It's just a question."

"Sounds more like an interrogation. Always does with you." Her voice rose. "Because you're a cop and that's the way you roll."

"So you don't like cops now. You tell your dad that yet?"

"Shut up, Raul." She rubbed her eyes. "Just shut up."

From the couch, Tremont began to breathe hard, one hand scratching a leg continually, his usual reaction when they fought.

"The charity ball. Let me guess," Raul said. "You took the twentysomething douchebag."

"And you're living in a monastery these days?" She looked up, voice angry.

"What's that supposed to mean?"

"I hear the stories," she said. "If it's got a pulse and votes Democrat, you've mounted it."

Tremont jumped up. He rushed over to Junie, pulled on her arm. "Stop it. P-please. Stop f-f-fighting."

She pushed him away.

"How much do you need?" Raul asked. "What's it gonna cost this month?"

"How much do you have?" Her face was flushed with anger.

He wanted to tell her that he wouldn't bail her out anymore, but they both knew this would be a lie. He was always there when Junie needed something. Always had been, always would be.

He realized that at one point he had been in love with her, but he wasn't anymore. He felt bound to Junie, however, a twin to her suffering for reasons he couldn't, or wouldn't, articulate. A dark secret that was buried in the black loamy soil of Bobby's ranch nearly thirty years ago. A secret that ate at him every day.

"I'll pay you back." She undid the top button of her blouse. "Maybe we can figure out a trade."

Her words were icy, movements and demeanor anything but enticing.

Tremont opened the back door and went outside. He usually wandered off when they fought. Today was no different.

No one spoke for a moment. Then:

"Why are you so angry?" Raul's voice was soft. He wished he could just hold her.

She didn't respond. Her breathing was labored. Eyes welling with emotion.

"You're so pretty," he said. "You have so much going for you. I just don't understand."

"*Why?*" She clenched her fists. Tears streamed down her face. "You are asking me *why*?"

He took a step toward her, held his arms out. After a moment she accepted the embrace.

They stood together like that for a while, the fight and the anger draining out of both of them.

"Doesn't it ever get to you?" Her voice was small against his chest. "What we've done. Who we are."

"Shh." He knew that she was referring to Wayne. "We don't talk about that."

She pushed herself away. "Why?"

"Because we don't."

She shook her head, expression flat and empty.

"You came to my rescue, Raul. My knight in shining armor."

He didn't respond. They stared into each other's eyes for a period of time, long enough for more tears to trickle down her face.

She said, "But did you ever consider that maybe I wasn't being raped?"

# - CHAPTER FORTY-FIVE -

The Trinity River ran along the west side of downtown Dallas, splitting the city in two. The muddy ribbon shadowed Stemmons Freeway for a few miles, the highway where moments before I found myself traveling in the back of Raul Delgado's police Suburban.

Levees kept the flood waters at bay, forming a large channel with the river itself in the middle.

In many parts of Dallas County, the land between the levees was much like it had been for millennia—overgrown with post oaks and saw grass and honeysuckle. Swampy, guarded by a furry militia of beaver, nutria, and raccoons.

In the middle of a major metropolitan area, the geographical center of nearly six million people, the Trinity River and accompanying lowlands were wilderness, remote yet easily accessible to the rest of the city if you knew the right roads to take.

Which clearly Deputy Chief Raul Delgado did.

I was still in the back, Piper in the front passenger seat.

Delgado headed south on Inwood past a warehouse district that was slowly being gentrified as development pushed outward from downtown.

The street ran across a four-lane bridge that spanned the river, headed toward West Dallas.

Delgado stopped before getting to the bridge, pulling onto a dirt road that ran behind a warehouse, an alley of sorts, nearly invisible unless you were looking for it.

The rear of the warehouse abutted the levee, and a gate blocked the dirt road.

Delgado exited the SUV, unlocked the gate, and then drove us through. Once past, he got back out and secured the gate.

Then he followed the road through a small grove of trees, and a few minutes later we emerged on the top of the levee, elevated above the city by about sixty feet.

The river lay to our right, downtown to the left.

No trees grew here. The mounded earth formed a small man-made mountain in a city known for its flatness, offering a particular view that few had ever seen.

Delgado drove south on the elevated dirt track that ran atop the levee. He passed the jail and the courthouse, several blocks away and lower. A few hundred yards later he stopped.

Below us, at the foot of the levee, sat the cop bar, Sam Browne's, between a strip club and a bail bondsman's office.

A chain-link fence ran along the base of the levee to keep people out.

Beyond the cop bar and Riverfront Boulevard, the buildings of downtown were visible. From our position the dominant structure was American Airlines Center, the original location of Little Mexico and the deserted field where the police killed Raul Delgado's brother years before.

Delgado stared at the view for a long while, the car idling.

"Sam Browne's," I said. "You know the guy that owns that place, don't you?"

"Yeah." He spoke without turning around, voice flat. "I know him."

An ex-cop, the bartender I'd smarted off to a few days before, when I met Piper there. His name wasn't really Sam, though everyone called him that. There was a thread between the owner and Delgado that eluded me for the moment.

"Bobby, that's his real name, right?" Piper said. "He's the guy that took care of you after your brother died."

No one spoke.

"I remember the stories now," Piper said. "I just never made that connection between that guy and Sam Browne's before."

Delgado ignored her. He turned down a narrow track that led off the levee, toward the river. The SUV bumped and swayed over the uneven surface.

"Bobby McKee," she said. "That's his real name. Retired as a captain, oh, maybe fifteen years ago."

*McKee,* I thought. The name mentioned by Mason Burnett in the back of the chopper.

The road, if it could be called that, was canopied by hackberry trees, meshed together with a thicket of poison ivy and stinging nettles. Branches and thorns scratched at the side of the SUV.

After a hundred yards or so, he cut back on a slightly wider path that paralleled the river. Vegetation on the side opposite the water was as thick as a wall, impenetrable.

The Suburban bounced along for a minute or two as the brush gradually became less dense. At a clearing by the river about the size of a tennis court, he slowed down to a crawl.

"McKee?" I remembered where else I'd heard the name before. "Is he any relation to the woman who runs the Helping Place?"

"Hannah J. McKee," Delgado said. "The *J* stands for June."

He parked by an ash-filled fire pit and exited the SUV. He walked to the river and stared into the flowing water. The surface was brown and choppy. After a moment, he pulled a cell phone from his pocket and appeared to make a call.

Piper and I got out as well. The air smelled like dead fish, cut grass, and old ashes.

Raul ended his call and walked back to where we stood by the Suburban.

"Hannah's missing," he said. "Not at her home or office. Her cell phone's turned off."

We stood in a loose circle near the back of the SUV.

"She's important to me," he said. "I need to find her."

Piper cocked her head. "She's more important than Tremont?"

Raul didn't answer.

"What's her connection to all this?" Piper said. "And to you?"

"She's like a sister to me," he said. "I wouldn't expect you to understand."

*Chug-chug-chug.*

From down the road we'd just traveled came the sound of a sputtering exhaust, a vehicle years past its prime.

A moment later, an elderly Ford pickup appeared out of the vegetation.

"Speak of the Devil," I said.

The bartender from Sam Browne's sat behind the wheel. Bobby McKee, known to most as Sam.

The truck stopped behind Delgado's SUV, and the older man got out.

He wore khaki work pants, Roper boots, and a faded denim shirt.

At first he appeared surprised by what he saw. Then wary.

"What's going on here, Raul?" He pointed to Piper. "What are you doing with her?"

"Hey, Bobby. Thanks for coming." Delgado smiled. "This is Piper. She's a friend."

The old man squinted at me. "And why the hell are you here?"

"Have you heard from Hannah?" Raul asked.

Bobby McKee shook his head. "Why you asking?"

No response.

The old man said, "Is something wrong?"

"What's your daughter doing in West Dallas?" I asked.

McKee looked at me and then Piper, a puzzled expression on his face.

"Apparently, she's MIA," I said. "Not answering her phone."

"She shouldn't be in that part of town," Bobby said. "Not if she's by herself."

No one spoke for a few moments. Then:

"The little creek that runs through your ranch," Delgado said. "I wonder if it feeds into the Trinity. What do you think?"

The old man frowned but didn't say anything.

Raul pointed to the water. "Everything's connected, Bobby. Somehow, some way. You can't get away from what you are."

The old man looked like he was going to say something but didn't.

A helicopter flew overhead.

I watched it bank far to the south and come back for another pass. "Raul, give me your phone."

Delgado ignored me. "Do you believe in divine retribution, Bobby?"

"What the hell are you talking about? Where's my daughter?"

Delgado continued. "What if something's happened to her because of what you and I did?"

The helicopter swung around, and I wondered who had been paging me. If it had been Theo Goldberg and he thought I was in a jam, we might have a problem.

"Either one of you," I said. "I really need a phone. If my boss gets it in his head that I'm in trouble, it's not going to be pretty."

The old man glanced at me and then turned his attention back to Raul. "Listen, son. I'm not sure what you're getting at, but let's don't talk about it now."

A second helicopter appeared in the north. It hovered, maybe a thousand yards away.

Theo Goldberg had the attorney general, the director of the FBI, and the secretary of defense on speed dial. He would drain an ocean to get one of his people out of harm's way if they were there due to law firm business.

This was not out of loyalty. He was deathly afraid of the liability. He once arranged for a drone strike in Somalia because a junior associate had strayed across the Ethiopian border and gotten himself kidnapped. The associate had been released unharmed an hour later.

"My people will track Delgado's cell phone from our last known location," I said. "Then they'll rewind satellite coverage like it's a DVR."

Bobby said, "What's he talking about, Raul?"

I continued. "They'll send a team to get us. To get me. Probably from Homeland Security. Maybe the FBI."

As if on cue, the sound of footsteps crunching through undergrowth.

"Are you packing?" I looked at Bobby.

He nodded after a moment of hesitation.

"Put it on the ground," I said. "That will make everybody less nervous."

More movement from the underbrush.

"It's okay," Delgado said. "He's right."

Bobby hesitated for a moment and then pulled a gun from his waistband, a Glock.

"Old-school guy like you," I said to Bobby, "carrying a plastic gun?"

Law-enforcement officers of a certain age didn't trust Glocks or their knockoff cousins.

"I gave my old backup revolver to Jun—to Hannah," the old man said. "Besides, change is good for a body."

"That's the kind of gun being used by the vigilante killer," I said.

The old man didn't respond. He stared at me, a blank expression on his face.

"You, too, Raul," I said. "I'd put your gun down before whoever's out there gets too close."

Raul pulled his piece, another Glock, but didn't drop it.

"Whatever happened to Wayne's family?" Delgado stared at the old man. "Do you think they know how it all played out?"

Bobby's eyes grew wide, his face pale. He flexed his left hand.

"The guns," I said. "Seriously. I'd put them down."

Piper said, "Who's Wayne? What are you talking about?"

Bobby's breathing was ragged, face ashen. "Let's not get into that, Raul."

"You okay?" I took a step toward the old man. "You're not looking too good."

He dropped his gun and clutched his chest with both hands, looked at Raul. "Where's my daughter?" he said. "What have you done to her?"

Raul didn't appear to notice the older man's distress. "Can you imagine what it's like, never to find out what happened to your child?"

Piper spoke to me. "I think he's having a coronary."

"Bobby." I touched his arm. "Sit down and we'll call an ambulance."

The old cop didn't move. He looked at his gun on the ground, his face white, mouth open, gulping for air.

"Wayne's parents," Raul said. "They had a right to know."

The old man held up one hand like he was trying to deflect Delgado's words.

Raul shook his head. "I didn't mean to hurt him. I just wanted him to get off of Junie."

The old man fell to his knees as the first FBI agent burst through the underbrush, a submachine gun aimed our way.

"Drop your weapon." The agent aimed at Delgado.

Raul hesitated. Then he pitched his weapon in front of him. The gun fell on top of Bobby's firearm.

More agents followed the first.

Piper and I raised our hands.

"B-Bobby?" Raul Delgado seemed to snap back to reality, realizing something was wrong with the old man.

I spoke to the lead agent. "He's having a heart attack. We need a medical team."

"*Bobby!*" Delgado knelt beside the old man.

High above us, the sound of a helicopter. On the marshy dirt by the river, Deputy Chief Raul Delgado began to weep.

# - CHAPTER FORTY-SIX -

They medevaced Bobby out, taking him to Parkland Hospital.

The FBI agents choppered us out, too, a very short trip, setting down in the parking lot of Sam Browne's, Bobby's bar, which was at the base of the levee.

Before the rotors of the helicopter stopped spinning, several Dallas police squad cars squealed into the bar's parking lot, followed by the same number of black SUVs full of feds.

Everyone congregated on the hot asphalt until someone pointed out there was a nice cool bar a few steps away.

Piper and I stood a little ways apart from the group, and, without talking about it, began to ease away, heading toward the street, putting distance between ourselves and the strange, uneasy mix of cops and feds. I wanted to regroup, call Theo Goldberg, and continue the search for Tremont Washington.

No such luck.

An agent flanked us and held up one hand. Then he pointed toward the bar. "They want to debrief you."

"What if we don't want to be debriefed?" I asked.

"It's hot out here and I'm sweating my nuts off," he said. "Let's don't make this hard, okay? Just go inside."

Piper and I looked at each other and then followed a dozen or so FBI agents and about the same number of DPD officers into Sam Browne's. Raul Delgado, who'd pulled himself together, was at the head of the group.

I sat in the same booth we'd been in a few days before and decided to order an iced tea and a cheeseburger while I waited for whatever was coming next. Piper moved to the rear to confer with the lead FBI agent and several senior staff from DPD headquarters.

Halfway through the burger, I noticed Lieutenant Hopper, the chief's assistant, milling about by the dartboard. He glanced at me several times but didn't approach.

A few minutes later, the waitress took my empty plate and refilled my glass of tea.

I was worried about a repeat of the near-riot earlier that day at the building in North Dallas, but this time apparently everybody decided to play nice.

Another ten minutes went by before Piper came over and told me why.

"The two Glocks at the scene." She slid into the booth. "Feds have this new ballistics system. Fits in the back of a panel van."

"Yeah?"

"They ran a preliminary test on both guns. Got a ninety percent match that one of them was the weapon used in the vigilante killings."

"Which one?" I asked. "Bobby McKee and Delgado both were carrying the same kind of gun."

A moment passed.

Piper said, "They don't know."

I tried not to raise my voice. "What the hell do you mean they don't know?"

"They were found next to each other. Neoprene grips. No usable prints."

I tried to remember the details of what had gone down only an hour or so before.

Bobby had finally dropped his weapon when his heart attack began, and Delgado had tossed his when the FBI agents arrived. It had fallen on top of Bobby's. Everything had occurred in a relatively small area behind the SUV.

"So what does Delgado say?" I asked. "Which one was he carrying?"

Piper glanced from side to side, then leaned close. "Nobody knows where he is."

*"What?"* I looked around. "He was just here."

"He's a deputy chief. Apparently, he just walked off and nobody stopped him."

I took a moment to process that information. "What about serial numbers?"

"They're working on that now," she said.

It didn't really matter at this point. One of the men—a retired captain or an active-duty deputy chief—would be held responsible for the killings. The feds possessed the evidence, so of course the DPD was playing nice. They had laundry they needed to clean.

Before I could say anything else, the front door to the bar opened and a whirlwind of activity entered, causing a momentary lull in the crowd noise.

At the head of the whirlwind was a man about five foot five. He moved awkwardly in pointy-toed snakeskin boots that appeared to be out-of-the-box new. He was in his late forties, wearing an oversized cowboy hat with a huge feather band and a shirt that looked like something Porter Wagoner might have owned, but not as tasteful.

Behind him were several people in blue Windbreakers—federal agents—and two men I recognized as being attorneys from the Dallas office of Goldberg, Finkelman, and Clark.

The man in the cowboy hat looked around the room and then made a beeline to my booth.

"Who's the rhinestone cowboy?" Piper asked.

The man bounded over and held out his arms to me.

"Jonathan Cantrell. We finally meet." He leaned over and gave me a big hug. "It's me. Theo Goldberg."

"Welcome to Dallas, Theo." I shook his hand. "The wardrobe department from *Urban Cowboy* called. They want their clothes back."

"You like, huh?" He ran a finger around the brim of his hat. "I went to a mall in McLean, told them I needed some duds for a trip to Dallas. Told them I needed to, you know, fit in."

"You look great." I smiled. "Like a native."

"I have a meeting with the mayor tomorrow." He beamed. "I want to make a good impression."

His entourage fanned out, the attorneys huddling with a group of feds. One of the FBI agents appeared to be a high muckety-muck from DC, so there was much genuflecting from everyone with a federal badge.

I settled back in the booth. "What brings you to the provinces, Theo?"

"And this must be Sergeant Westlake." He touched Piper's elbow. "I've heard so much about you."

"Charmed, I'm sure." Piper held out her hand.

"Pictures don't do you justice, my dear." Theo kissed her fingers and slid into the booth next to me. "You are a rose of exceptional beauty, blossoming on the plains of the Lone Star state."

In spite of herself, Piper blushed a little.

"We needed to do a little cleanup in regards to the mess with the shipment," Theo said. "Flew down this morning on the assistant director's Gulfstream."

Little-known fact. The largest consumer of private jets— Gulfstreams, Lears, Citations, et cetera—was the US government.

"So, Jonathan." Theo turned toward me, nearly hitting me in the eye with his oversized Stetson. "You've had a busy day."

"An understatement of epic proportions," I said. "How did you find us?"

"Things were obviously going downhill," he said. "So I asked a friend at the State Department to activate Snoopy on Delgado's phone."

"Of course. Snoopy." I smacked my forehead. "And you 'asked a friend.'"

Theo shrugged innocently. "I had to ask, Jonathan. As a civilian, I certainly wouldn't have access to such an invasive program as Snoopy."

"Okay, I'll bite," said Piper. "What's Snoopy?"

I explained briefly.

At the request of the State Department, a Northern California technology company, one who shall remain nameless, had developed a program that allowed a telco to remotely access a phone's camera and microphone even if the device was turned off. Neither the owner of the phone nor anyone in the vicinity would have the slightest idea what was going on.

The State Department wanted the software in order to track kidnapping victims. Obviously, it didn't take long for some of the other alphabet agencies to see the benefit of this particular technology. The official name of the program was so complicated that no one remembered it. Everybody called it Snoopy.

"Hence." I finished my story. "Why I never carry a cell phone."

"That's really scary," Piper said. "Isn't there a law against that?"

"Probably." I shrugged. "But that's never stopped them before."

"Hey." Theo pointed a finger at her. "Do you want the terrorists to win?"

Piper rolled her eyes.

"Do you still have access to Delgado's phone?" I asked.

Theo shook his head. "He threw it in the river."

"Maybe he's been micro-chipped?" Piper said. "You know, like a dog?"

"Are you trying to be funny?" Theo looked at me. "Is she trying to be funny, Jonathan?"

"She's asking if you know any other way to find him," I said. "Apparently, he's gone missing."

"Oh yes. The thing with the ballistics match and the vigilante killer."

I nodded.

Theo didn't respond.

After a moment, I said, "So . . . any ideas where he might be?"

Theo frowned. "Why would I care about some schmuck in Dallas?"

I tried not to sound exasperated. "Because you wanted me to keep track of him. Remember?"

Theo nodded. "Yes. But that was before we found out he was bat-shit crazy."

I sighed, tired all of a sudden.

"What do I want with a crazy politician, Jonathan? We have enough of those already in DC."

This point, I had to concede.

"I'm here to meet with the mayor and the district attorney," Theo said. "Smooth things over after the problem with that shipment."

"Problem?" Piper said.

"Best not to ask." I shook my head.

"I don't care about Raul Delgado anymore," Theo said. "I never really did that much in the first place. He just seemed like a good person to have in your back pocket, you know what I mean?"

"Like a comb?" I asked.

"You're funny, Jonathan." Theo slapped my cheek lightly. "That's why I like you."

I smiled.

Theo continued. "That's also why it causes me great pain to have to fire you."

I cocked my head. "Say what, cowboy?"

Piper smirked. "Dogs and fleas, Jon. Lie down with one, get the other."

"The shipment," Theo said. "I have to sacrifice someone on the mayor's altar tomorrow."

"You're firing me?" I tried not to sound incredulous.

"Poor choice of words on my part. We are allowing you to resign. The HR department will work out a generous severance package."

I didn't reply. The idea of being away from the nine-to-five grind as well as the unseemly nature of the contracting business was not unappealing.

A figure crept into my peripheral vision, oozing across the room like mist from a witch's cauldron.

Lieutenant Hopper, the chief's assistant, approached our booth. He cleared his throat and stared at Theo.

"I don't believe we've met. Who are you?"

Theo sighed dramatically and said his name. "I am a lawyer, and I represent the United States, specifically, the Department of Homeland Security."

"What about the US attorney?" Hopper asked. "Where's he?"

"I had breakfast with the attorney general in DC this morning. That would be the local guy's boss." Theo paused. "Told him I would handle things."

Hopper nodded and then looked at Piper. "Sergeant Westlake. I need to have a word with you."

Piper stared at Hopper for a few moments longer than necessary and then slid out of the booth. They walked to a corner of the room. Ninety seconds later, she returned.

"I got shit-canned, too." She slid back into her side of the booth.

"I'm sorry." I patted her hand.

"Not like I didn't see it coming," she said.

Theo clucked his tongue. "What a horrible thing. You should come work for the law firm. We have an opening."

"Shut up, Theo." She shook her head. "You're starting to annoy me."

"Spunk." He smiled. "I like that."

"When is my termination effective?" I asked.

"Immediately," Theo said. "Sorry. But I have to tell the mayor and DA tomorrow."

"My severance package. I need access to the databases for a couple of weeks."

"This could be arranged." Theo stroked his chin.

Piper said, "You're still trying to find Tremont, aren't you?"

I nodded. "And Bobby's daughter. Hannah June McKee."

# - CHAPTER FORTY-SEVEN -

In the makeshift orphanage in West Dallas, Lysol watches Hannah McKee cradle the baby, a bottle of formula in the infant's mouth. Both she and the child are cooing, looking at each other with contentment.

Hannah is naked except for a pair of black panties, Lysol's measure to keep her from running away. As time has gone by he's realized she wouldn't run even if given the chance. But he doesn't tell her to put her clothes back on. Nor does she ask to.

Something about a woman with an infant, especially an attractive woman who's nearly naked, gets a man's blood going.

Despite wanting Jamal's help in feeding the babies, Lysol banished him to the backyard after the formula was warmed. Jamal is just a boy, but there's no sense getting his hormones cranked up any earlier than necessary. Lysol helps with the feeding, surprised at how easy it has all come back to him.

The baby gurgles. The woman pats his back while staring at Lysol, her expression seductive without meaning to be.

Lysol shakes his head, trying to force those particular thoughts of Hannah McKee from his mind. He turns her cell back on, debates who to reach out to. Realizes there's no one except his lawyer, the phone call of last resort.

"What happens after I'm done feeding the babies?" Hannah says.

"I'm gonna figure a way out of here." He peers through the window.

The cop is still there but he has company now. A Dallas County sheriff's deputy has just pulled up. The cop and the deputy talk for a moment and then the cop leaves. This is an odd occurrence and Lysol doesn't know what to make of it.

The five-oh are obviously still looking for him, but they are apparently stretched a little thin if the county's getting involved.

"The babies, they're gonna need to be changed in a little while." Hannah puts the child down.

"So get to it." Lysol is all good with feeding the kids. Changing them, that's another story.

"We're about out of diapers. There're more in my car."

"And where would your car be?"

She walks over to the window, seemingly unashamed of her nudity. It's late afternoon and the light is growing dim in the living room of the house south of Singleton.

She stands next to Lysol, reaches in front of him, and lifts one slat of the blinds. Her arm brushes against Lysol's shoulder; he steps back.

"There." She points to the right. "Down the block."

Lysol doesn't want to open another slat and risk the po-po seeing too much movement from the house. So he moves closer to the woman, peers over her shoulder.

A late-model BMW sits in front of the home next door.

He can smell the odor of shampoo and baby powder on Hannah McKee, not an unpleasant combination. That, combined with her body, makes his head swim.

"The car registered to you?" He moves away.

"To a leasing company. My name's on the lease, though."

"Is it hot?"

She doesn't answer.

"Anybody looking for the car? Or you?"

"No." She turns back from the window and stares into his eyes. "No one is looking for me."

"Can Jamal and his little crew change the babies?"

She hesitates, then nods.

Another sheriff's car pulls up behind the first one. The two deputies stand on the sidewalk, conversing. They are relaxed, not anxious. For now at least.

"You can't leave by the front," she says.

"I need your car. In the alley."

"Then I'll have to put my clothes on and drive it there."

Lysol doesn't reply.

"But that would mean you'd have to trust me." She puts one arm on his shoulder, a finger rubbing his neck. "Do you think you can trust me?"

Lysol struggles not to stare at her body, to control the involuntary reactions from his own.

"Is your leg okay?" Hannah glances down at the flesh wound. "Want me to change the bandage?"

Lysol looks down. She's standing right in front of him, so his eyes traverse the length of her body, the breasts, the smooth flesh of her belly, the front of her panties, a triangle of black silk.

"My leg's fine." He slips away from her, heads down the hall.

She follows him to the bedroom.

Lysol dashes to the window, bumping the bed as he goes, knocking Hannah's purse to the floor. Her wallet falls out, flops open.

Lysol moves one side of the blinds a fraction, peers outside, looking for an escape.

The children are in the backyard, kicking a basketball. Their weapons are not visible. Beyond the yard lies the alley where he first encountered Jamal.

He realizes he'll never make it on foot. He has to have a car.

Hannah lies on the bed, head propped up on one arm.

"You ever been with anybody like me?" she says.

Lysol stares at her. A cray-cray white ho, hot-looking, built for speed. Usually this is his favorite combination.

Not now, though.

He glances at her purse and wallet on the floor. He picks up the wallet. Earlier, he'd searched the money compartment and read the info on her driver's license, which was on the outside in a plastic sleeve.

He had not searched the entire wallet, however.

After dropping off the bed, the wallet had fallen open to the picture section, a throwback to a different era. Who keeps pictures like that anymore when you have a cell phone?

Two photos are visible. One is a black kid, maybe twelve or thirteen. The kid has eyes that aren't slow but aren't right either. The other picture is a much younger Hannah McKee, maybe a decade before, standing by a Mexican man in a Dallas police uniform.

"This is Tremont Washington." Lysol points to the first photo. "I recognize him from the neighborhood."

Hannah doesn't reply.

"People are looking for Tremont," Lysol says. "You know where he is?"

She shakes her head. "We had a fight, me and—it's not important. He always runs away when we fight."

"We who?"

"He always comes back, too." She paused. "Except this time he didn't."

"The cop." Lysol points to the second picture. "You had a fight with him?"

Hannah grabs an end of the comforter and covers herself.

"Is the cop your boyfriend?"

She pulls the comforter to her chin.

"If you tell me where Tremont is," Lysol says, "then I can get someone to pick me up and I'll go away. You won't have to see me again."

Jonathan Cantrell. He's still connected to the feds. He can call off the local heat if Lysol can give him info about Tremont Washington.

Hannah shakes her head. "I don't know where he is. He just took off running and we never saw him again."

Tears fill her eyes.

Lysol throws the wallet against the far wall, angry and frustrated.

Cantrell will be of no help then. Lysol is alone. The weight of that simple fact hangs on his shoulders like a lead blanket.

Time for the escape plan. He's been putting it off for too long.

Lysol sits on the bed and, using Hannah's cell, dials the number of his attorney, an ethically challenged gash-hound named Stodghill.

Stodghill, a criminal-defense specialist, answers his cell after a long time. Lysol can hear 1980s hair-band music blaring in the background. He figures the man is in a strip club since it's after lunch and all.

Without going into any incriminating details, he explains quickly what's happened.

Stodghill understands immediately, says he'll ready Lysol's escape plan, which is really quite simple.

A chartered Learjet will be standing by at Love Field. In the passenger compartment will be a bag of cash, a passport, and a key to a safety deposit box in Houston. Three million euros are in the safety deposit box, enough to start a new life somewhere else.

They discuss the details for a few moments. Then Stodghill says, "You really leaving Dallas?"

Lysol stares at the wall of the bedroom for a long time.

Stodghill says, "You still there?"

"Stand by," Lysol says. "Just keep it all on hold."

He hangs up before the attorney can respond.

He looks at Hannah. "Do you want to come with me?"

"Where?"

"Away."

Neither of them speak.

A helicopter flies overhead. Low and fast.

On the dresser is a small flat-screen TV. Lysol turns it on.

The local anchors with their puffy hair and plaid sport coats are talking fast, like they get paid by the word and they better get as many out as possible.

A gunfight on Singleton Boulevard several hours before. A picture of Lysol appears on the screen.

There is another story, too, though.

A suspected serial killer, responsible for what the police are now calling the Vigilante Murders, has been taken to a local hospital after suffering a heart attack.

Another picture flashes on the screen, this one of an older man, a retired cop named Robert McKee.

Hannah weeps softly as Lysol calls his attorney back.

# TEN DAYS LATER

# - CHAPTER FORTY-EIGHT -

### The Loan Shark

The thing about borrowing money is, you have to pay it back.

An important lesson, one that Donny Ray Holecek always tries to impart to his clientele.

You take money from Donny Ray, you gotta make payments. With interest. Lots of interest.

Simple concept, right?

This fine morning Donny Ray is in his South Dallas office, a picnic table in a park a few blocks from the crumbling Cotton Bowl.

The park backs up to a cemetery, which makes for some interesting visuals when instructing a reluctant client on how important it is to keep current with his payments.

Across the street from the park lie block after block of small wood-framed homes built in the 1920s, most of which suffer from what could be termed "extreme deferred maintenance."

Peeling paint, weed-filled lawns, broken windows. The only modern features most have are satellite dishes and the occasional late-model luxury car in front of the home of the local drug dealer.

In other words, nobody in the neighborhood is going to give a shit about what goes on in this particular park.

Ergo, why Donny Ray has chosen it as his office.

At the moment, he's in a meeting with a client who is late on his interest charges.

The client, who Donny Ray affectionately calls "Fuck Stain," is lying on his back on the picnic table, held down by Donny Ray's assistant, a seven-foot-tall African American gentleman named Mr. Phyllis.

Fuck Stain—a stockbroker with a drug problem—has been ignoring Donny Ray's calls, something that is almost worse than not making your interest payments.

Communication, Donny Ray likes to say. That's the important part of any successful business venture. And Donny Ray Holecek—a pudgy high school dropout from Kosse, Texas—is very successful in his field. In fact, Donny Ray is so successful that he's considered the biggest purveyor of street money in all of Dallas County.

Donny Ray takes pride in this fact, an accomplishment for which he credits two things: good communication (see above), and passion for the job.

Another lesser element of his success comes from choosing just the right tool for the task at hand. In this instance, a ball-peen hammer.

"Mr. Phyllis," Donny Ray says. "Refresh my memory. How behind is Fuck Stain?"

The stockbroker groans and cradles his left hand, the one with the two broken fingers, knuckles smashed by the ball-peen hammer.

"Four payments now plus the vig," Mr. Phyllis says. "Twenty-five hundred."

Donny Ray clicks his tongue. He points at the stockbroker with the business end of the hammer.

"You got two and a half on you, Fuck Stain?"

"N-no." The man shakes uncontrollably. "But I can get it for you. I promise."

"That's what you told me last week. Isn't that right, Mr. Phyllis?"

Mr. Phyllis nods.

Fuck Stain looks back and forth between his two captors, hyperventilating.

"And then you quit answering your phone." Donny Ray shakes his head.

"See, I got a new cell," Fuck Stain says. "I was gonna call you with the number."

"But you didn't," Donny Ray says. "Which means, before we even talk about the money, I gotta break another finger."

"*Nooo!*" Fuck Stain struggles to get away from Mr. Phyllis's meaty arms.

"Hold him still, will ya?" Donny Ray grips the hammer.

"I'm trying, boss, but he's a wiggly sonuvabitch." Mr. Phyllis reaches for the client's injured hand but stops. He stares at the street, which is partially obscured by a row of cedar trees.

Donny Ray follows his assistant's gaze.

A battered navy-blue Crown Victoria has stopped. The driver's door opens and a man in a black tracksuit gets out.

# - CHAPTER FORTY-NINE -

I have a thing for cemeteries.

The solitude and stillness. The desolate sense of peace, brooding yet calm, surrounded by long-forgotten actors from the world's stage, the bare nuggets of their life story encapsulated on the weathered tombstones.

The magnificent melancholy of it all.

Midmorning. The humidity wasn't too bad yet, though precious little wind stirred among the oaks and pecans in the graveyard by Fair Park, a few blocks away from the Cotton Bowl.

Old weather-gnarled trees formed a canopy over my family's plot, a small rectangle surrounded by a wrought-iron fence and set apart from the rest of the dead.

I sat on the tombstone of my father, Frank Cantrell. His final resting place was a few yards away from my grandfather's.

My cell phone, a disposable model, chirped with a text message from Piper. *R u there??*

I replied in the affirmative, gave an exact location. Then I waited.

The gate to the graveyard was visible in the distance, bracketed by a pair of oleander bushes.

The cemetery was in an area that had been lower-middle class a hundred years ago. Now it could best be termed as a neighborhood for the working poor, except there wasn't much work to compensate the poor. There were, however, a lot of crack houses, people on food stamps, and single mothers interspersed with shotgun shacks, tin-roofed blues clubs, and exotically named Baptist churches.

It was a perfect location for a meeting away from prying eyes.

A few minutes later a white Ford stopped at the gate.

The driver's door opened, and Piper exited, scanned her surroundings.

She peered over the tops of the tombstones, saw me, then opened the rear door of her car.

A man in handcuffs stumbled out. He was lanky to the point of emaciated, wearing a white jumpsuit with "Dallas County Inmate" emblazoned on the back.

She grasped him by the elbow and together they threaded their way through the tombstones to where I sat on my father's grave.

Piper stopped a few feet away and mopped sweat from her brow with a forearm.

"Spending a little quality time with the family?" she asked.

I shrugged.

The man stumbled against a tree root but didn't fall. He stared at the ground, not speaking.

His name was Stephen Duane Chalupnik, alias "Stoma Steve" due to the breathing hole in his throat from the tracheotomy.

He was well over six feet tall and weighed about as much as a grade-schooler. The reasons he looked like a concentration-camp escapee were myriad: HIV positive, screwed-up metabolism, bad jail food—take your pick.

"Any problems getting him out?"

Piper shook her head.

Steve Chalupnik was East Texas hillbilly, what in less polite circles would be referred to as white trash, that of the trailer variety. He had an arrest record as long as the Rio Grande. His criminal history read like the Molesters' greatest hits album and included such gems as "Sexual Contact with a Child," "Indecency with a Child," and the always-popular "Continued Sexual Abuse of a Child."

He fit the profile of the person Lysol Alvarez had told me about. And sure enough, he'd been arrested in front of the Iris Apartments on the day that Tremont Washington had gone missing.

Stoma Steve glanced around the graveyard for a moment. Then he returned to staring at the ground, not making eye contact with either of us.

"Tremont Washington," I said. "That name mean anything to you?"

Stoma Steve didn't reply.

"Let's don't make this messy." I smiled. "Tell me what you know about Tremont and then you can get back to lockup in time for your bologna sandwich."

"Are you a cop?" Stoma's voice was croaky from the trach hole.

Piper chuckled.

"No." I shook my head. "But I'm a guy who can get your child-raping ass brought to a deserted cemetery just because."

"You hadn't oughta taken me here. I want to talk to my lawyer."

"What do you think this is?" I said. "An episode of *Law and Order*?"

Sweat trickled down Stoma's face, dripped from his nose.

"Your public defender's in rehab," Piper said. "Besides, you violated probation."

"You know who Tremont Washington is?" I said.

He continued to stare at the ground and shook his head.

"How come I don't believe you?" I stood.

"'Cause I don't like niggers."

"Watch the language, cocksucker." Piper pulled a black plastic object from her pocket. "Or I'll Taser your ass."

"Yet you were hanging out by the projects in West Dallas." I cocked my head. "Not exactly the yacht club."

Stoma Steve stared at the business end of the electric device, licked his lips.

I arched an eyebrow. "And how do you know Tremont is black?"

Stoma frowned, muttered under his breath. The sharpest tool in the shed, he was not.

"Let's try again," I said. "Think back. What's it been, three wee—"

*Bam-bam.*

Two gunshots in rapid succession, close by. Hard to tell the direction because the noise echoed off the tombstones, muffled by all the vegetation.

I dropped to my knees, right on top of Dad. Swiveled my head in a 180, scanned the tree line. No one was visible.

Piper shoved Stoma to the dirt and dropped a few feet behind me, checking out the opposite field of view, gun drawn.

*Bam.*

Another round, a larger-caliber gun or the same one fired closer.

I reached for my hip, grabbed for the pistol I'd started carrying again.

Silence.

Nothing but the screech of the cicadas and the thump of my heart.

# - CHAPTER FIFTY -

Donny Ray knows the five-oh when he sees it.

The old Crown Victoria, the way the man in the black track-suit moves, the tilt of his head.

In the fourteen years he's been in business, Donny Ray has pissed off a number of people—dozens of cops, several judges, too many lowlifes to count. He's been beaten up, stabbed twice, shot at a half-dozen times, run off the road, and banned from three different strip clubs.

But he's never had anybody aim a silenced weapon at him before.

The man in the black tracksuit pulls the Glock out from under his jacket as he walks through the cedar trees, maybe thirty feet from Donny Ray's office/picnic table.

In the brief amount of time it takes Black Tracksuit to raise the Glock, Donny Ray calculates his best play.

It's all very simple really. The law of self-preservation.

This is a hit, a professional one. From this range, the shooter is not likely to miss. Ergo, Donny Ray is likely to die.

And the only thing you can do that's worse than shooting a cop is to die.

Therefore, Donny Ray's best bet is to pop a cap in the man in the black tracksuit even though he's a police officer. Because he doesn't want to die.

To that end, he drops behind the picnic table as Black Tracksuit fires a single shot, which hits Fuck Stain in the leg.

Donny Ray pulls a Ruger .38 Special from his waistband. Aims at the only target available, the shooter's legs. Jerks the trigger twice.

Mr. Phyllis, himself no stranger to the ways of the street, has evidently reached the same conclusions as Donny Ray.

From one side of the picnic table comes the roar of Mr. Phyllis's weapon, a four-inch .44 Magnum.

Donny Ray doesn't wait to see if any of their shots have found their mark. He rolls away from the table, jumps up, and sprints toward the thick line of vegetation that serves as a boundary to the cemetery.

A tingling sensation on his shoulder. He touches the spot. His hand comes away wet with blood. Black Tracksuit is still in the game.

He pushes through the bamboo, turns, fires twice more.

Then he runs as fast as he can.

# - CHAPTER FIFTY-ONE -

Two more shots, closer.

Sweat trickled down the small of my back. The cemetery seemed to have gotten hotter. The air held less of a breeze.

"You see anything?" Piper whispered.

"Nuh-uh. You?"

"Nope. I think it came from your direction."

A bush on the fence line in front of me rustled slightly, maybe twenty yards away. An animal or the returning wind? Or the shooter?

"You gonna call it in?" I stared at the bush, knuckles white around the grip of the pistol.

"Wasn't planning to," she said. "Since I'm not really a cop anymore and I used someone else's badge number to get Stoma out of lockup."

The bamboo next to the bush twitched.

I stared at the leaves, focused all my attention.

Movement behind me, then swearing.

"Dang you, Stoma Steve." Piper's voice was a loud whisper, angry. "Don't you dare run on me."

I glanced away from the bushes, lowered the gun.

Stoma Steve, hands cuffed behind him, was galloping away, long legs making good time with each stride.

Piper holstered her weapon, stood, ran after him. And tripped. She fell face-first, disappearing behind a grave marker.

I looked back to the shrub line.

The man had emerged in the few seconds I'd been turned around.

He was in his midforties, Caucasian. He wore a black tracksuit and a matching ball cap, brim low. The jacket of the tracksuit was zipped up all the way, obscuring the lower half of his face. The way he moved and his overall appearance seemed familiar, but I couldn't place him, my attention being drawn to the silenced pistol in his hand.

I didn't move, didn't speak. He glanced at me for a quarter of a second and then melted back into the vegetation, leaving me to wonder if he'd ever really been there.

# - CHAPTER FIFTY-TWO -

*Fifteen minutes later*

No more gunfire. And no sign of Stoma Steve.

Piper called a friend at dispatch to see if there had been any calls about shots fired in the Fair Park area. So far nothing. Given the usual number of weapons discharged in this particular locale, and the innate distrust most of the inhabitants had for the police, the fact that there had not been a report didn't seem too unusual.

So Piper and I drove around the area surrounding the cemetery in her borrowed unmarked squad car.

It was nearly eleven in the morning, the day heating up.

Malcolm X Boulevard, the main drag through this section of town, was not open for business yet. The only place that appeared to have any activity was a convenience store that advertised discount cigarettes and lottery tickets. The store was next to a fried chicken joint and a bar called TJ's Adult Playtime Club.

TJ's looked like the kind of place you would go if you wanted to learn firsthand about knife fighting and syphilis.

Piper stopped in front of the bar and got out. I stayed in the car. She knocked on the door of the club, got no answer, then went inside the convenience store and the chicken joint only to emerge a few seconds later from each, shaking her head.

After that we drove slowly down the side streets, where we saw a lot of old men sitting on front porches smoking cigarettes, several stray dogs, a Vietnamese guy driving an ice cream truck, and a kid pushing a lawn mower down the sidewalk.

What we didn't see was a redneck child molester with a blowhole in his throat wearing jail whites, hands cuffed behind his back.

Piper, as one might imagine, was a tad nonplussed.

"Stoma's a freaking pedophile." She turned a corner. "And I let him go."

We were cruising down a street a few blocks south of the cemetery, windows open, letting the sounds and smells of the city wash through the squad car.

"Don't worry," I said. "We'll find—"

A hulking figure knelt in the middle of the next block, crouched over something that looked more than a little like a dead body.

"What the heck?" I squinted.

Piper eased off the gas. "Is that Mr. Phyllis?"

"I thought he and Donny Ray got blown up in a car bomb," I said.

The loan shark and his number-one enforcer were legendary in North Texas law-enforcement circles.

"Nuh-uh. That was his cousin." Piper shook her head. "Over in Fort Worth."

The figure glanced up, saw us, and stood.

It was indeed Mr. Phyllis. He appeared to be injured, blood staining his white guayabera shirt. He also appeared to be angry.

"Crap." Piper jammed on the brakes. "He's got a gun."

We were maybe forty feet away. Mr. Phyllis pointed what looked like a small cannon at our car.

Piper yanked the transmission into reverse, mashed the accelerator to the floor.

Mr. Phyllis turned away from us, his gun aimed at the side of the street. The weapon erupted—a plume of fire the size of a watermelon and a roar like a howitzer.

Then a strange thing happened.

Mr. Phyllis's head snapped back, and he fell to the ground. Like he'd been shot by a silenced weapon.

Piper stopped.

No movement on the street.

She put the car in park.

"What the hell are you doing?" I said. "Let's get out of here."

"What if it's somebody who's seen Stoma?" She opened her door, gun drawn.

I swore under my breath. She was right; we had to do whatever it took to find Stoma Steve. I exited as well and took cover behind an old Honda parked a few feet in front of our vehicle.

Piper dashed to the other side of the street and hid behind an oak tree.

Mr. Phyllis was obviously dead. The figure on the ground, apparently Donny Ray, was the same or nearly so.

A few seconds passed.

About fifty feet away, a man emerged from between two parked cars.

The shooter in the black tracksuit. His ball cap was gone, the jacket unzipped, face clearly visible.

He walked hunched over like something was wrong with his side. As he approached Mr. Phyllis, I could see that a portion of his abdomen had been blown away. One hand was clutching a tangled mess of flesh and jacket. The other held the silenced pistol.

The man stared at the two bodies for a moment and then fell to the ground himself.

Piper stepped from behind the tree. She holstered her gun.

Her face was ashen. Arms and legs shaking. I realized I was in the same condition, terrified, and not just from the gunfight we'd witnessed.

"C'mon. Let's roll." I headed toward the car.

"Did you see?" She pointed to the man in the black tracksuit. "He was using a silenced Glock."

"The ballistics on Bobby's or Raul's gun," I said. "It was only a ninety percent match."

"That's—" She kept pointing. "He—he—"

"Hurry up. We need to get out of here."

She shook her head as if to rid herself of the images on the street. Then she jogged to our vehicle.

Once behind the wheel, she cranked the ignition, turned around, and sped away, going in the opposite direction of the three dead bodies.

Two thugs and a guy in a black tracksuit.

The latter was Lieutenant Hopper, the chief's assistant.

# - CHAPTER FIFTY-THREE -

We didn't speak for a couple of blocks. Shaky from adrenaline. Silent from the shock of learning who the man in the black tracksuit was.

Old houses and overgrown yards blew past the windows.

I turned the AC to high.

We stopped for a light at Hatcher Street.

Piper looked my way and said, "What the hell?"

"I don't know. Maybe Hopper was doing his own one-man crime-reduction program."

"Figured him for an asshole. Not crazy."

"Everybody's got layers," I said. "Like a dysfunctional onion."

I wondered where Deputy Chief Raul Delgado was at the moment. He'd disappeared in the aftermath of the incident by the Trinity River where Bobby McKee had died.

A group of people ran past the front of the car. Maybe six or eight. Men and women, varying ages, all moving fast, pointing to the other side of the street. Everybody had a cell phone in their hand. We'd left the gunplay far enough behind us that the hubbub had to be for some other reason.

"Speaking of assholes," Piper said, "where do you think Stoma Steve has run off to?"

Hatcher was a main thoroughfare south of Fair Park, three lanes each direction.

Old apartments lined one side of the street. The other side, across from us, was a strip mall. The businesses there were pretty typical for the area—a beauty supply store and a dialysis office, a pawnshop.

And a day-care center.

The group of people crossed the street en masse and headed toward the day-care center where another, larger group was clustered.

Piper took several deep breaths and leaned her head back against the rest. "You don't think he's over there, do you?"

Where else would a child molester seek refuge? A place to which he is irresistibly drawn.

She hit the switch for the red and blue lights in the grill and peeled across the street.

A few seconds later, the borrowed car screeched to a stop in front of about twenty people circled around an inset of the strip mall, a corner where the day-care center connected with a tax-refund business.

Badge-less, Piper and I pushed our way through the crowd like we were cops.

Stoma Steve huddled in the corner, kept at bay by an old man wielding a rake like it was a spear. Stoma was still handcuffed but his jumpsuit was filthy.

"Step away, partner." I grabbed the old man's arm. "We'll take over from here."

Grumbling from the crowd.

"Show's over, folks." Piper whistled once, a piercing tone. "Please clear the area. This is police business."

"He's a damn pedophile," the old man said. "My pastor told us about him."

"Your pastor's right." I walked toward Stoma. "And now we're taking him back to lockup."

"What's he doing out here anyway?" The old man pointed a finger at me. "He's wearing jail clothes."

"It was a, uh, clerical error," Piper said.

Stoma stood up, eyes frantic. He addressed the crowd: "These aren't real police. Somebody call 911."

"Shut up, Stoma." I grabbed his arm, leaned close. "You want us to leave you here?"

Stoma squinted at me while the crowd continued to grumble. He tried to pull free from my grip.

I shoved him toward our vehicle while Piper carved a path through the angry people.

Thirty seconds later we were barreling down Hatcher Street, Stoma in the back.

I looked in the rear. "Start talking. Tremont Washington, everything you know."

"I coulda died back there," he said. "I wanna go back to jail."

I punched him in the nose.

He caterwauled. Bounced up and down on the seat.

Piper pulled into the parking lot of a self-serve car wash. She stopped the car. Turned around. "You want me to take you back to those people? Cuffed? In your jumpsuit? They'd love to see you."

Stoma cowered in the backseat, pressed against the door.

"Begin at the beginning," I said.

He took several deep breaths.

"That day. I saw three people," he said. "Two adults and Tremont."

"Keep going," I said.

"One of 'em was the po-po. A Mexican in a black Suburban."

I looked at Piper. That had to be Raul Delgado.

Stoma continued. "The Mex was fighting with this woman. She was the third person."

"What did the woman look like?" I said.

Stoma shrugged. Women weren't his thing.

"They was like a family or sumpthin'. Bitchin' at each other." Stoma shook his head. "My mama used to chase Daddy around the hog holler with a garden hoe. I know from fightin'."

"Black or white?" Piper said. "The woman. What color was she?"

"She was white. Maybe in her forties." He licked his lips. "Rich-looking."

Hannah McKee.

"So the Mexican cop and the rich lady are fighting," I said. "Then what happened?"

"Tremont. He ran away."

No one spoke.

"And?" I said.

Stoma frowned at us, a little jailhouse lawyering going on in his ninety-IQ brain.

"This isn't gonna come back on you," Piper said. "Everything's off the record. We'll even take you to Burger King on the way back to lockup."

Stoma nodded. "I, uh, followed him."

I stifled my natural revulsion to the implications of that statement.

"Then what?" Piper asked.

"We were on Hampton." Stoma's eyes were animated. "I was getting close, about to start talking to him." He paused. "Then a squad car stopped."

"Because there was a warrant out on you," Piper said. "And you don't exactly blend in."

"The last warrant, that was all a misunderstanding," he said. "See, I was just—"

"No one cares, Stoma," I said. "What happened to Tremont?"

"The police arrested me." His voice was whiny. "They put the cuffs on too tight."

Piper rolled her eyes. "Cry me a river, ass-munch. Now tell us what happened to Tremont. Where did he go?"

Stoma looked out the window of the borrowed squad car. The sun was shining, traffic moving along Hatcher Street.

"He went back to the Iris. On the other side of the property, there's a side gate."

"And you saw him go in there?" I said.

Stoma nodded. "With that colored fellow. The one with the diamond grill, the one that talks like he's from England."

I turned back around and slumped my shoulders.

Tremont never left. He was in the Iris all along.

# - CHAPTER FIFTY-FOUR -

We didn't take Stoma Steve to Burger King like we'd promised. Instead we dropped him off at the jail.

Literally.

Piper drove slowly by the intake entrance as I climbed in the back and tossed Stoma out the rear door. The car never stopped.

He was still in his jail whites, still cuffed. He rolled a few times and ended up in the gutter. Hopefully, somebody would find him and get him where he belonged.

I shut the back door, and we drove to the Iris Apartments.

Once there, Piper parked in a handicap spot, and we strode to the building to where Tremont's unit was, the one he shared with his grandmother.

The courtyard was empty, no thugs standing around drinking beer. Nobody acting tough.

Piper rapped on the door of the grandmother's place.

No answer.

She hit harder.

I peered through the window.

One of the curtains was open a fraction, giving me a view of where the sofa had been.

"It's empty," I said.

"Now what?"

I kicked in the door.

"That's one option," she said. "Not necessarily my first choice, but hey, I can go with the flow."

I stepped inside.

The apartment was empty, furniture and personal items gone. In the kitchen, there was nothing in the refrigerator except a box of baking soda.

"She's an old lady with no money," I said. "Where could she be?"

———

The manager's office was in the front building, a ten-by-ten cube that smelled like copier toner and cigarette smoke.

The manager, a hard-looking woman in her sixties with a Misty Ultra Slim 120 dangling from her lip, told us that Alice Simpson had left no forwarding address.

"Any guesses where she might have moved to?" I said.

The manager shook her head. "I'm not sure she even knew. Most days she couldn't tell you where she lived even if she was standing in her living room."

"When did she leave?" Piper asked.

The woman blew a stream of smoke toward the ceiling. "Three, four days ago."

"Who moved her?" I said. "She had to have help, right? Especially with the dementia."

"Some moving company. I don't remember the name." The woman shrugged. "Maybe you could ask that Mexican guy."

"What Mexican guy?" Piper said.

"That one that was always around. He worked for the city or something."

Piper shook her head, muttered under her breath.

"They were together on the day she moved out?" I asked.

The woman nodded.

"Thanks." I headed toward the door.

"The old lady, Mrs. Simpson. She said something about the ocean." The manager lit another Misty. "She and the kid wanted to see the beach."

"What kid?" Piper said.

"Her grandson. The one that lived with her."

The office got very still except for the cigarette smoke curling upward. Piper and I looked at each other.

"Her grandson was with her?" I said. "When she moved?"

The woman nodded again.

"He ran away a lot. Used to hide in those vacant units on the ground floor." She coughed, a deep rattle like marbles in a can. "Had to chase him out a bunch of times."

"Did his grandmother know he used to hide out there?" Piper said.

"I told you. She didn't know what year it is most days."

One of those ground-floor units was where I had encountered Lysol's girlfriend trying to buy drugs. Sawyer, that was her name. She died in the mysterious explosion a few blocks away, the one that left Lysol Alvarez missing, presumed dead.

Tremont had been hiding in plain sight. Staying at the stash house. He would have made a perfect scout for the crew that ran the Iris, a little off, so no one suspected him of anything.

Or maybe they just let him stay there. Who knows?

Piper and I stepped outside.

"They've left, Jon. Out of our jurisdiction, so to speak."

I didn't say anything.

She touched my arm. "Let it go."

"I knew the kid's father." I pulled a disposable smartphone from my pocket. "I need to find him."

The smartphone had an app that was connected to the databases used by law enforcement. Theo Goldberg had allowed me to have access. I was glad to find that the access had yet to expire.

I ran the same search I'd been performing the past few days—Raul Delgado, his social, DOB, last known address, et cetera.

Nothing. Again.

Then I tried Alice Simpson. No results.

"He's a cop with a lot of money," Piper said. "He can disappear pretty easily."

"Do you think the kid's with him?"

Piper nodded.

"Do you think he's safe?"

"Safer than here." She massaged her stomach.

"You okay?"

"I feel like crap." Her face was pale. "Let's stop by the drugstore on the way—"

She put a hand to her mouth, then ran around the corner of the building. A moment later, a retching sound.

I dashed after her.

She was leaning over, hands to her stomach, a pool of bile at her feet.

"What's wrong, Piper? Talk to me."

"Nothing." She waved me off. "Let's get out of here."

"You think it's food poisoning? Something you ate?"

She didn't reply.

I put an arm around her shoulder. "Let's find a pharmacy."

She nodded.

I said, "Maybe an antacid will help."

"I doubt it." She looked in my eyes for a few seconds. "What are you saying?"

"I'm saying I don't think an antacid is gonna help what I've got."

I didn't reply, my mind racing with the implications.

"When I broke up with Raul. Couple months ago." She said, "I shouldn't a quit taking the pill."

"The pill? What pill are you talking about?"

"The pill-pill, you idiot."

My mouth was hanging open. We'd been together since then, several times, the last being in her rented house right before she'd gone to ground.

"Let's go to the drugstore, Jon." She took my hand, pulled me toward the car.

———

*Port Isabel, Texas*

Cesar Diaz considers himself the mayor of Jefferson Street. He watches over the homes on his block like a shepherd does his flock. Quietly, without seeming to. Missing nothing.

Jefferson is a tranquil residential street that dead-ends in the marina. The houses are old and small, occupied by working-class people or retirees.

You can't see the ocean from his house on Jefferson, but you can smell the salt and hear the gulls trill overhead.

The marina is a few blocks away from Cesar's place, South Padre Island maybe a three-minute drive over intercoastal waterway via the Queen Isabella Causeway.

Cesar is sixty-three years old, an ex-Navy mechanic and former letter carrier for the postal service. He's worked hard all his life and is now content to pass his time as an observer of the activity on Jefferson Street.

He sits on the front porch of his wood-frame house, drinking coffee in the morning, beer as the afternoon wears on, watching people come and go.

The stucco house across the street from Cesar's is set back from the curb, under a pair of palm trees, a "For Rent" sign at the end of the sidewalk. A porch runs the length of the front, a swing at either end. Cracked shells and weeds make up most of the yard, encased in a waist-high fence that matches the material of the house.

Port Isabel is near the Rio Grande Valley, a peculiar slice of North America that is a strained mixture of two vastly different cultures, a place where people keep to themselves and don't ask many questions.

This is why Cesar doesn't immediately walk across the street and welcome the mixed-race family that moved into the stucco house one hot summer night.

So many strange occurrences on the border, things that don't seem to fit together.

Men are enemies one day, friends the next.

People drop out of view regularly, only to surface in another town with a different name. Usually. More often than not, they disappear and are never heard from again.

Hard to tell what is normal in these trying times.

Maybe the strangeness is due to the heat. Perhaps it's the *brujas*, the Mexican witches who sell potions and spells from their shacks by the Rio Grande.

Or maybe it's the narco-traffickers, the shadowy people no one likes to talk about.

Who's to say?

In any event, Cesar doesn't bother the new arrivals. He just watches.

Two African Americans—a boy in his early teens, and a woman in her late seventies. And a handsome Latino man with hard eyes and a trim physique.

The man is the one who walks with the boy to the marina every day to look at the boats.

They stop at a little shack by the Catholic church for tacos and coffee, and then they continue on to a bench by the water, where they watch fishing trawlers leave for the Gulf.

A few days after they move in, another, even odder pair joins them.

Cesar sees them arrive one morning as he is reading the *Brownsville Herald,* a story from Dallas about a group of babies found in an abandoned house not far from where Bonnie and Clyde grew up.

The new arrivals come in a late-model sedan, a Japanese import, gray and nondescript.

A pretty woman in her late thirties, a Caucasian, with hair the color of mahogany. Her companion is a light-skinned black man in his forties, who walks with a slight limp. The man is dangerous-looking, the type of person you cross the street to avoid.

Cesar watches them get out and then continues reading. It's a sidebar story about the skeletal remains of a young man found on the ranch of the Dallas vigilante killer, a former police officer named Robert McKee.

The authorities had been alerted to the existence of the makeshift orphanage by an anonymous call from a cell tied to McKee's account. At the moment, they were trying to piece together the connection, but were not having much success.

The light-skinned black man and the Latino do not greet each other. They keep their distance from one another like two tomcats aching for a fight.

They all go inside and after a while the lights in the stucco house click off, one by one.

The next morning, as Cesar is having his second cup of coffee, the black man leaves the house, gets into the gray import, and drives away.

Cesar never sees him again.

The woman stands on the porch and watches him go. After a few moments, the Latino man joins her.

By the way they stand, Cesar surmises they are lovers or used to be. The status of their relationship now is hard to determine, though Cesar spins all kinds of wild tales in his head, most based on the soaps his wife watches on Univision.

Perhaps they are bank robbers on the lam. Or spies hiding from the government. Cesar wishes he could ask, but that is not the way on the border.

For the next few weeks life is serene on Jefferson Street.

Cesar and the man nod hello to each other and occasionally visit about the weather and how the redfish are running.

The man tells Cesar his name but it is so obviously a fake that Cesar only thinks of him as the guy across the street.

He has family nearby, that much is obvious. Cousins in Brownsville and Matamoros. From time to time, the cousins come over and there's a big cookout in the backyard of the stucco house.

Smoked brisket. Ears of corn on the grill. Coolers of beer. Bottles of white zinfandel.

The old black lady stays inside for these events, her health precarious.

The man and the boy seem to enjoy themselves, but the pretty white woman sits by herself off in a corner of the yard, drinking her wine. She smiles when people approach, but by the way she holds her shoulders, Cesar can sense her sadness.

One evening, as a get-together is in full swing, the woman storms out of the backyard and sits on the low wall in front of the stucco house.

The shadows are long, so she doesn't see Cesar on his porch.

A few moments later, the Latino man joins her.

He is angry; she is drunk. The predictable happens. They argue, voices raised, fingers pointed.

Cesar hears certain words that are louder than others.

Wayne and Junie.

And, from her: *Hannah! Why can't you fucking say Hannah?*

He doesn't know if those are the real names of the couple or not. He really doesn't know anything. After a few moments, the man and woman look up and down the block as if suddenly realizing they are arguing in public. They go inside and the party breaks up soon after.

As the months go by it becomes increasingly evident that the woman doesn't fit in.

The neighborhood is not to her liking. More and more she comes back from the mall in Brownsville with shopping bags from expensive stores, places that the other residents of Jefferson Street would never consider patronizing.

She drinks more.

A glass of wine on the porch in the afternoon becomes a bottle or sometimes two.

The man is concerned; this much is evident. He takes her to church but she doesn't like the ritual, Cesar hears via another argument—the priest in his vestments, the confession booths, the candles.

Her downward spiral continues.

There is a car crash and a fight, each delivering and receiving blows. Both the crash and the fight are smoothed over with the local police by generous amounts of hundred-dollar bills that the man has in abundance, according to a friend of Cesar's who works at the city.

Finally, in the fall, nearly six months after they moved in, the woman goes away. One day she is there, the next not.

The man and the boy and the old lady remain.

Cesar wonders if perhaps she joined the black man, but he knows better than to ask.

This is the border country, and people disappear all the time.

# - ACKNOWLEDGMENTS -

Creating a book for public consumption is an oddly communal effort. The raw material may have been mine but the finished product is the result of a group effort, a dedicated team of professionals who are as much responsible for what you hold in your hand as the author is. To that end I would like to thank the incredible team at Thomas&Mercer: Alison Dasho, Jacque Ben-Zekry, Gracie Doyle, Alan Turkus, Tiffany Pokorny, and David Downing.

I would also like to offer my gratitude to Jan Blankenship, Amy Bourrett, Victoria Calder, Paul Coggins, Peggy Fleming, Fanchon Knott, Brooke Malouf, Clif Nixon, David Norman, Glenna Whitley, and Max Wright.

Special thanks to Richard Abate for helping me navigate the waters leading to this book being published.

And finally, last but never least, thanks to my wife, Alison, for all her love, patience, and support.

# - ABOUT THE AUTHOR -

Harry Hunsicker, a fourth-generation native of Dallas, Texas, is the former executive vice president of the Mystery Writers of America. His debut novel, *Still River*, was nominated for a Shamus Award by the Private Eye Writers of America, and his short story *Iced* was nominated for a Thriller Award by the International Thriller Writers. Hunsicker lives in Dallas, where he works as a commercial real estate appraiser and occasionally speaks on creative writing. *Shadow Boys* is his fifth novel.